Lethe fell. . . .

The last crimson rays of the waning sunset painted the walls of Hells Canyon. The dark scar of the Snake River below grew thicker as Lethe plummeted toward it. He willed himself to follow cyberzombie Burnout into the abyss.

In one hand, Burnout clutched the Dragon Heart—an artifact that glowed gold and white-hot in the astral. It was very powerful magic.

Lethe willed himself into Burnout's body of metal and flesh. He possessed the cyberzombie and overwhelmed the man's spirit, which flickered like a weak candle, barely tethered to the meager amount of natural flesh that remained inside the machinery.

I must protect the Dragon Heart. I can still save Thayla. This was Lethe's last thought as the canyon walls closed around him. . . .

SHADOWRUN

CLOCKWORK ASYLUM

Book 2 of the
Dragon Heart Saga

Jak Koke

A ROC BOOK

ROC
Published by the Penguin Group
Penguin Putnam Inc., 375 Hudson Street,
New York, New York 10014, U.S.A.
Penguin Books Ltd, 27 Wrights Lane,
London W8 5TZ, England
Penguin Books Australia Ltd,
Ringwood, Victoria, Australia
Penguin Books Canada Ltd, 10 Alcorn Avenue,
Toronto, Ontario, Canada M4V 3B2
Penguin Books (N.Z.) Ltd, 182–190 Wairau Road,
Auckland 10, New Zealand

Penguin Books Ltd, Registered Offices:
Harmondsworth, Middlesex, England

First published by Roc, an imprint of Dutton Signet,
a member of Penguin Putnam Inc.

First Printing, November, 1997
10 9 8 7 6 5 4 3 2 1

Series Editor: Donna Ippolito
Legend of Thayla: Tom Dowd
Cover art: Doug Anderson

 REGISTERED TRADEMARK—MARCA REGISTRADA

SHADOWRUN, FASA, and the distinctive SHADOWRUN and FASA logos are
registered trademarks of the FASA Corporation, 1100 W. Cermak, Suite B305,
Chicago, IL 60608.

Printed in the United States of America

For Frances Cogan,
who showed me love for the written word,
and for Thomas Lindell,
who encouraged me to try it myself.

This book would not have been possible except for the generosity of Jonathan Bond. The effort he put forth for me was indispensable, especially on the outline and the first draft. Credit should also go to Mike Mulvihill for his great help with the plots and characters in this trilogy.

I'd also like to thank Tom Lindell, Nicole Brown, Seana Davidson, Don Gerrard, and Marsh Cassady for their insightful critiques of the manuscript. My appreciation also goes to Donna Ippolito at FASA, who originally made it possible for me to play in this wonderful universe, and who has kept me focused on character and clarity.

NORTH

CIRCA 2057

TSIMSHIAN

ATHABASKAN COUNCIL
Edmonton
Lake Louise

ALGONKIAN-MANITOU
COUNCIL

Saskatoon

Vancouver
Calgary

SALISH-SHIDHE
COUNCIL

Pacific
Ocean

Seattle
Spokane
Regina

Winnipeg

Portland
Salem
Eugene

Helena
Butte

SIOUX
NATION

Fargo
Duluth

Hell's
Canyon
Boise

Billings
Bismarck

TIR
TAIRNGIRE

Sheridan

Rapid
City

Sioux Falls
St. Paul

Idaho Falls

Minneapolis

Eureka

Reno

Salt Lake
City
Provo

Cheyenne

Des
Moines

Omaha

San
Francisco

Boulder

Denver
Colorado
Springs

Kansas
City

CALIFORNIA
FREE STATE

UTE
NATION

Las
Vegas

Pueblo

Topeka

Wichita

Bakersfield
Santa
Barbara
Los Angeles

PUEBLO
CORPORATE
COUNCIL

Santa Fe

Tulsa

San Diego

Tijuana

Phoenix

Albuquerque

Amarillo

Oklahoma City

Little
Rock

Tucson

Roswell

Ft. Worth

Dallas

Shreveport

El Paso

San Angelo

Pacific
Ocean

San Marcos
dig

Austin
Houston

Chihuahua

San Antonio

Corpus
Christi

North America

- National Capital
- Seattle • City
- - - - International Boundary
- .... State Boundary
  (U.S.A. circa 1990)

AZTLAN

Monterrey

Culiacan

Durango

Ciudad
Victoria

AMERICA

CIRCA 2057

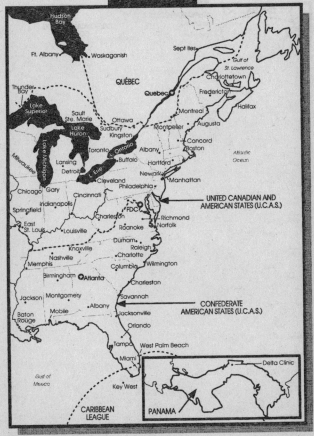

Hudson Bay

Ft. Albany • Waskaganish

Sept Iles

Gulf of St. Lawrence

Charlottetown

QUÉBEC

Quebec

Fredericton

Thunder Bay

Montreal

Halifax

Lake Superior

Sault Ste. Marie

Ottawa

Montpelier

Augusta

Sudbury

Kingston

Concord

Boston

Milwaukee

Toronto

L. Ontario

Albany

Lansing

Buffalo

Hartford

Atlantic Ocean

Lake Michigan

L. Erie

Detroit

Cleveland

Newark

Manhattan

Chicago

Gary

Cincinnati

Philadelphia

UNITED CANADIAN AND AMERICAN STATES (U.C.A.S.)

Springfield

Indianapolis

FDC

Richmond

East St. Louis

Charleston

Roanoke

Norfolk

Louisville

Durham

Memphis

Knoxville

Raleigh

Nashville

Charlotte

Wilmington

Birmingham

Columbia

Atlanta

Jackson

Montgomery

Charleston

CONFEDERATE AMERICAN STATES (U.C.A.S.)

Baton Rouge

Mobile

Albany

Savannah

Jacksonville

Gulf of Mexico

Orlando

Tampa

West Palm Beach

Miami

Delta Clinic

Key West

CARIBBEAN LEAGUE

PANAMA

The year is 2057 . . .

And magic has returned to the earth after an absence of many thousands of years. What the Mayan calendar called the Fifth World has given way to the Sixth, a new cycle of magic, marked by the waking of the great dragon Ryumyo in the year 2011. The Sixth World is an age of magic and technology. An Awakened age.

The rising magic has caused the archaic races to re-emerge. Metahumanity. First came the elves, tall and slender with pointed ears and almond eyes. They were born to human parents, just as were dwarfs shortly thereafter. Then later came the orks and the trolls, some born changed, like elves and dwarfs, but others goblinized—transformed from human form into their true nature as the rising magic activated their DNA. Manifesting as larger bodies, heavily muscled with tusked mouths and warty skin.

Even the most ancient and intelligent of beings, the great dragons, have come out of their long hiding. Only a few of these creatures are known to exist, and most of them have chosen a life of isolation and secrecy. But some, able to assume human form, have integrated themselves into the affairs of metahumanity. They have used their ancient intellect, their powerful magic, and their innate cunning to ascend to positions of power.

One is known to own and run Saeder-Krupp—the largest megacorporation in the world. Another—Dunkelzahn—is the most controversial creature to ever to have been elected to the presidency of the United Canadian and American States. Dunkelzahn was assassinated in a mysterious explosion on August 9, 2057—the night of his inauguration.

The Sixth World is a far cry from the mundane environment of the Fifth. It is exotic and strange, a paradoxical blend of the scientific and the arcane. The advance of technology has reached a feverish pace. The distinction between man and machine is becoming blurred by the advent of direct neural interfacing. Cyberware. Machine and computer implants are commonplace, making metal of flesh, pulsing electrons into neurons at the speed of thought. People of the Sixth World are a new breed— stronger, smarter, faster. Less human.

The Matrix has grown like a phoenix out of the ashes of the old global computer network. A virtual world of computer-generated reality has emerged a universe of electrons and CPU cycles controlled and manipulated by those with the fastest cyberdecks, with the hottest new code.

It is an era where information is power, where data and money are one and the same. Multinational mega-corporations have replaced superpower governments as the true forces on the planet. In a world where cities have grown into huge sprawls of concrete and steel, walled-off corporate enclaves and massive arcologies have super-seded two-car garages, vegetable gardens, and white picket fences. The megacorps exploit masses of wage-slaves for the profit of a lucky and ruthless few.

But in the shadows of the mammoth corporate arcolo-gies live the SINless. Those without System Identification Numbers are not recognized by the machinery of society, by the bureaucracy that has grown so massive and complex that nobody understands it completely. Among the SINless are the shadowrunners, traffickers in stolen data and hot information, mercenaries of the street—discreet, effective, and untraceable.

The Sixth World is full of surprises, not the least of which is the recent discovery of a Locus by Aztechnology, a megacorporation with a dark and bloody core. The Locus serves as a focus for metahuman sacrifices. It gives the puppeteers who control Aztechnology the power they need to construct their metaplanar bridge to the tzitzi-mine—demons who live off torture and suffering. When the bridge is completed, the demons will come into this world and ravage it. Aztechnology believes it will be rewarded as the tzitzimine scourge the land, bringing a millennium of pain.

Only Ryan Mercury can stop them. He is an undercover operative who worked for the recently assassinated great dragon, Dunkelzahn. Ryan must take the Dragon Heart— a magical item of immeasurable power—to the meta-planar bridge and give it to Thayla, the woman whose song protects the world from the demons she calls the Enemy. The Dragon Heart will give Thayla the power to destroy the bridge.

Recently, Thayla's power over the bridge was breached by Aztechnology. And at the same time Ryan Mercury struggled to overcome the selfish personality inside that inspired him to keep the Dragon Heart for himself. The evil part of him that allowed the cyberzombie, Burnout, to steal the artifact.

Ryan defeated Burnout, throwing him into the depths of Hells Canyon, but the cyberzombie reached out and snatched the Dragon Heart. Burnout plummeted into the chasm, taking the salvation of the world with him.

Now, Ryan Mercury must get the Dragon Heart back.

Prologue

Lethe fell.

The last crimson rays of the waning sunset painted the walls of Hells Canyon. The dark scar of the Snake River below grew thicker as he plummeted toward it. He willed himself to follow Burnout into the abyss, pushing his spirit close as the cyberzombie dropped. The cliffs on either side narrowed, and the universe contracted around Lethe as he fell after the cyberzombie called Burnout.

The cyberzombie looked human for the most part, but Lethe felt a cold, inhuman radiance from him. In the physical world, Burnout was very big, at least two and a half meters, with a density to him that spoke of cybernetic limbs and torso. His bald head was perfectly symmetrical and looked tiny on his massive shoulders and chest. His legs were strangely proportioned, with elongated shins and shortened, overly muscled thighs.

This . . . creature is perhaps the opposite of me, Lethe thought. Lethe was pure spirit, and unable to manifest in the physical world at all.

In the astral, Lethe saw that most of Burnout's spirit was gone. His aura was a dark shadow amid a glowing constellation of magic and spells. His true spirit was somehow separated from his body. Out of phase.

Lethe had never seen anything like it. He noticed a slight hazing in the astral wherever the cyberzombie passed. This creature was polluting astral space by its mere existence. Highly unnatural.

In one hand, Burnout clutched the Dragon Heart—an artifact that glowed gold and white-hot in the astral. Very powerful magic.

Lethe willed himself into Burnout's body of metal and

flesh. He possessed the cyberzombie and overwhelmed the man's spirit, which flickered like a weak candle, barely tethered to the meager amount of natural flesh that remained inside the machinery.

I must protect the Dragon Heart, Lethe thought. *I can still save Thayla.*

Burnout's body crashed into the cliff wall, bouncing off with a grinding crunch. Lethe tried to extend his will into Burnout's cybernetic arms, to make the man bring the Dragon Heart close to his chest. To protect it. Despite massive exertion, Lethe could not influence the creature's metal parts.

That brought the first wave of panic. Lethe was a powerful spirit, a creature of will and energy who was not bound by flesh and could not influence the physical world except by possessing the bodies of living creatures. He had only tried it twice before, that he could remember, and only in emergencies, but each time he had gained full control over the host body.

Here he was merely an observer. A passenger.

The canyon walls closed around him. Narrower and narrower. It was pitch dark; Lethe didn't know when he would hit bottom. Burnout was falling like a bullet now, his metal growing hot from the speed. He impacted on the rock again, smashing his left shoulder. And again, scraping a wide patch of skin off the shiny metal sheathing.

Still he did not drop the Dragon Heart. Lethe felt its power close. Saw it through the cyborg's artificial eyes. Somehow that visual information made its way into the organic brain and Lethe could tap into it.

Burnout hit the black water and should have died. Water like duracrete. His hot metal casing warped under the impact, and Lethe knew that much of his cybernetics were destroyed. But whether it was Lethe's presence or the Dragon Heart, the man's spirit decided to stay with his remaining flesh.

As Burnout's body sank into the depths of the Snake River, Lethe panicked once again, not in fear for his own existence, but because he couldn't imagine anyone finding Burnout's body in time to get the Heart to Thayla at the magical spike.

The memory of Thayla came to him as he sank. He remembered when he had first awakened and been named by her, the goddess of the light and the song. Thayla had stopped her singing to speak to him. A song so perfect, so painfully wonderful that he could not move.

She had stood on the hard, cracked ground of a stone outcropping, framed by a colorless sky. A deep chasm surrounded her on three sides, the chasm dropping away in front of her precipitously. Lethe had no concept of the depth of this chasm; he could not see the bottom. The outcropping thickened into a broad arc as it stretched away behind them, widening ever so slightly as it extended. Until finally it connected with solid land in the distance.

"This outcropping is the result of unnaturally high magic," Thayla had said. "The Chasm, here, is the gap between our worlds and those of the . . . the . . ." She faltered, pain evident in her speech.

Lethe remembered looking out across the abyss. In the absence of Thayla's song, wind roared around them, throwing her hair across her face. The far side of the chasm was barely visible in the blowing distance, but Lethe could make out a similar cliff at the reaches of his perception. He could see a similar outcropping protruding toward them from the land on that side. Darkness clung to the distant cliff, and as Lethe looked across that space, revulsion rose inside him. A desperate nausea as he glimpsed the creatures writhing on the other side.

"I am here to prevent them from completing their bridge," Thayla continued. "They are evil and horrifying and more powerful than we can imagine. If they can finish the bridge, they will come in droves. And when they come, they will destroy everything they can touch. They will torture us. They will make us all do things . . ." Again her voice wavered.

Lethe shivered at her distress. Her voice was powerful even in shock.

Thayla took a breath and composed herself. "As the natural cycle of mana increases, the Chasm will grow narrower. But these outcroppings are unnatural—spikes above the normal mana level. The result of blood magic. Our worlds are not ready."

"But your singing . . ."

She smiled at him, the light beaming from her and warming him. "My song stops them. You see, they cannot stand to hear it, and my voice carries even across the Chasm."

Lethe knew it to be true: her song was the light.

"There are those on our side who are working to accelerate the completion of the bridge, those who are puppets of the Enemy and who are trying to hasten their coming. Look." She pointed back down the outcropping.

At first Lethe didn't see it because it was so small, a shadow among shadows. But when Thayla began to sing again, filling the world with light and beauty, a tiny blemish of darkness remained. It was almost insignificant, and it lasted only briefly, but Lethe had seen it—a flaw in her song.

"They have found one who can withstand the song," she said. "She is not strong enough to stay long, but I fear her strength will grow. And when it does, others will come. They will kill me."

Lethe's spirit sank as Thayla's song died away.

"Unless you stop them," she said.

"How?"

"You must find the great dragon called Dunkelzahn. He came to me not long ago and told me that I would not be able to hold off the Enemy's forces for longer than a few hundred years. He said they would find a weakness in my song. He said he needed more time.

"Dunkelzahn promised to create an item that would keep the Enemy from crossing over prematurely. The Dragon Heart."

Thayla bowed her head. "But that was some time ago, and the dark spot is growing. I fear something has happened. Will you go and find Dunkelzahn? Will you bring the Dragon Heart to me?"

"I will," Lethe had said. "I promise."

Now, trapped inside Burnout's metal husk, sinking toward the cold heart of the river, Lethe wondered how he would be able to keep his promise. He couldn't move the cyberzombie and he had no one to help him.

Ryan Mercury certainly couldn't be trusted. Lethe had seen the human claim the Heart for his own. Mercury had succumbed to the power of the Heart; he had simply jettisoned any pretense of carrying out the quest Dunkelzahn had given him. He had refused to take the Dragon Heart to Thayla, and Lethe would never trust him again.

Perhaps the other gifted one, Nadja Daviar, could be convinced to help him get the Dragon Heart to Thayla. She had always helped him in the past. *Yes,* he thought, *I will go to her.*

Lethe willed himself to flee Burnout's body.

Nothing happened. He couldn't move.

By the goddess! What is going on?

Lethe kept sinking inside the unconscious metal corpse. Then he noticed a spectral mesh of magic, barely visible. Like a gossamer web of fine strands, the mesh held Burnout's spirit to his body. The web kept Burnout's spirit from leaving the too little flesh. It was part of the cybermancy that allowed the man to be alive even with all this hardware.

Now that same magic blocked Lethe from getting out.

Lethe struggled, exerting all his power against the magic that held him. The gossamer strands stretched and bulged, but they would not break. Lethe was trapped.

An inmate inside this metal asylum. This clockwork prison.

20 August 2057

1

The air in Hells Canyon blew hot and dry even in first rays of the morning sun. The fiery ball crested the peaks behind him as Ryan Mercury walked along the edge of the cliff face. The sun battered down on him with its relentless scorching blaze.

Ryan stood on the edge of the Assets Incorporated airstrip, a hidden ledge of rock cut into the eastern cliff face of Hells Canyon—deep in Salish-Shidhe Council lands on the border of what used to be Oregon and Idaho. The compound included a modest underground shelter, an old corrugated metal hangar, and some ramshackle storage sheds. Ryan had commissioned the expansion of the underground facilities, but so far only the command room had been completed. There was a lot of work to be done.

He looked over the edge of the cliff and down at the thin line of the Snake River a thousand meters below, taking a long drink from his water bottle and forcing himself to chew a soy protein bar. He wasn't hungry, and his stomach hurt so bad he wasn't sure if he was going to be able to hold anything down.

Ryan was two meters and 130 kilos of well-conditioned muscle, magically enhanced and accelerated flesh. No cyber, no bio. He swallowed, knowing he needed to eat in order to keep up his strength.

The buzz of Dhin's drones came to his ears. The ork rigger was remote-piloting the surveillance vehicles, scouring the canyon floor. *Burnout must be down there,* Ryan thought, *and he must have the Dragon Heart with him. But why can't we find him?*

Ryan and the Assets Incorporated team had been

searching for the cyberzombie's body and the Dragon Heart for almost three days, with no progress. It was as if they had simply disappeared, swallowed into astral space or disintegrated into their constituent atoms and blown away in the hot wind.

The memory of his final battle with Burnout flashed into Ryan's mind. The colors of sunset, the sounds of wind. The canyon walls glowed deep crimson in his memory, and Burnout's chromed parts reflected the blood-colored light.

It was two days ago in the memory. A hurricane of wind blew through the open side door of the Hughes Airstar helicopter as Ryan had fought with the cyberzombie. As Ryan's final kick sent the overlarge metal body sailing out into the air.

Burnout plummeted, falling into the black fissure of Hells Canyon, an expression of sheer hatred flashing across his inhuman face.

At the last second, the cyborg's telescoping fingers had shot out from his bloodied hands. The prehensile metal snakes flashed toward Ryan. Aiming for Ryan's belt. They curled their sharp and mangled ends around the nylon net bag that held the Dragon Heart. And when they snapped taut, the whole weight of Burnout's body came down like an anchor.

Ryan jerked forward at the waist, pulled off his feet, flying for the door. He scrabbled for a hold, frantically grabbing for anything. He found nothing but grooved flooring. He fell out the side door, the hot air of Hell baking around him as he followed the cyberzombie down.

The helicopter's runner caught Ryan in the gut, knocking the breath from his chest. But it slowed him enough so that his hands found purchase, wrapping around the hot metal. Then he slid over, and their combined weight pulled at his grasp, his sweaty fingers slipping on the runner. White-hot needles jabbed the back of his hands and arms as he tried to focus, tried to hold on.

"I will have your magic, Ryan Mercury," said Burnout from below, his voice the grating of metal on metal.

Ryan looked down. Below him, Burnout hung suspended, his metal parts tinged with the pink of the dying sun. Framed by the impenetrable black of the abyss. Ryan felt his fingers giving way, slipping on the smooth round metal as his strength waned.

Then the nylon web bag tore, ripping away from his belt. And Burnout fell into the dark canyon below. He made no sound as he fell. He simply disappeared, a dark silhouette melting into the inky void. The Dragon Heart went with him, his chrome fingers still clutching it. Still gripping the one thing Dunkelzahn had said could save the world.

The Dragon Heart was an orb of solid orichalcum, shaped like a real four-chambered heart. It was a magical tool of such awesome power that Ryan couldn't even comprehend its true purpose. Dunkelzahn had left Ryan with instructions to take it to the metaplanes, to the site where the magic level had spiked artificially high after the Great Ghost Dance. He was supposed to give the Dragon Heart to the woman who protected the site, to Thayla.

Now, standing on the cliff edge, and breathing in the hot morning air, Ryan gave a harsh laugh. *Dunkelzahn couldn't even save himself,* he thought. *If a great dragon can't prevent himself from being assassinated, how does he expect a simple human to save the whole fragging world?*

Ryan hard-swallowed a bite of his protein bar and tried to push all the images and distractions from his mind. Dunkelzahn was dead and no amount of bitterness and anger would bring him back. It was better to try and stay focused on the task at hand.

Burnout's body will show up, he thought. *Can't hide that much metal forever.*

In addition to Dhin's drones, the decker Jane-in-the-box was using satellites to scan for the machine corpse. Plus the two samurais, Axler and Grind, had set up remote surveillance sites.

We'll find him when he drifts into a shallow area.

But it was hard to stay focused. The mood around the compound was starting to get ugly. Even though Axler and company were some of the most pro-level mercenaries it had been Ryan's pleasure to work with, they

were shadowrunners, not a search and rescue team. They
wanted action, not the numbing task of trying to find the
proverbial needle in the fragging haystack.

Ryan couldn't agree more. The last thing he wanted
was to waste any more time in the search for Burnout and
the Dragon Heart. He wanted to finish the construction on
the Assets compound, hire some more mercs and runners,
and get his forces gathered. He wanted to organize and
begin delving into the assassination of Dunkelzahn. So
far, no one had any clue to who did it.

And it slotted Ryan off that he was stuck here when he
could be helping bring the assassins to justice.

His wristphone beeped, pulling him from his angry
self-recrimination. He looked at the small screen, which
indicated that it was Jane-in-the-box on the line. Dunkelzahn's decker and a sometime member of the Assets, Inc.
team. He took a breath and punched the connect.

Instantly, the tiny vidscreen filled with a cartoon
image—a tangle of lion-blonde locks, doe-innocent blue
eyes, and a set of the largest breasts this side of a BTL
porn chip, barely covered by a black leather halter laced
up the front with tiny silver chains. The icon was a sharp
contrast to the Jane-in-the-box Ryan knew from real
life—a plain-looking human woman of about thirty-five
with scraggly brown hair and a skinny body.

Ryan knew that Jane's physical location was deep
inside Dunkelzahn's lair in Lake Louise. She rarely left
the lair, nestled deep in the stone heart of the old Canadian Rockies, now part of the Athabaskan Council. Frag,
she rarely left the cavernous room where she had decked
for Dunkelzahn all those years. She even had food deliv-
ered—when she ate at all.

Ryan had seen her custom set of decks and gadgetry; he
had seen her enter the trance that allowed Dunkelzahn to
see the Matrix through her mind, telepathically. He had
even ridden along once.

"Hello, Jane," he said.

Jane's Matrix icon smiled at Ryan, flashing perfectly
white teeth. "Ryan, it's good to see you eating something." Her full, gloss-black lips turned downward in a
sneer. "Even if it is that soy-supplement drek."

Ryan looked down at the remainder of his protein bar and absently shoved the last of it into his mouth. Through chews, he spoke, "You're advising me on diet? That's rich."

Jane laughed.

"What's biz, Jane?"

"Couple bits. First, I followed up on the magical support you requested, though the pickings are slim right now. All the top names on my A-list are otherwise occupied, but I managed to contact one of the top names on my B-list. I think you know her actually."

"What's her name?"

"Miranda."

Ryan thought. "I don't know any runners by that name."

Jane smiled at him. "She has only recently joined the ranks of the independently employed. Which is the main reason she hasn't been moved up to my A-list. By all accounts, she can light up the mana with the very best of the best, but she's green about the shadows. Up until a month ago, she worked as a high-placed wage mage for Fuchi IE."

"Miranda Everli?" Ryan asked.

"Just Miranda now," Jane said.

Ryan took a breath, remembering his two-month undercover stint at Fuchi under the false name of Travis W. Saint John. He recalled working alongside some of the best scientists and mages in the corporate world. One of those mages was Miranda Everli, a petite human with Nihonese features.

Ryan had liked her, and under other circumstances, they might have been close. But he was an undercover operative, and knew better than to form emotional attachments to anyone.

Miranda hadn't been a typical corporate. She had a wild, independent streak to her. And perhaps that was why they had become friends. After several weeks of working closely together, she had finally confessed her frustration with the corp bureaucracy.

Ryan's cover hadn't allowed him to admit he sympathized. Hadn't allowed him to tell her he was planning to be extracted by shadowrunners and placed inside Aztechnology.

Ryan was glad she'd made it out. He'd be happy to see her, but he was concerned about her ability to perform outside the corporate environment. He looked at his wrist-phone. "Is she the best you can come up with?"

Jane nodded, sending her blonde locks flying. "I know this isn't a good time to be breaking in someone new, but with McFaren gone, you need a magical arm."

Ryan knew she was right. McFaren had been the Assets mage until a few days ago when he'd died in the run against the Atlantean Foundation—an organization reportedly searching for the lost city of Atlantis, but that seemed more interested in recovering all kinds of magical artifacts. By whatever means necessary.

Members of the Atlantean Foundation had stolen the Dragon Heart from Dunkelzahn's lair, and McFaren had been instrumental in helping Ryan get it back.

Jane went on. "Miranda's the best you're going to get right now. The shadows are hot in the shakedown from the Big D's death, and good mages are even rarer than normal since they have their pick of assignments."

Ryan nodded. "Thanks, Jane. Any news on Lethe?"

Lethe, named after the river of forgetfulness, was a powerful free spirit with a mysterious past. He had also helped Ryan recover the Dragon Heart from the Atlantean Foundation. Lethe had been missing for several days now.

"Sorry, chummer," Jane said. "I haven't heard a frag-ging thing."

Ryan wasn't sure what to make of that, but Lethe was a spirit. Who knew why a spirit might suddenly up and dis-appear? "Okay, what else?"

Jane's frown turned into a soft smile. "I have a message from Nadja."

Ryan winced as the pain in his gut doubled. "All right, give it to me."

Jane nodded, then vanished. In her place, the delicate oval of Nadja Daviar's elven face filled the screen. Her emerald eyes were set wide, compelling and beautiful. Honest. Her long raven hair hung loose over her pointed ears. Her magenta-tinted lips curved into a delicious smile. "Ryan," she said, "I'm sorry this message had to be recorded. Things have gotten hectic, and it's very early in the morning here. I haven't slept yet and probably won't get to bed tonight."

To Ryan, the tenor of her voice was like the seductive sound of a slow-moving stream, gentle and caressing. He couldn't take his eyes from her.

"Ryan, I know you're troubled about what happened a few days ago. I *know* you; you're not going to rest until you come to terms with what you did. About what it has done to us. So I think it would be best if you let the others continue the search and you came to Washington. We need to talk."

Ryan shook his head. She was right. They needed to have a serious heart to heart about what he had done to her. But right now? He couldn't even let himself think about leaving. The temptation was too great.

On the screen, Nadja's face smiled softly. "Ryan, I know you think this is a bad idea, but you need some closure on this issue. We need to get it behind us, and . . . and there are other needs we should talk about. Like *my* need to have you near. If you've seen the news, you know things have gone over the top around here, and I need to talk to you, face to face."

Ryan's heart was breaking. Since Nadja had returned to Washington a few days ago, he hadn't been watching the news, had actually been trying to avoid any thought of her at all. He had been trying to convince himself that nothing mattered but his mission, nothing mattered except finding Burnout's body and recovering the Dragon Heart. Still, he hadn't been able to stop thinking about Nadja and the fact that he'd nearly killed her for the Heart. His thoughts were filled with shame and regret, but it seemed as if there was nothing he could do about it.

"Ryan, I know it would be hard for you to leave right now, but please consider my proposal. A break might be just the thing you need to put yourself in the right frame of mind to find the Heart and accomplish your goal."

Ryan found himself listening not so much to her words, but to that soothing tone. Maybe she was right.

"I *am* right about this. Think about what Dunkelzahn would have advised if he were here."

That was the key, Ryan knew. Because he didn't have any slotting clue what Dunkelzahn would have advised.

Perhaps Nadja's right, he thought. *Perhaps she knows what the dragon wanted better than I.*

Nadja leaned in close, the screen filling up with just her eyes, sparkling like dew-covered drops of green glass. "Please, for both of our sakes, come back for a few days."

The screen went dark, and Ryan found that he held his wristphone very close to his face. Instead of Nadja's face, he caught his own reflection in the black screen. Huge, bruise-colored crescents seemed to swallow his silver-flecked blue eyes, telling of days without sleep. His rugged face held the beginnings of a beard, but that did nothing to hide the gaunt hollow of his cheeks and the tight grimace that chiseled lines into his mouth and jaw.

Ryan's wiry auburn hair was unkempt, and he ran thick, callused fingers through the tangle to smooth down some of the more errant strands. He looked like someone who needed a break.

Suddenly, Grind's raspy voice came over the Phillips tacticom earphone—a tiny unit that fit snugly into his ear and linked by mimetic tape to a flesh-toned throat mic and transmitter unit at his belt. The Phillips was a military-type system capable of scrambling transmissions with encryptions that were very hard to break. "Quicksilver," Grind said, calling Ryan by his code name. "We got company coming."

Ryan looked around, concentrating on his magically heightened sense of hearing. There, just over the rush of wind roaring through the canyon, he could make out the distinctive rhythmic thrum of helicopter rotors. "Number and distance?"

Grind was a dwarf, a combat and weapons expert who had served in a number of mercenary efforts before catching the attention of Dunkelzahn a few years ago. He was currently manning the compound's defenses. "Three bogeys just passed the southern radar. They're coming fast, attack formation, heading directly for us."

Ryan started running back to the entrance to the underground compound. "Have Dhin pull back his drones. Get Axler out of the canyon. I don't know who these slots are, but I want to be ready for them."

"Copy," Grind said, with just a hint of excitement in his voice.

Ryan made it to the newly cut entrance to the compound just as Axler swept up over the lip of the cliff in the Northrup Wasp single-man chopper. Axler landed the helo and climbed out. She walked to meet Ryan at the entrance.

Axler was a human woman of about twenty-five. Very attractive with shoulder-length blonde hair and doe-brown eyes. Ryan knew she bore a great many cybernetic enhancements under her plycra bodysuit, but none were visible on the surface. All very discreet.

Axler's usually hard-set expression was slack from fatigue. "I got the buzz from Grind," she said. A hint of strain behind her words told Ryan just how hard she'd been pushing herself. She was nearing the edge.

Grind appeared at the door next to Axler. The black-skinned dwarf came up to her elbow, but was easily as wide. He was heavily muscled with obvious cyberarms painted the matte-gray color of old navy ships. Grind's afro hair was cut close to his head.

"You two ready to lock and load?"

"I was ready the day they cut me out of my mama's belly," said Grind, with a laugh.

"Axler?"

Her tone was cool. "Ready if you are."

Ryan didn't bother to respond to the subtle insult behind her words. She hadn't given him her complete trust since he'd tried to take sole possession of the Dragon Heart and had faced off with Nadja. And Axler was slotted off because he had taken the leadership of Assets Inc. away from her. She hadn't said anything overt, but Ryan knew. Axler was an excellent general, but not such a good soldier.

Ryan put all that out of his mind and got to biz. "All right," he said. "We've got three unknown bogeys in an offensive posture. If they attack from the air, we'll blow them out of the sky. Dhin?"

The ork rigger's voice sounded calm and steady over the tacticom. "Ready to go drones-up at your signal."

"Copy. If they're hostile, Dhin's drones will take point, and we'll smoke them in a standard one by two, starting with the lead craft."

"Copy," said Grind and Axler in unison.

"If they land, we'll play it straight. Remember, Jane has registered us as an official weather observation station. So we'll take that angle."

Suddenly, the three helicopters broke the horizon, coming up over the rim of the canyon wall. And they weren't ordinary helos. Ryan recognized all three as Aztechnology Aguilar-EX military choppers. Very high-powered, lots of weapons and extremely expensive. They had ridden with sound suppression and had come in against the wind so that Ryan hadn't known they were so close until it was too late.

These people are professionals.

"Frag it!" Ryan keyed his wristphone. "Dhin, you got them?"

Dhin's rumbling growl wasn't quite as calm as it had been. "Yeah. What the frag are they doing here already?"

"I got a bad feeling about this, folks. Stay sharp. Especially you, Dhin. If things get ugly, you need to put enough firepower in the air to stop that drek from getting anywhere near us."

"Making no promises, Bossman. The Azzies build one tough bird, but at the very least, I'll be able to slow them down."

Ryan watched as the three attack helicopters made their first pass. Like giant insects they buzzed past the cliff face, the red jaguars painted on their sides glittering in the sun. They broke from their attack formation. The lead helicopter made for the landing pad, while the other two took up defensive positions, hovering near the far wall of the canyon.

Dust from the landing pad twisted into a small cyclone as the big chopper settled its weight on the duracrete. The pilot cut the engines, and the flying dirt settled back to earth. The small hatch on the near side of the chopper popped upward, and a small man stepped out, followed by two other humans.

Ryan concentrated, and his vision shifted to the astral. *Chromed, almost beyond the pale,* he thought as he watched the dead parts of their aura. He relaxed and his vision shifted to normal.

"Smiles, everybody," he whispered. "We're playing it straight. If things get sticky, go to diversion plan beta."

With Axler and Grind at his back, Ryan stepped forward, forcing his lips into a wide grin.

The man in front was short, less than a meter and a half, stocky and muscled like a very large dwarf, but he was human. He walked briskly, his spine straight, his shoulders back, and he wore a black jumpsuit that didn't quite cover the heavy body armor underneath. The red Jaguar patch looked like a spot of dried blood over his heart.

Everything about him screamed military, as did the bearing of the two warriors behind him. The shorter man stepped up to Ryan, his charcoal eyes sizing him up in much the same way Ryan was doing to him.

His weather-burned face was dark, swarthy, and his toothy grin was wide, even though there was no humor behind those black eyes. The man stretched out his hand. "I'm sorry for disturbing your work, Señor," he said in a deep voice, heavy with an Aztlan accent. "This won't take long."

Ryan shook the man's hand, which was dry and warm, the grip relaxed and friendly. Ryan forced himself to match the man's grin. "I'm in charge of station security. We don't get too many visitors. It's a nice break from the routine. How can we help you?"

They both dropped the handshake at the same time. Ryan looked over the man's head to the two guards, who were scanning the area like professionals. Their body posture held a high-tension stiffness. They were ready for battle at the slightest provocation.

Ryan just hoped Axler and Grind were pulling off the relaxed look better than their counterparts.

The man's smile dropped. "This is a very delicate situation, and I hope I can count on your discretion."

Ryan looked over at the Aztechnology attack chopper

and nodded. "Seems like you've come quite a distance, maybe a bit *too* far, but I'm sure we can keep this visit quiet. As long as you're not here to . . . acquire any information regarding our weather satellites."

The short man laughed, a clipped, strangled sound, as if his throat was unused to the action. "I am General Dentado, and I can assure you, Mister . . ."

Ryan forced his grin again, "Deacon, Phillip Deacon."

The smaller man smiled, a slow secretive gesture that indicated he saw through Ryan's facade. "I can assure you, Mister Deacon, that we have no interest in your satellites." He looked at Azler and Grind. "May I have a word with you . . . in private?"

Ryan nodded, and the two walked to the edge of the cliff.

"Mister Deacon, my country has lost a very valuable piece of hardware, and I'll be honest with you, our last trace of him was near this very site. I have no idea what he was doing here, or why, but we do know he was here."

Ryan shook his head. "I thought you said you lost a piece of hardware."

"I did."

"Then why are you referring to your hardware as a 'he'?"

Dentado's smile was tight and dangerous. "Once again, I'm going to be forced to rely on your discretion. Have you seen anyone out of the ordinary around here in the last couple of days? He would be hard to miss, as he is quite large."

Ryan stopped walking. "I still don't get it. Did this guy *steal* some hardware from you?"

The smaller man's face took on a look of impatience. "Just answer the question, Mister Deacon."

Behind him, Ryan heard the rustle of clothing and the distinctive sound of an automatic weapon's slide being pulled. Both he and the Azzie turned, the smaller man just a bit slower than Ryan.

The picture before Ryan was a still tableau of impending violence. Axler and one of the Aztechnology guards stood face to face, the muzzle of Axler's Predator digging a groove in the man's neck as the guard's pistol jammed into her sternum.

Grind had dropped to one knee, his Colt Manhunter dead-set on the second guard's forehead. The second guard was trying to play it cool, but Ryan could tell he was jumpy.

"Nobody move!" yelled Ryan.

"At ease!" said General Dentado.

Ryan turned to the small man. "Have your men back off. We don't want any trouble."

The swarthy man looked up at him with a cocked eyebrow. "For a man who is so large, you seem to have a fear of direct confrontation. Tell me what I wish to know or I will have all of you killed. It is as simple as that."

Ryan nodded. "All right, yeah, your guy was here. About three days ago. He stole a chopper and bugged out before we could catch him."

Dentado looked Ryan over, and for a second Ryan felt that his aura was being scanned. Then Dentado nodded and turned to his men. "Rico, stand down."

The man who was face to face with Axler didn't take his eyes off her as he said, "But, General, this woman is—"

"I don't care, Captain. Stand down!"

The man slowly removed his pistol from Axler's chest.

"Axler," called Ryan. "Back off."

With a deadly smile, she lowered the Predator. "This is a dangerous place, Captain," Axler said. "It would be a shame if something happened to you."

Both Axler and Grind stepped back to a little more than five meters, but both still held their weapons at the ready.

General Dentado turned back to Ryan. "I appreciate your cooperation, and I apologize for the overzealousness of my officers. You should also count yourself lucky that you were not able to intercept the man in question, otherwise I would have been having this pleasant little discussion with a corpse."

Ryan shook his head. "You got what you came for, now get the frag out. If I see your ships on the radar again, I'll be on the horn to my government so fast they'll take you down before you hit the canyon."

General Dentado smiled. "I'd expected nothing less. By

the way, I hope your . . . weather research goes well. Good day, Mister . . . Deckerd."

"Deacon."

"Of course. My apologies." With that, the short man headed for the chopper, followed closely by the two guards, who walked backward, weapons still drawn.

Within minutes, they were gone.

Ryan walked over to Axler and Grind, who were talking and laughing. "Nicely played, you two."

Grind turned. "Thanks, Quicksilver. I think we were about a half beat too late, but it was difficult to read your body language."

Ryan shook his head and smiled. "No, any sooner and he would have known something was up. You were both right on."

Axler shook her head. "Those boys were good. When we made our move, I would stake all the chrome I've got that they were just waiting for us to make a play."

Ryan nodded, and looked at the skyline where the choppers had disappeared. "I got the same feeling."

"They were looking for Burnout, weren't they?" said Grind.

"Yeah. Probably want to recover his tech. That drek is expensive." Ryan winced. "They know we were lying about this being a weather station," he said. "But I think they bought our story about him hitting us and disappearing."

Axler shook her head again. "I got the distinct feeling we'll be seeing those boys again."

"Me, too," said Grind.

Ryan turned his back on them, the familiar pain working at his gut. Fatigue hitting him suddenly in the pouring sunshine. He was tired of the unending search for Burnout. Tired of staring into the unchanging maw of Hells Canyon. He was tired of the mission Dunkelzahn had left him.

Maybe Nadja's right. Maybe I should take a break from this place and settle things with her. Maybe that's what Dunkelzahn would have told me to do.

In the sky, the sun rose high into the washed-out blue above the mountains. *But can I afford to leave now? What if General Dentado finds Burnout before I do? What if Aztechnology gets the Dragon Heart?*

He didn't know what to do. He was unused to indecision; he was a man of focused action. A weapon, guided by Dunkelzahn.

Nadja will know, he thought. *She will help me think this all through.*

Provided she doesn't hate me for almost killing her.

2

It had been a long and rough trek from the depths of Hell, beginning several days ago. Lethe would never forget it. The sensation of drowning as Burnout's body sank to the bottom of the Snake River, until his compressed air supply automatically kicked in to keep the organic parts oxygenated.

It was incredible that this body was still alive, if barely. The cyberzombie had a number of built-in devices like the air tank nestled into his artificial torso, all designed to keep it going under adverse conditions. In fact, as far as Lethe could tell, the only natural tissue remaining were Burnout's spinal column and part of his organic brain. His limbs were mechanical, his torso was man-made, and all his internal organs had been replaced with a battery pack and a system of some sort to deliver food and oxygen to the organic nervous system.

A dull sound had come then to Burnout's cybernetic ears, and Lethe had heard it. Lethe listened to the muted throb and realized that it was a boat. If he could move the metal limbs enough to push to the surface, perhaps he could latch on and save the Dragon Heart.

Lethe discovered that, with Burnout unconscious, the body obeyed his will. He pushed off the bottom and succeeded in latching onto the jet boat. They traveled nearly forty-five kilometers upriver in less than an hour. It was dark when the boat docked, and Burnout's compressed air supply was quickly vanishing.

Lethe had made the body stagger onto a gravel beach and hide among a jumble of boulders. The moon rose a few hours later—a bloated, blood-colored thing that clung to the horizon like a maleficent boil.

Burnout had slowly drifted back into consciousness. And as the man's spirit awakened, Lethe lost control over the machine. He became a trapped passenger again, an inmate in the body of a chrome killing machine. Burnout seemed confused, lost, for the first few minutes after he regained consciousness. He had no idea where he was or how he had gotten there.

It took Lethe a moment to realize that the cyberzombie believed himself to be dead, that the machineman had fully expected the fall to kill him. Even though Burnout had come to rely on the near indestructibility of his metal coil, his mind still found it inconceivable that anything, even a being such as himself, could survive that fall.

Lethe sensed a great feeling of relief in Burnout at this thought, that some great weight had been lifted from the man's shoulders. But then Burnout became fully aware of his surroundings, exerted his will, and called up an internal mechanism he referred to as his GPS—Global Position System.

Within seconds, Burnout had his exact coordinates, took in the entire situation, and formulated a crude plan. That was when the Dragon Heart made its presence felt, still clutched in the twisted chrome remains of Burnout's telescoping fingers.

For a moment, Burnout remained rigidly still, then began to laugh. It started as a low chuckle and gradually grew to a shrill whooping screech until Lethe couldn't tell if it was laughter or a cry of pain. It continued for long enough that Lethe began to wonder if the fall had not somehow unhinged the creature's frail mind.

Lethe nearly panicked again. Being trapped was torture enough, but to be prison mates with an insane animal . . . It was horrifying. Lethe focused his will and tried to exert control over the body, and actually managed a faltering half-step before Burnout's laughter stuttered and wound down to a dry chuckle.

The man didn't seemed to notice his own involuntary movement, but simply lifted the Dragon Heart and held it before him at arm's length. The blood light of the moon shone on the heart-shaped orb of golden orichalcum. "So I beat you after all, Ryan Mercury," Burnout said softly.

"I'll give you credit—you were the closest thing to a challenge I've had in years, but in the end, I stole your magic."

Then something changed in him. Lethe could sense a coldness radiating from the man's aura, a sense of flowing rage. "No. I came away with the prize, but you still beat me, didn't you?"

Lethe couldn't understand the icy hatred he felt coming from Burnout. After all, Burnout had defeated Ryan, and in the final counting he had the Dragon Heart. Suddenly, it came to him, almost as if he could discern the intense thoughts in Burnout's mind. Burnout had snatched this victory from the jaws of defeat, and the man hadn't known defeat in combat since becoming this nightmare of magical metal contradiction. To him, victory was almost more important than gaining the Heart.

Lethe also understood one thing more, something he guessed was just sinking into Burnout's mind. Ryan was still out there, in possession of resources, manpower, and weapons that even the cyberzombie, killing machine that he was, couldn't hope to match. Burnout was on his own, while Ryan had a veritable army with which to trace, track, and finally run to ground even the most formidable enemy.

Burnout was beginning to realize he hadn't come close to winning yet, and victory would never truly be his until Ryan Mercury had been ground to dust beneath his heel. Quickly, Burnout wrapped the Dragon Heart in a strip of camouflage that he tore from his vest and lashed to his belt. He then took a rapid inventory of himself, discovering that he was in surprisingly good shape, all things considered. His telescoping fingers were jammed or sheared off, essentially useless, and his left shoulder showed a slight limit in motion due to a bent servo. His magnetic generator wasn't functioning, either. In the places where his body plating showed through the ruin of his black outer garments, his vat-grown skin had been abraded down to the dermal sheathing, which gleamed red in the light of the full moon.

"Not too slotting bad," he muttered to himself. "In fact, I feel more coherent and human than I've felt since . . .

since I sold my soul to those Azzie hatchetmen. Maybe it's the Heart."

Burnout continued checking himself over. "What's this?" he said. "I have access to my articulate arm." Lethe felt a thrill of excitement pass through Burnout as a third arm tore itself from the fabric covering the man's back and arced into position above his head. A rotor-barreled weapon sat on the end of it, the cartridges of ammo full and ready to fire. "That fall must have short-circuited the lockout."

The cyborg activated the weapon, and the barrel whined as it spun, but he didn't fire any bullets. Then he seemed to notice something else, and he shut down his arm and stowed it away into its cavity in his back. "Need to power up soon," he said. "Battery reserves will only last another few days of travel. Considering the terrain, that should be just about enough."

Lethe found it comforting when Burnout spoke his thoughts aloud. It gave the spirit a way to judge the man's constantly shifting aura.

They had begun to travel then, making incredibly fast time, given the rough ground they were forced to cover. Swiftly, they journeyed up a narrow crevice to the top of the canyon's precipice.

They had traveled day and night, without rest. Only pausing when Burnout's hypersensitive hearing told of an air vehicle passing overhead. At these times, Burnout burrowed into whatever soft earth was available, digging himself in like an animal, covering himself in as much vegetation as possible to mask his presence from sensors that could detect his heat, from magic that could trace his aura. He knew such efforts were feeble at best, but thought every possible measure might just be the one that left him undetected.

By the second day, they had come over the mountains and down to the edge of the Salmon River, a broad expanse of water sluicing by the lush bank like a serene serpent. Burnout hesitated long enough to fill his liquid reserve tank. And as he bent to the languid water, Burnout got the first clear picture of what was left of his face. What stared back at him out of the dark water didn't resemble anything living. It was a gruesome mixture of scarred chrome and bits of dried, hanging vat flesh.

The sight horrified Lethe, but for some reason Burnout found the picture grimly amusing. "All right, Mercury." Again, his voice was soft, dangerously gentle. "You've thrown your best at me, and I'm still here. But the next time we come face to face, it won't be Burnout you're looking at. I'm the boogie man now. I'm your worst nightmare, come to life. One look at me, and you'll know Death has come knocking."

Then he laughed and continued filling his tanks.

It seemed to Lethe at the time that he had become mere baggage. Any chance he had of controlling Burnout only occurred when the man's consciousness was gone or when his focus slipped so much that he ceased to be aware of his surroundings. Only then could Lethe slip through the neural connection to make contact with the silicon interface.

However, as they crossed the river, Burnout's attention focused on moving as swiftly as possible over the long stretch of open ground to get back under the cover of the dense pines. In those moments, Lethe sensed something approaching them, something traveling on the astral, something dark, dangerous, and malignant.

When Lethe turned to face the presence, he knew it for what it was. It was a two-legged creature that seemed to be formed of clotted blood. The thing came after them in a low, shuffling crouch.

Where the monster's skin showed cracks, dark blood oozed like crimson oil from the crevices. It was a blood spirit, summoned from the sacrificed remains of a living metahuman. As spirits went, it was paltry, especially in comparison to Lethe, and with free movement, banishing it would have been a simple task. However, trapped within the confines of the spirit net, Lethe could not bring his power to bear.

"Be gone," Lethe told the spirit. "This being is none of your concern and soon will be gone. Let us pass in peace."

It must have been sent to find Burnout, he thought. Lethe realized that the spirit had been able to track them by the smudge of polluted astral space Burnout left behind him wherever he traveled.

"Be gone," Lethe told the spirit. "This being is none of your concern and soon will be gone. Let us pass in peace."

A dry, barking roar was all the response he got.

Burnout still ran across the asphalt, moving at extreme speed, dodging deep craters and broken rock with grace and ease. He was totally oblivious to the spirit swiftly overtaking him. Unaware that he was being hunted by a power that could destroy him no matter what physical prowess he had.

As the creature approached, Lethe became desperate. Desperate to let Burnout know what was happening, hoping the wily human had just one more trick he could pull out of thin air. Lethe exerted his will on Burnout, trying to alter the cyberzombie's path so he would be able to take notice of what was gaining on them, but Burnout was too focused, too intent on his goal.

The stench of the spirit threatened to overwhelm Lethe with its palpable reek of pure evil, and it was just a few meters from Burnout, manifested in the physical planes, its long rock hands outstretched to grab, rend, and destroy.

"Burnout! Behind you!" It was an involuntary cry. And like a distant echo, Lethe heard the ringing of his words deep in Burnout's mind.

The cyberzombie didn't even hesitate. With action faster than thought, he threw himself to the side, mid-stride, and rolled, coming to rest into a crouch. Chrome blades snapped from his forearms, and his articulate third arm emerged from its cavity and swept up into position above his head. The machine gun began to whine, and suddenly the still air was filled with the roar of gunfire as the weapon belched rounds in an almost continuous spray.

The blood spirit roared. It was a sound of surprise and anger, but held no note of pain, despite the barrage of heavy rounds disappearing into the gelatinous red flesh. Then it was on them. In one ungainly leap, it landed on the spot where Burnout had been crouching moments before.

The cyberzombie moved, anticipating the attack, dodging away in a reverse one-handed cartwheel. He slashed at the blood spirit with the blade of his cyberspur as he retreated. The machine gun quickly rotated to keep up its punishing barrage of lead.

While bullets seemed to have minimal effect, Burnout's blades swept along the surface of the inside of the spirit's thigh, and Lethe saw a thin gash appear, and more dark ooze seeped from the wound. This time when the creature howled, the true sound of pain was unmistakable.

The creature counter-attacked in a burst of blinding speed. The blood spirit dove at Burnout, its arms outstretched. It caught Burnout around the waist.

Suddenly every part of Lethe was on fire. The evil burned at his core, tortured his very essence. He screamed, and his cry was matched by Burnout's as the spirit began to squeeze, ignoring the swift mechanical slashing of Burnout's oral spurs along its neck and face.

Lethe struggled, pushed like never before, straining to get away from the pain. The putrid evil. He pushed at the confines of the gossamer mesh that held him inside Burnout. Lethe focused his entire being in one direction, straining to break even just one of the magical strands.

The strand didn't break, but instead, it stretched. Pushing away from the physical confines of Burnout's body, away from the pain. Lethe concentrated his effort, and suddenly he came into contact with the Dragon Heart.

Like cool water in the desert, the Heart soothed his parched being, filling him with its glorious, pure power. Without thinking, Lethe used the Heart as a conduit for his power, lashing out with a blaze of pure energy, searing the blood spirit into bits, scattering its essence to the astral wind.

Burnout dropped to the earth, and lay still for a moment. Then he spoke, loudly. "I know a banishment when I see one. Where are you? Show yourself."

Lethe was slowly pulled back into the confines of the magical net. He tried to remember just what he'd done to communicate his earlier warning to Burnout. He directed his speech into Burnout's memory. "There is no need to fear."

A cybernetic circuit kicked in this time, and Lethe sensed his words dropping into the man's mind via the interface.

Instead of relaxing, this only made Burnout roll into a crouch again, the weapon on his third arm turning this way and that, searching for his nonexistent opponent. "How the frag are you activating my IMS? I don't take kindly to people fragging with my mind, or my cyber. Now show yourself."

"I am called Lethe, Burnout, and am incapable of showing myself because I have no physical body."

"A damn ghost." Burnout muttered as he stood. "Never heard of a damn ghost wielding that kind of power before. Well, wherever you are, I guess I owe you one, both for the warning, as well as the banishment."

The machine translated. "I'm no ghost, and I'm guessing you might be less thankful when you learn the real truth."

"Don't frag with me, you ethereal slot. I gave my thanks, now I'll be on my way. Stop me if you can, otherwise leave me alone."

Lethe sighed, not really expecting the machine to translate the sound, but wasn't surprised when it did. "I can neither stop you, nor can I leave you alone. Had I suspected I could use this IMS device inside you to communicate, I would have made my presence known days ago."

"Invoked Memory Stimulator," Burnout muttered as he pushed himself into motion again.

"What?"

"The IMS," Burnout said. "It stimulates my memories when my spirit starts to drift. Or at least that's what they said it does. Hasn't kicked in since the fall."

"Maybe that's because of me."

"Tell me about it."

As they moved, Lethe unraveled the story of the fall. How he had possessed Burnout to protect the Dragon Heart. How he was trapped inside. Lethe spoke about being able to move Burnout's body when the cyber-zombie lost consciousness, about latching onto the jet boat and pulling them out of the river.

"So that's how I escaped Mercury. I guess I owe you

more than just one." Burnout's tone was happy for the first time. But he didn't speak again for a long time, and it seemed to Lethe as though the man was thinking.

"Burnout," Lethe said. "I think that blood spirit was sent to find you. But I don't think it was sent by Ryan."

"So the Azzies are looking for me, too," Burnout said. "That scans true. The spirit was trying to knock me out. I'm worth a lot to them."

"I've started to mask the trail you leave in the astral," Lethe said. "It's not invisible, but it'll be a lot harder for spirits and mages to find us."

"You can do that?"

"My strength is limited in here, but I'll do my best."

"Thanks," Burnout said. "Though I don't like owing debts to anyone."

For the first time, Burnout made a camp of sorts that night at the bottom of a sheer rock face that stretched several hundred meters up into the air. They talked until almost dawn, speaking of how to best evade discovery by Ryan Mercury or Aztechnology. They also discussed where they could find a safe haven, but never strayed too far from the topic of the Dragon Heart. Burnout was fascinated by the artifact, by the power that he could feel, could almost touch, but that remained just beyond his grasp.

"When the blood spirit got me," Burnout said, "and you banished him, I felt the power. Almost like I was part of the magic. I haven't felt that familiar tingle since . . ."

Burnout sat bolt upright. "Of course. I should have thought of that before."

Lethe sensed excitement build inside Burnout, anticipation.

Burnout stood, and looked up at the stars. "I wasn't always like this. That sounds obvious, but the truth isn't. You see, I used to be a mage. I used to talk with spirits like yourself, used to control those spirits."

This admission stunned Lethe. He knew that the metal in Burnout's body decimated magical ability and couldn't understand how any mage would sacrifice magic to become this abomination. "Why did you change?"

Burnout's voice turned far away. "It wasn't purposeful.

Just a progression of small adjustments, each seemingly innocuous. Until my magic was as dry as the desert wind. I've always been the best at what I do, so when all I had left was my physical abilities, I taught myself how to kill with my hands. I learned how to use weapons, and eventually, I sold myself to Aztechnology in exchange for . . . for this life. If you can call it that." Burnout shook his head. "I haven't thought about it much since the cybermantic operations. In fact, I haven't thought much at all."

"I'm sorry."

Burnout's voice was harsh with furor. "Don't pity me, spirit. I can't stomach it."

"But you feel some of the magic now?"

"Yes, it feels the same as just before I first learned to tap into my Art. And that is why we're going to Pony Mountain. To see the Kodiak."

"The Kodiak?"

"Yes. He is a very powerful shaman who follows the Bear totem. He was the first to recognize the magic in me. I lived with him for a few months when I was a child."

Lethe was confused again. "A few months? Seems too short for a student to learn magic."

Burnout shrugged, and sat again, propping his back against the cliff face. "Well, things didn't work out quite like the Kodiak had hoped. Even though I tried my best, I couldn't contact any form of totem. Something seemed off kilter about his methods of magic. Finally he told me I would have to leave. Almost broke my heart. I thought I was a failure. But he took me by the hand, and led me to top of Pony Mountain. We looked out on the deep valley, and he told me that there was more than one avenue to power. That my gift was different from his, and if I wanted to tap that gift, I would have to find a new teacher. One who practiced my form of the craft."

Lethe sighed. "Why do you wish to go back now?"

"Don't you see? The Heart is like this universal piece of magic, something either shaman or mage can tap into. Maybe all I need to do is relearn the path. Maybe the Kodiak can teach me a new path so I could tap into its power."

Lethe remained silent, but he was deeply troubled.

Burnout was talking just like Ryan Mercury now. However, a glimmer of hope remained. If this shaman was as powerful and kind as Burnout had suggested, perhaps he could be persuaded to help extricate Lethe from Burnout's body or even to take the Dragon Heart to Thayla.

"What you say has merit, though it also seems as if you are setting yourself up for disappointment."

Burnout didn't respond.

"The Dragon Heart is powerful, perhaps the most powerful magical artifact that exists in the world today. But there is so much dead material inside you . . ."

Burnout nodded, and Lethe realized that if the cyber-zombie had human eyes still, he would be crying. "Yes. I kissed it all away. But I have to try. Even if there's only the slimmest chance, it'd be worth it.

"Besides, I'm up against a wall here. This is the only path that would give me an edge over Ryan. I know his type. He's not going to stop. He's going to keep coming, with more and more firepower until I go down. I have to do this."

Just then, the sun peeked over the edge of the cliff, sending brilliant light into the chilly, crystalline clear air smelling crisply of pine trees. Burnout climbed to his feet, extending thirty-centimeter blades from his forearm as he reached for the rock. The blades shot into the rock and anchored. Burnout put one foot up against the rock and held it as a long spike shot out of his heel and anchored into the rock.

"Time to move," said Burnout. Then he pulled himself up, and anchored the next step, beginning his assault on the cliff face.

They were about halfway up when they heard the unmistakable subsonic thrum of approaching helicopters.

3

In the approaching Lear-Cessna Platinum III, Ryan looked through the scratched macroglass. The flight from Hells Canyon had been uneventful and relatively smooth, giving him time to get nervous about seeing Nadja.

Can we ever be close again? he wondered.

The endless city sprawled over the land below. Corporate arcologies and Federal high-rises of blue and silver glass clustered together in the distance as the jet approached, their shine dulled by the haze of blood-colored smog. Darkening in the late-afternoon sun.

Surrounding the cluster, the sprawl lay like a tiger . . . brought down by a pack of hyenas. The huge beast had been harried and scarred by a thousand tiny wounds, until it lacked the strength to fight or flee. It merely lay there bleeding its life into the rust-colored Potomac.

Riot-caused fires burned all over the ruined areas of the city, sending black smoke into the air. Outside the central cluster, tenements and low-slung office buildings were boarded up. Few residents walked the streets in the aftermath of Dunkelzahn's assassination. The only pedestrians to be seen were rioters, tight groups of heavily armed Federal police, and corporate security.

Ryan knew this city was not unique; it could be any of a thousand just like it. A thousand individual names— Newark, Philadelphia, Baltimore—but all one stretch of concrete and rebar. One never-ending metropolis that ranged from Boston to Atlanta.

It could be any city, but it wasn't. It was Washington FDC, the seat of government for the United Canadian and American States. The city where Dunkelzahn was assassinated. Until his untimely death two weeks earlier, the

great dragon Dunkelzahn had been Ryan's master—his
benefactor, teacher, father figure, and friend. Ryan missed
the old wyrm.

"Bossman, we're going in to National Airport. Heart of
the Federal cluster, and it looks like there are limos
waiting on the runway. Miss Daviar must have pulled
some serious strings to bypass security like that." Dhin's
tusky growl was full of good humor this afternoon. Happy
to have a break from the exhausting routine of Hells
Canyon. "I just love having friends in high places."

Ryan nodded, though Dhin couldn't see him. Nadja,
sweet Nadja, with all the shakedown from Dunkelzahn's
will, she had enough clout to pull strings all over the
world. Before Dunkelzahn's death, she had been the
dragon's voice, translating his telepathic speech into
vocals for the world. She had also managed his presiden-
tial campaign with intensity and extreme intelligence.

But now, in the aftermath of the assassination, Nadja
had become the head of the Draco Foundation, a new
megacorporation founded from the dragon's major hold-
ings. She was also the current nominee for vice-president
of UCAS. One tiny tug from her immaculately manicured
fingers, and people in the farthest corners of the Awakened Earth jumped to do her bidding.

Ryan smiled as he thought about Nadja, the beauty of
her face, her curvaceous body, her hard-line sense of duty,
her keen intellect and ordered mind, her aura of command.
All these things she had, and all of these things she had
offered to him without reservation, with a deep abiding
love and trust that threatened to take his breath away. It
stunned him that a woman of such personal prowess could
turn so gentle, so tender in those few moments they had
alone together.

At least that was the way it had been before . . .

With a dull thump and the high whine of braking jets,
the Platinum III kissed the tarmac. Ryan gathered up his
suitcase, and stood, buttoning his double-breasted shark-
skin suit coat. On the outside, he looked like any other
high-powered exec, but underneath the corporate broker
disguise, Ryan was unadulterated flesh and magically
enhanced muscle. Beneath the Armanté tailoring was an

arsenal to make a weapon-fetishist drool with envy. Guns and darts, grenades and knives, all hidden from view.

The jet rolled to a stop, and Ryan moved to the front of the cabin, meeting Dhin as the ork exited the cockpit. In Dhin's gnarled face, Ryan saw a mirror of his own exhaustion. Dhin was dressed in a brown suit that seemed a bit too small for the big ork, straining at the bulge of his chest and arms, but Ryan knew that was deceptive. The suit very effectively hid the twin nickel-plated Savalette Guardian pistols under each armpit. Dhin's scarred lips cracked into a grin, showing yellow fangs and a broken left tusk. "End of the line—everybody off."

The big ork pressed the stud that triggered the pressure door. Dull, wet heat swam into the cool cabin, bringing a familiar stench to Ryan's magically enhanced sense of smell. It was the stink of the battlefield, a burned, dead scent that bespoke tremendous violence and suffering.

Dhin wrinkled his flat nose, wide nostrils flaring. "Smells like something died out there."

Ryan nodded. "Something did." Then he stepped into the humid, oppressive afternoon.

As he descended the short steps to the hot tarmac, Ryan was aware of Dhin following closely behind, could picture the ork's body posture, eyes scanning the runway for possible trouble, one meaty hand buried in his suit jacket, ready to pull a Guardian at the first sign of something amiss. Playing his corporate bodyguard role to the hilt.

Ryan reached the ground, training and instinct sending his body into full alert, his senses testing every turn of the foul breeze, cataloging every possible vantage point from the nearby buildings where a sniper could find an attack position, infrared vision scanning for heat signatures in places where there shouldn't be any. His hearing automatically tuned out the dull background noises that come standard with a bustling airport, searching for that elusive sound, the one that didn't belong, the one that spelled danger.

Ryan concentrated as he stepped toward the two limousines, and his vision shifted into the astral, searching and scanning for threats. He found nothing out of the ordinary.

The limos were jet-black Mitsubishi Nightskys, their sleek bodies glossed to a high shine that fractured the sunlight into a rainbow of reflection. The side doors were embossed with the Draco Foundation logo, the image lasered and holographic, making it three-dimensional.

Ryan shook his head. He would rather have landed at one of the smaller, less prestigious airfields, and journeyed to Dunkelzahn's Georgetown estate in something a little less flashy. Like an armored step-van. But in corporate and federal dominated downtown DC, this cover was less conspicuous than anything else.

The near passenger door of the lead limo opened, and a thin human with white hair stepped up to meet them. The man was dressed in a suit similar to Ryan's, though it hung loose on the older man's whipcord frame. He smiled. "Mister Mercury?"

Ryan nodded and took the man's outstretched hand, which gripped his own like a dead fish—limp, damp, and soft.

"I'm Maxwell Hersh, assistant to Miss Carla Brooks. She wanted to greet you personally, but her new position on the Scott Commission has made her extremely busy. She sends her regards, and hopes your trip was smooth and uneventful."

Ryan grinned for the first time that day. Carla Brooks, a.k.a. Black Angel—Dunkelzahn's former head of security—had never composed a sentence half that long which didn't contain at least six expletives. Now, Carla served as chief of security for Nadja and the Draco Foundation as well as being part of the Scott Commission—a primarily political committee that was investigating Dunkelzahn's assassination. Ryan was glad of it. There was no one better.

Maxwell returned the grin as though he understood Ryan's thoughts about the political correctness of his boss. "She also left me some instructions, though she said you would probably countermand them, saying that I should persist, just up to the point where you are about to beat me half to death, then allow you to do whatever you feel is best. If it's all right with you, we'll skip the verbal sparring and get right to the point where you do what you want. Agreed?"

Behind Ryan, Dhin's barking laughter carried in the sluggish air.

Ryan smiled again; he felt better than he had in days. "Agreed," he said. "What were your instructions?"

Maxwell gestured to the limo. "The cars each come with a rigger. Under no circumstances am I to allow your companion to drive the limos. Miss Brooks seems to believe that if you're left to your own devices, you'll get into mischief of some kind. And . . ." Maxwell looked from Ryan to Dhin, sizing the ork up in one casual sweep, "And she also seems to think that if your companion is allowed in command of the controls, the Draco Foundation will soon be minus a very expensive luxury auto."

Dhin snorted. "Like they couldn't afford it."

Ryan stepped up to Maxwell and put his massive arm around the thin man's shoulders, turning him in the direction of the limo. "I'll be sure and tell your boss that you did your best to dissuade me from deviating from her schedule, and that you even threw your body in front of the limo to prevent us from doing anything foolish. However, as Carla correctly anticipated, my companion will drive. I assume you can find your way in the other vehicle."

Maxwell nodded and opened the rear door of the lead Nightsky for Ryan.

Dhin had already stepped to the driver's door, opened it, and motioned for the waiting driver to exit, which the woman did without so much as a blink.

"Many thanks, Maxwell. It was a pleasure meeting you."

"Likewise, Mister Mercury. May your journey be swift and its rewards be great."

Ryan smiled and closed the door. Within seconds, the heavy limo was exiting the front gate and pulling out into the sparse traffic of the corporate cluster. Alone in the rich interior, nestled into the plush seat that seemed to mold to every contour of Ryan's body, his good feeling started to fade. His mind refused to shut down, refused to let him relax.

Everything had gone wrong with the recovery of the Dragon Heart, and for the first time since the death of his parents, Ryan had failed. It was not a feeling he was used to, one he did not want to get used to. His stomach was in knots, and dull pain wracked his gut.

Dunkelzahn's message came back to him. The message relayed to Ryan several days ago by a spirit that had somehow been bound even after the dragon's death.

"Your mission," the spirit had said, speaking in a voice like Dunkelzahn's, "is to take the Dragon Heart to the metaplanes and give it to the one whose song protects the spike created by the Great Ghost Dance. She is called Thayla. I will repeat this once, Ryanthusar, because it is so important. Retrieve the Dragon Heart and deliver it to Thayla—the bridge must not be finished.

"In order to complete your task, you must enlist the service of a powerful mage who knows the ritual that can carry you and the Dragon Heart into the metaplanes. This mage must also be absolutely committed to this endeavor. Of all my friends, only two fit these criteria . . .

"I have taught you of the cycles of magic, but no one has dared manipulate them as our enemies do now, bringing this age to the brink of destruction so early in the mana cycle. The discovery of the Locus by Darke may be the single most devastating event in all of history. If the metaplanar Chasm is breached before we are ready, we will all suffer. All beings will die.

"*All* beings."

"My fellow dragons are overconfident, thinking they can hide in their lairs as they have always done. But when the Enemy comes, the monsters will be able to use the technology of our own time to locate and breach our lairs. No sentient creature is safe this time. When the mana level gets high enough, the chasm will grow narrower and narrower until the Enemy can cross without any bridge. But there will be no hiding this time. Technology changes everything. No magic can protect against it.

"This time there will be no hiding. There will only be war. We must build up our defenses; we must gain the time we need to build up *our* technology so that we have the ability to fight the Enemy when it can cross. But to gain that time we must protect our natural defenses. They must not be allowed to fail, and the Dragon Heart will ensure that they don't. Thayla will know how to use it. Get it to her before it is too late."

The spirit had vanished then, its task completed. And Ryan had been stunned. How could he be entrusted with such a responsibility?

I don't want it.

Ryan took a deep breath and sank into the cushions. The mission was too much, too daunting a task, and one he had no idea how to even begin.

Ryan had always been a weapon, wielded with extreme precision by the great dragon Dunkelzahn.

Now Dunkelzahn was dead. Gone in a massive explosion. Vaporized.

And while Ryan's edge was still sharp enough to cut, there was no hand to guide him. No hand but his own.

Ever since his ordeal with Roxborough, Ryan had been thinking on his own more and more. Thinking about what *he* wanted from life. Thinking about the comforts of life that other people had. Comforts like a home, a loving and stable relationship.

Comforts that Ryan had never allowed himself.

Dhin's voice cut the air of the limo's cabin. "Were you expecting company, Bossman? Seems we've picked ourselves up a tail."

Ryan sat upright. He took a breath and said, "Thanks, Dhin. Keep them in sight."

He touched his wristphone, punching in the code for Carla Brooks. After a second, the tiny screen filled with the platinum white hair, black skin, and sharp elven features. Her smile was warm, even though her tone was dry. "Well, well, Quicksilver, I see you still like to do things your way. I just got off the line with Maxwell—"

"No time for chat, Black Angel. Did you anticipate my actions and assign covert escort?"

Carla's smile faded, and her eyes narrowed. "You know me better than that. Those are not the kind of games you and I play with each other. I take it by the look on your face that you've picked up some unwelcome company."

Ryan nodded.

Carla's face took on a look of concern. "You want me to send an intercept team?"

Ryan shook his head. "We'll take care of them. Dhin's going to feed you the vehicle specs and all the info he's got on it. Track it from your end. If I don't hear back from you in three minutes, we'll move on them."

"Got it, Quicksilver. Good hunting." Carla's face faded from the screen.

Ryan took a second to remove his suit jacket, roll up his shirt sleeves, and pull the matte-black Ingram Warrior machine pistol from its trim pouch at his waist. He checked the slide clip, thirty rounds ready, one in the chamber. Ryan slid the silencer from its holster and screwed it onto the Ingram's barrel. As a physical adept, he followed the Silent Way, moving with silence and stealth whenever possible.

Ryan set the silenced Ingram on the seat beside him, then reached into the inner pocket of his suit coat for his MGL mini-6 grenade pistol, again popping the clip and checking the load. Six high-explosive rounds. By feel, he pulled another grenade clip from the pocket. Six white phosphorous grenades.

He jammed the WP clip home, and stuffed the clip of explosive rounds into the pouch that had held the Ingram. Ryan still had his usual bandolier of narcotic throwing darts that he would use preferentially. But if things didn't go the way he expected them to, the white phosphorous would burn his pursuers out of their vehicle, and the Ingram would do the rest. He just hoped it didn't come to that.

Three minutes passed without a word from Carla Brooks. Ryan looked into the front seat and spoke, "Dhin, status."

"They're still with us."

"Range?"

"They're hanging back about a quarter-klick."

They hadn't closed the distance; that in itself was strange. They must have known Ryan had tagged them.

Something nagged at the back of Ryan's mind, something he wasn't getting. He rubbed his eyes and cursed himself for not getting more sleep. He wasn't as sharp as he needed to be, and in the world of covert ops, a dulled edge was as good as a quick death.

In their place, Ryan would have done one of two things. Either split off and let a back-up team take over, provided there was one, and Ryan had to assume there was. If no back-up team was available, Ryan would have moved into strike position before the quarry had time to set up a defensive posture.

That nagging itch refused to go away, a familiar twitch he couldn't pin down. Almost a feeling of déjà vu. This set-up tasted familiar, but Ryan just couldn't place the flavor.

"Is there any chance of losing them?" Ryan asked.

Dhin's chuckle was cold and humorless. "In this boat? They're driving a modified Eurocar. Sleek, fast, and surprise, surprise, lightly armored. No chance we'd outrun or outmaneuver it."

"Do we have any drones aboard?"

After a pause, "Yeah. One."

"Surveillance or assault?"

Dhin laughed again. "Well, I guess assault would sum it up, 'cause that's all it can do. It's a modified Stealth Sniper II, but somebody with a firepower fetish has stripped all its armor off and replaced the sniper rifle with a minigun. She's packing hot loads, which should cut that Eurocar in half, armor or no armor, but one hit with so much as a fly swatter, and the drone will go down."

Ryan smiled.

"Bossman, you want me to force them off the road?"

Ryan gave that option quick consideration before discarding it. "No, the outcome would be too uncertain. Besides, in the downtown cluster, that's going to attract a lot of very unwelcome local heat."

Ryan leaned forward to the telecom and called up a street map of the heart of the DC sprawl. The contour grid appeared, showing their position on the George Mason Memorial Bridge. If Ryan took the time to look out the Nightsky's window, he knew he would see the smog-clouded sunlight sparkling off the polluted waters of the Potomac.

"All right, Dhin, here's the plan. Just after the Jefferson Memorial, take Fourteenth up past the White House."

"You going to have the Federal Police take care of them?" Dhin's voice held a note of incredulity.

"No, continue on up to K Street."

Dhin slaved his screen to Ryan's telecom display so that he could see what Ryan was talking about.

"See the corner here, right at Fifteenth?"

"Got it."

"Just before we get there, punch it. Take the corner as fast as this boat will travel. If I've got their MO down, they'll accelerate to try and keep pace. As you round the corner, pop the drone. The high-rise should shield the action. Round the far corner here." Ryan highlighted the next corner one block up, which crossed toward Fifteenth. "But make sure you do it slow enough for them to play catch up. At that point, hit this alley."

"Playing cat and mouse, Bossman?"

"Yeah, but this time the mice have very sharp teeth. The instant you hit the alley, stand on the brakes, and I'll bail out. Then punch it to the far mouth of the alley and stop, blocking the exit. When they round the corner, we'll have them in a vice. On my signal, hit them with the drone's minigun. Disable the car, but make sure the occupants are still able to walk and talk when you get through with them."

Dhin whistled. "Poor slots aren't even going to know what hit them."

"I hope you're right."

A minute later, Dhin spoke. "We're closing in on target area. Tail vehicle running true to form."

"Ready."

"Here we go!"

Ryan heard the dim squeal of tires on pavement as the acceleration pressed him back into the cushions. With one hand he grabbed the Ingram off the seat beside him, with the other he lifted the mini-6 from his lap.

"First corner!"

Even leaning into the turn, Ryan found himself slammed into the door as the limo fishtailed around the corner. Then he heard the sharp click as the drone was sprung from the trunk.

"Tail vehicle accelerating. Second corner!"

Ryan grabbed the door handle and prepared himself to bail.

"Alley entrance!"

Ryan rocked sideways and forward as Dhin took the corner and slammed on the brakes. Ryan pulled the handle and rolled with the motion of the limo out into the dim, dirty alley. He kept rolling until he crashed into a trash dumpster. Pain wracked his shoulder, but he ignored it and scurried behind the dumpster, using magic to mask himself and blend with the dank surroundings.

He did a quick weapons check as Dhin accelerated down the alley. Everything was still in its proper place.

A second set of tires squealed as the nimble Eurocar shot past him. Ryan saw two figures in the vehicle, and from their heat signatures, he guessed the driver to be an ork and the passenger to be human.

Dhin screeched to a halt at the far end of the alley, causing blue-gray smoke to pour from the tortured tires of the limo. The Eurocar did the same, and for a long moment, everything was silent.

Then the back-up lights on the Eurocar glowed white, and the little car shot backward.

Ryan keyed his wrist phone. "Now!"

The high-pitched whine of the minigun's rotating barrel screamed from five meters overhead as Ryan stepped into the middle of the alley, weapons raised. The thunder of hot rounds hitting armor roared through the narrow confines of the alleyway, deafening Ryan.

He watched as the front of the Eurocar disintegrated before his eyes. Metal and sparks showered the flanking buildings as the minigun perforated the car's engine compartment like hail through thin glass. In less than five seconds, it was all over. The Eurocar's engine surgically separated from the rest of the vehicle.

Ryan heard the minigun's barrel whine to a stop, and once again silence filled the alley. The after-echo of violence rang in his ears.

He stepped forward, Ingram raised. "Occupants of the

vehicle!" he shouted. "Step out of your car and keep your hands where I can see them."

There was a long pause, and slowly, the passenger-side door opened, and out stepped a tall, heavily built man of about forty-five, gray hair closely cropped to his skull. He wore light body armor covered by a short trooper's vest. The man's hands were above his head, and his brown eyes danced with a humor that was mirrored by the delighted grin on his face.

"Mister Mercury!" he said with a laugh, his familiar voice relaxed, comfortable. "It's lucky for us you happened by. There seems to be something wrong with our car. I told the management boys not to buy foreign—the damn things always seem to break down."

Oh, drek, thought Ryan as he lowered the Ingram. Suddenly he knew what that nagging itch had been trying to tell him. That sense of déjà vu.

4

Lucero's spirit walked the metaplanes with her master. She paced around inside a stained circle on a cracked plane of rock. The outcropping of magic that was protected by the song of the goddess.

She was the dark spot in the sea of light. She was its nucleus, its genesis. And somewhere in the recesses of her mind, she knew the stain of shadow could only exist against the onslaught of white because of her.

Earlier, she had thought that perhaps it was the voice of Quetzalcóatl singing, trying to cleanse her innate evil. But she doubted that even his power could rid her of the taint, the curse of her blood desire. Her yearning for its power.

Her blood addiction.

That dark stain on her soul refused to be washed away.

Lucero was in her astral form, much like her physical body. Naked skin covered with runic scars, shaved head. Once beautiful, now hideous.

She stopped pacing at the center of the blood-blackened earth. It was a tiny island of silence amid a sea of song. Beautiful music on an arching outcropping of stone.

The ground under Lucero's scarred feet was soaked with sticky, thick fluid that drenched her skin up to her ankles. Everything around her held the iron stench of the freshly dead.

A smooth, lifeless hand touched her leg with an almost erotic sensation, and she shuddered as she looked down at the grinning wound beneath the dead girl's throat. *So young,* thought Lucero. *So much life unlived.*

Lucero was drawn by a dark fascination. She knelt by the young girl and touched her fingers to the gaping wound, which still pulsed with the last quaver of life. This was the freshest victim, and her body radiated heat.

Lucero watched in detached, morbid fascination as her own fingers touched inside the viscous slash on the girl's neck. She felt slick warmth, and drew her hand back almost against her will, her fingers rising to her lips. Fingers covered in what was left of the child's blood.

A thrill of ecstasy shimmered through her as she smelled the iron tang, as she felt the dwindling life energy in the child's blood. Lucero could resist no longer and she plunged her fingers into her mouth, sucking greedily at the metal-tasting liquid that covered them. A hunger consumed her, and she found her fingers dipping again into the wound, found herself licking desperately at the blood that spilled down her hand.

As if in response, the music outside the small, dark shell rose to a crescendo so beautiful, so painful that Lucero stopped herself so that she could listen. The song spoke to her like the voice of goodness, revealing the horror of what she had been doing. It choked the hunger out of her.

Lucero stood, quickly, not risking a look down at the scatter of dead bodies that stretched around her. She was not alone in the circle of the dead. Señor Oscuro, her master, was with her, working feverishly. His blood-drenched blade flashed across throat after throat as the sweat streamed down his forehead and cheeks to drip into his dark beard.

Power radiated from his black eyes. His raven hair reflected the red glow of the blood power he drew from the victims he summoned from the physical world. Transporting them here by magic before making a sacrifice of their life energy.

Lucero watched as Oscuro approached and pulled the young girl's body up by the feet. He dragged her to the furthest edge of the circle, positioning the girl's head so that the blind, lifeless eyes looked outward, guarding the perimeter.

Lucero stood, numb. In her heart, she longed for the searing beautiful pain of the music. The purity that let her forget about the dark blotch on her soul, the cancer of her addiction.

Oscuro returned to the center of the circle, and called to her. "Lucero?" His soft voice seemed to ooze over her flesh, making it crawl. Yet part of her was comforted by the sheer evil she felt there. Hearing his voice made her corrupted soul feel more at ease.

She stepped forward, until she could smell the stench of blood and sweat that poured off the bearded man. "Yes, Master," Lucero said, with head bowed.

He touched a blood-smeared hand to her cheek. The feeling brought revulsion, even as the smell of the blood woke her hunger again, tearing at her mind, her sanity. "I must return to the physical world now," he said, tracing blood along both her cheeks, then her forehead, and lastly to her lips.

He seemed to be tempting her deliberately. She strained not to open her mouth, to lap at the fluid that stained his fingertips. "Yes, Master," she whispered, and slowly licked her bottom lip.

"The Gestalt has weakened to the point of collapse. The Locus is only partially active and it can only help them sustain me in this metaplanar location for so long. Now is the time for the test. I believe that I have done enough of the work to keep you here, but you must concentrate. You must keep the link open."

Lucero nodded.

"Be strong, child. Our work is nearly complete. Soon we will have reached the tip of the outcropping. And when we do, we will feel the power of the *tzitzimine*. They will help us finish the bridge and bring our allies across." His voice grew forceful. "Ah, that will be a glorious day. Our allies from across the Chasm will help us rule the world."

With that, he vanished. Traveling back to the physical world.

Lucero longed to be with him. Her master. She knew where he went in the physical world. He would appear in his body, high inside the step-pyramid *teocalli* in San Marcos. The temple's rock surface would be radiating warmth from the day's heat. The night hanging still and hot.

In Lucero's memory, the old amusement park tower stabbed up into the sky directly across from the *teocalli,* like a stiletto dipped in black blood. And below that was the spring-fed lake; it glowed a blue-green from the submerged floodlights. In the center of the lights was the Locus, a sharply chiseled stone of obsidian black.

Power emanated from the Locus. Even partially active, its force was palpable and crisp.

Lucero longed to tap into the stone's strength. An untainted magic that brought her hope that she might wield the mana again. That she might be as she once was, a manipulator of life energy. A mage.

If only I had another chance, she thought. *I would not accept the taint. The addiction to blood magic. The desperate need that stains my soul.*

Now, in the metaplanes, anchored on the bloody cracked rock in the middle of a black circle of corpses, Lucero collapsed. She stumbled and fell, landing on the first ring of bodies, her cheek resting on the childish breasts of an older girl. Her mouth just centimeters from a drying dollop of blood that rested on the girl's collarbone.

The music came again, roaring over the darkness. It punished her as it pleased her, its white heat purging all thoughts of evil from her mind. *Oh, great spirits,* she thought. *If only it could go on forever.*

The light cast garish shadows among the dead, its flickering making the young bodies seem to sway and dance in time to the music. To Lucero the shadows meant the piecemeal destruction of the light and the music—something so perfect, so painfully beautiful that she felt unworthy to be in its presence.

It's my fault, she cried silently. *I've done this to you through my blood lust. Without me, you would be safe, whole.*

Tears ran down her face. She cursed the darkness in her, and for the first time in her life, she prayed to something other than Quetzalcóatl, the great feathered one. She prayed now to the light. She prayed for it to kill her before Oscuro could use her to create more destruction.

Something happened in that moment. The pain of the song diminished, though the song itself grew louder. Her breathing eased. She gazed about in wonder. The dead were even more revolting than they had been a moment before, but the light . . . the light was glorious.

Her mind and heart rang with the beauty of it. It was still painful, but the pain had lessened to the point where she could think of other things besides her own delicious torment. She looked inwardly, and saw what she already knew to be true. The dark spot of her addiction was still there, perhaps it always would be, but it was different now.

The song was cleansing her soul. Turning her black heart to gray.

5

"Dhin," Ryan called to the far end of the alley. "Home the drone. Everything's chill."

Ryan watched as the sunlight flashed off the drone's carapace. The thing looked like a huge beetle, buzzing in the dirty air. Dhin guided it smoothly into a compartment in the trunk.

"Uh, Mercury?" The voice was deep southern molasses now. "You mind if I put my hands down? I'm not getting any younger, and I think all the blood is rushing to my heart. Be a tragedy if I keeled over before we had a chance to catch up."

Ryan turned to the speaker. The broad grin had turned into a wry, crooked smile, and the deep brown eyes held a certain intensity Ryan found vaguely disturbing.

"Frag you, Matthews. What's the Secret Service trying to do? Get you killed? If I'd played this differently, you'd be dead, and I'd be up to my short hairs in bureaucratic drek."

Matthews lowered his meaty hands, and dropped the smile as well. "Got to hand it to you, Mercury. You learned everything I taught you, and then just a mite more. Almost made a mess of my suit when I saw that limo come to a stop."

Suddenly Ryan felt tired. More tired than he could ever remember. The adrenaline rush was wearing off, and the shakes were setting in. His shoulder hurt, his gut hurt, and he felt an uneasy nausea creep into his stomach. "Yeah, whatever. I'm just glad this situation didn't get too ugly."

Matthews' smile was grim. "Well, actually, old friend, it's a tad uglier than I think you—"

He was interrupted by the sound of the Eurocar driver's

door opening. An ork stepped out, and Ryan watched in mild wonder. For her metatype, she was huge. It seemed like more and more of her just kept coming until Ryan couldn't believe she could possibly have fit into the car in the first place.

Well over two meters, she dwarfed the vehicle, and wore an outfit similar to Matthews. On her, however, it stretched and bulged, showing rippled muscles. She had a deep, ugly scar that stretched from the left corner of her mouth and traveled up to the ruin of her left ear. It looked like one of those wounds that should have killed.

"Ah, Mercury, I'd like you to meet my new partner." Matthews gestured from Ryan to the huge ork. "Mercury, this is Agent Phelps. Phelps, this is the infamous Ryan Mercury. Best student I ever had, even if he doesn't seem to realize it's bad form for the student to show up his teacher."

"New partner?" Ryan grinned. "So Edgefield finally got that elusive Secret Service desk job he kept talking about."

Matthews turned back to Ryan with a slow deliberate motion of his head. The intense look had returned.

Ryan's grin faltered.

"We put Bob in the ground two weeks ago. Had a big memorial service just day before yesterday. Should have been there, Mercury. It was real nice, lots of tears, lots of flowers."

The hair on the back of Ryan's neck started to rise, and some primal warning instinct flared. "I didn't know. I'm sorry."

Matthews arched one eyebrow. "You didn't know? I thought you were more in touch with the dirty underside of things in this fair city."

"I've been out of town for a while."

"You must have been far-side-of-the-solar-system out of town to have missed the trid coverage."

"He died in the assassination explosion?"

Matthews just nodded.

Ryan felt his shoulders sag. "Listen, I'm very sorry about Bob."

"Get the driver out of your vehicle." It was the first

time Phelps had spoken, and her deep ork voice dropped into the alley like a sheet of napalm. It was the voice of someone used to command, someone used to having those commands obeyed, and the implied threat in her tone made Ryan smile.

"We're going to wrap this up in a moment, Agent Phelps," Ryan said, "so just relax."

Then, in a movement so swift it was almost a blur, Phelps drew her Czech-made 88V assault rifle. A stubby, ugly weapon under the best of circumstances, the 88V looked even worse from the receiving end.

It took every drop of Ryan's control to stop himself from geeking her with a quick burst from his Ingram. She'd moved fast, surprisingly fast, but he'd caught the tiny back step, the bunching of her neck muscles. He could have dusted her, and almost had, on instinct.

Phelps spoke again, "I'll repeat myself only once. Have your driver step out of the vehicle." This time there was no menace in the tone, and her voice was soft.

Ryan turned to Matthews and gave him a pleading look.

Matthews just shrugged.

Ryan felt the rush of adrenaline hit him again. Instantly, his mind shifted into overdrive. The dumpster was still at his back. He knew he could move faster than the ork could follow. Could be behind cover before she could possibly track him and pull the trigger. Matthews' hands were empty, but Ryan knew that meant nothing. From personal experience Ryan rated Matthews, even open-handed, as a greater threat than the ork.

Once again, he forced himself to relax. He didn't have a beef with the Secret Service, and he wanted to keep it that way.

"Dhin! Step out into the heat. The nice Secret Service lady wants a look at you."

Dhin did as he was told and climbed out of the limo. Ryan noticed that his jacket was unbuttoned, and both hands were a tad far out to his sides. He was ready to rock and roll, and Ryan knew he had to be careful not to give Dhin any false clues, or two nickel-plated Guardian pistols would be blazing.

Ryan turned back to Matthews. "All right, we're

playing it your way, now let's cut the drek. Why were you following me? If you wanted to talk—"

Once again, Phelps interrupted. "If you would be so kind as to lose your weapons, Mister Mercury, we would greatly appreciate it."

Ryan looked at Matthews, who turned to Phelps. "Don't push him too hard, Phelps. He could have killed you when you pulled that damn rifle. Probably would have geeked you without even realizing it if he was any more tired. Besides, from what I've seen of him in action, he might be even more dangerous with his hands free. Leave it."

"Agent Matthews, I'm sure you think you're right, but I refer you to Suspect Interrogation Code six-eight—"

Matthews turned to face her, voice tight, angry. "Stow it! You've pushed Mister Mercury's patience, and now you're pushing mine."

Ryan felt the first real twinges of anger tighten the muscles in his shoulders. "Suspect Interrogation? Frag it, Matthews, is that what this is all about? You think I had something to do with Dunkelzahn's . . . with the assassination?"

Matthews turned back to Ryan. "Calm down, friend. I know how this must sound. I also know how loyal you were to the old wyrm, but you got to understand the Secret Service's predicament here. Somebody killed a dragon, chummer. A fragging great dragon."

Ryan shook his head. "That dragon was the closest thing I had to a father since I was ten. I'd have killed myself before I did anything to harm him."

"You're not getting my point, Mercury. No one can even figure just how the assassin killed President Dunkelzahn, let alone who might have been behind it."

"You're not telling me anything I don't know, Matthews, and you're beginning to slot me off."

Matthews held up his hands in a placating gesture. "Then let me break it down for you. With nothing to go on, we're left with one course of action—investigating anyone or any group with the ability to pull it off."

Ryan nodded. It made a lot of sense. Killing a dragon took more than just motive. It took exceptional talent and resources, magical as well as mundane. It would take cunning and intricate planning. Ryan had been too busy searching for Burnout to do any investigating himself so he had no idea how it had been pulled off.

The fact was, however, that very few people could have executed the assassination. After weeding out all those without the means, the Secret Service would be left with only a select few to investigate.

Matthews' smile was grim. "There are those who say you should head the list."

Ryan looked Matthews in the eye, saw the disturbing questions there, and returned the grim smile. "That's a pretty dubious honor; one I'd just as soon do without."

Matthews stepped close, close enough that Ryan could smell the man's sweat and aftershave. "Listen, old friend, I know you didn't do it. But you're one of maybe three individuals on this planet with the know-how, the skill, and the *cojones* to pull off something this massive. Not to mention that you were close to the dragon, and that gives you access. The clincher is that the Service's intelligence division has about eighty percent surety that the president received a call from you just before he drastically altered his scheduled itinerary—"

"Yes, I made that call. But I was out of the country at that time."

"Doing what?"

"Routine business."

Ryan could feel the sudden flash of anger from Matthews. "Don't lie to me, friend. You don't do routine."

"All right, then let's just say that my business had nothing to do with—"

Ryan's wristphone beeped. He gave Matthews a questioning look.

Matthews nodded.

Ryan hit the connect button, and the voice of Carla Brooks floated into the still, rotted air of the alley. "I just got off the line with Quentin Strapp, the special investigator for the Scott Commission. Whatever you do, don't slot around with that tail. It's Secret Service, and Strapp says it's routine."

Matthews threw back his head and laughed.

Ryan couldn't help but grin. "Uh, Black Angel? I already figured that out. But thanks for the scan."

"Frag me, Quicksilver, you haven't gone and done anything . . . regrettable, have you?"

Ryan looked at Phelps, who hadn't moved a muscle. The assault rifle was still centered on his chest. "Not anything irreparable. Thanks for your concern."

Carla's voice took on the dry tone of a doctor giving a terminal patient the bad news. "Don't thank me yet. When I talked to Strapp, he said for me to detain you until he arrived. He's on his way to the mansion right now."

"Detain?"

"Those were his words, not mine, Quicksilver."

"I don't like those kind of words, Black Angel."

"Me neither. Something's going down, and it looks like they want to take you along for the ride."

6

The afternoon sun shone down on the cliff face, warming the rock with its heat as Lethe listened to the unmistakable rhythm of helicopter blades. Getting louder.

Lethe fought down the urge to flee from the approaching helicopters. Instead he concentrated on making himself and Burnout invisible to both physical and astral surveillance. The cyberzombie pressed his huge and very noticeable body tight into a narrow rock crevice and looked out at the three Aztechnology Aguilar-EX helicopters that swooped past. Flying confident in attack formation. Sure of their own fire power.

"They are certain to see me," Burnout said. "I will try to take them down." He anchored himself into the crevasse with his heel spikes and brought automatic weapons to bear on the incoming helos.

"Wait!" said Lethe. "I have hidden us."

Burnout hesitated, and the three helos flew past and out of sight, never hesitating. Burnout waited twenty minutes before climbing out of the crack in the cliff face and continuing the ascent. "How did you keep them from seeing us?" he asked.

"I have the ability to mask myself to all but the most perceptive," Lethe said. "I simply extended that ability to include both of us."

"I am further in your debt." And that was the last Burnout would say despite all efforts by Lethe to continue the conversation.

They reached the top of the cliff and passed quickly down the gentle slope on the other side, covered with pines. "Just in time," Burnout said as he loped down through the forest.

"What do you mean?"

Burnout chuckled. "I've been running on reserve energy since the fight with that blood spirit. My cybernetic parts need electricity to function. That's most of me these days. Another day without charge, and this would have been a lot of work for nothing. We'd have froze up and died where we fell."

"You can get 'charge' here?" Lethe could see nothing around them but tall pines.

Burnout laughed. "Power, yes. Listen."

Lethe concentrated on Burnout's hearing, and suddenly through the soft noises of the wild, he could faintly hear the sound of someone blaring a horn of some kind. "Civilization."

"Ain't it sweet? But it gets better. According to my GPS, the town right in front of us is a tiny little fly speck called Kooskia. It sits right on the junction of Highways Thirteen and Twelve. It also happens to be a fuel depot for the automated truck trains that cruise the freeway. More charge than I would know what to do with. We can just go in and take as much as we need."

Lethe thought about that. "The depot will be manned, will it not? I doubt that the attendants will just give you power without some form of reimbursement."

Burnout laughed. "I'd like to see them stop me. One look at this face, and they'll probably go screaming into the night. The ones that don't will die."

Lethe didn't like the idea of hurting innocents, and was about to make his viewpoint very clear, when something else occurred to him. "Burnout, something troubles me. In my short association with the man known as Ryan, I learned that he is quite meticulous, smart, and extremely methodical. Isn't this just the sort of clue he'll be looking for?"

Burnout shrugged. "It's a risk I'm going to have to take. We've been lucky he hasn't found us yet, and I'll try to get in and out without anyone noticing, but I must have power to move. I have to get to the Kodiak soon. Besides, even if he does pick up the scent here, we'll lose him soon enough when we hit the open road."

A few minutes later, under the darkness of oppressive

cloud cover, Burnout approached the small town. They
circumnavigated the small cluster of houses and roads,
moving around to the southern end of the village where
the refueling depot rested in the white glare of lithium
lights.

Burnout scanned the lay of things, pointing them out to
Lethe. "Just there, on the far side of that big patch of
tarmac," he said, pointing to a small square building with
a red neon sign above the doorway. The sign read DEPOT
in fanciful curlicues. "Not a very original name for a
depot, but it must cut down on any potential confusion,"
Burnout said with a dry chuckle.

Lethe didn't understand why Burnout should find that
humorous. It seemed perfectly logical that a depot should
be called a depot. However, he decided not to make any
further comment.

"Look there. We got one guard by the building's
entrance, simple service pistol that probably has half a
kilo of rust in the barrel. No track-mounted drones and
only minimal video surveillance. Only three attendants.
All of them look very bored. Bored is good."

Burnout moved swiftly, circling around the huge pools
of cold blue light. Within minutes, they were at the rear of
the building. Moving along the wall in silence. He peeked
around the end of the structure, looking out onto the broad
expanse of tarmac.

One of the massive truck trains had pulled in for refueling. The unmanned tractor in the lead was a sleek black
Nordkapp-Conestoga Bergen and looked more like it
belonged on tracks than wheels. The tractor was controlled by a dogbrain neural network, and behind it were
seven self-propelled trailers, each the size of a boxcar.
The attendants were busy hooking up fuel lines to the
monstrosity.

Without warning, Burnout stepped into the light just as
a guard walked leisurely past them. The man turned
toward them in what seemed like slow motion. Burnout
had closed the distance before the man's expression
changed and had snapped the guard's neck a fraction of a
second later.

Lethe was stunned. Such sudden violence. How could it be necessary?

Burnout stashed the guard's body behind the building before anyone saw him. He searched the man's clothing and found an ID card. "This," he said, "should get me access to their power grid."

Burnout quickly moved out into the light again, dashed across the short space to the building's entrance, and scanned the card through the maglock scanner. The door popped and they were in a small room filled with machines and cameras and . . .

An alert guard.

Burnout and Lethe found themselves staring down the yawning barrel of an Ares Predator II.

The guard gave an involuntary start when he saw the ruin of Burnout's face, but the gun never wavered from its mark. "On your belly, freakshow. Now!" The guard's voice didn't even quiver.

Lethe knew what was going to happen, and even as Burnout moved, he screamed in the cyberzombie's mind. "No!"

Then the night lit up with a muzzle flash and the thunder of gunfire.

7

Ryan and Matthews made the ride to the mansion in relative quiet. Phelps had stayed with the destroyed vehicle, to wait for a Secret Service tow-truck, and Matthews didn't seem too interested in talking. That suited Ryan just fine. He wasn't at all happy being the target of any investigation, let alone one in which he might be accused of murdering Dunkelzahn.

The next thirty minutes would be very telling. He thought of Nadja, and his apprehension grew. They hadn't spoken directly since the incident at Hells Canyon, and the messages he'd received had been too short. Too businesslike.

Ryan's smile was grim. *Well,* he thought, *I guess having the man you love hold you hostage and nearly get you killed just might put a damper on the warm fuzzies.*

Matthews, sitting opposite him, caught the smile. "Don't worry, Mercury. Strapp's had a chip on his shoulder ever since he got off the booze, but for the most part, he's a good man. They pulled him out of retirement for this. His last major investigation was over ten years ago, and he's been a bit tense since this whole thing started. But he's no match for you when you turn on the charm."

Ryan rubbed his fingers in slow circles around his temples. "I'm not feeling too fragging charming right this minute."

Matthews grinned. "You? Not charming? Just look at the way you charmed me out of my car and right into your big old limo. You're not even my type."

Ryan laughed. "Thanks for the vote of confidence, Matthews. Believe me, it's appreciated."

"Null sheen, old friend. Just cooperate with Strapp, and everything will work out. Besides, you're not the most politically correct suspect."

Ryan leaned forward. "What does that mean?"

Matthews sighed. "Much as it bugs me, not to mention how much it bothers Strapp, politics are playing a big part in this investigation." People like you aren't even supposed to exist. Independent . . . *trouble shooters* like yourself are the megacorps' worst nightmare. The corp boys like to think they've got a lock on all the muscle; that all others are just puppets they can push around when they need a pacifier for the populace."

"That's supposed to make me feel better?" Ryan said. "That would make me the perfect fall guy. I can just see the trid talk shows screaming about a deranged operative, working solo."

Matthews nodded. "On the surface, you're correct. But the corps would much rather have it be some terrorist group, preferably someone big. If they could pin it on the Azzies, that would be a wet dream come true. But to have to *admit* that one man, no matter how well-trained, could slot things up like this, and leave an entire planet baffled, scares them even more than the possibility that it might be true. Even if you had done it, that story would never go to press. They'd still publicly blame it on some fringe group, like Alamos 20K, then kill you in your sleep."

Ryan sat back. "You can't imagine how much better I feel."

He looked out the window and saw that they were finally pulling up to the mansion's front gate. A Draco Foundation security team, undoubtedly trained by Carla Brooks, combined with a small Secret Service unit stopped them for a moment to double-check their identities before allowing them through the old-fashioned wrought iron gate.

Security here was heavier than it had ever been, and Ryan knew it was tighter even than it looked. There was an invisible monowire mesh interwoven with the iron bars while hidden cameras and drone weapons continually scanned the perimeter.

The gate pivoted, and Dhin rolled up the circular drive,

past the long grove of cherry trees that were still in full bloom. Ryan had never figured out how the mansion's gardener did that, keeping everything blooming well into the late summer and fall. The only thing Ryan could come up with was that the man must have some latent druidic ability because the things he did with plants were nothing short of miraculous.

Ryan's gut clenched up into a tight ball as the limousine approached the entrance to the main building. *She'll never be able to forgive me.*

Then the Nightsky limo was rolling to a stop, and Ryan stepped out into the warm sunshine. For the first time since arriving in the Federal District, the air smelled of something besides rot, death, and burned plastic. The smell from the cherry blossoms was a lurid, sweet fragrance that almost overwhelmed the delicate aroma of the lush Mr. Lincoln tea roses lining the marble steps of the mansion.

The mansion itself was a rolling colonial structure, made mostly of red brick, but re-faced in the front with huge marble columns. The steps leading up to the main entrance were shallow and very wide. They sprawled up to the front doors, which had been re-done when Dunkelzahn had bought the place. The doors were massive and made of real oak, inlaid with bands of wrought iron. Each door was nearly ten meters tall, extending to the roof of the high-ceilinged first floor, and three meters wide. Just the right size for a dragon to enter and exit without having to change form.

As Matthews climbed from the limo, Ryan stood transfixed. All worry forgotten.

Nadja, in a simple loose-fitting dress of emerald green, was walking down the steps. Tall and thin. Her elven features more gorgeous than he had remembered. She'd done something different with her hair; its ebony darkness curved around the china doll skin of her heart-shaped face.

Without thinking, Ryan was moving. His whole mind swam at the sight of her, watching for any kind of sign from her. Then, she was in his arms, and his face was buried in the curve of her neck, taking in the subtle scent of her skin.

"I've missed you," he said, as her arms went around his neck. "I'm so sorry."

Nadja's delicate hand stroked his head. "Shush now, my love. All is forgiven."

He pressed her supple body to his, nearly crushing her in an effort to touch all of her at once. She kissed him, a soft, intimate thing that made a mockery of his rugged embrace.

The moment was ruined by a voice from further up the steps—a slow drawl that bespoke a childhood spent in the Confederate American States. "Well, y'all, I hate to break up this touching scene, but time is short."

Ryan pulled back from Nadja. On the top step stood a man of about forty. Thick black hair, marred with a single shock of white sprouting from his sharp widow's peak. His face was broad, with a strong jaw and chin, and very thin lips. Bushy eyebrows grew together in between dark-brown eyes that were constantly moving, looking everywhere. Not missing a thing.

Suddenly, those eyes focused on Matthews. "Ah, Agent Matthews. I see you're taking your surveillance duties seriously, though I had assumed you would tail Mr. Mercury in a separate vehicle. And what has happened to your partner?"

Matthews, squinting in the sunlight, shrugged. "Had some trouble with the car. Mister Mercury was kind enough to give me a lift while Phelps stayed with the vehicle."

Quentin Strapp's thick eyebrows narrowed. "We'll talk more about this later."

Matthews smiled. "I'm sure we will, sir. I look forward to it."

Nadja took Ryan's hand and led him up the steps. Up close, Quentin Strapp was a short man, but broad and powerful. Without thinking, Ryan's vision shifted to the astral, where he was surprised to see that Strapp's aura was whole. With the exception of a datajack just behind his right ear, the man was completely unenhanced. *Perhaps he's a mage.*

"Quentin Strapp," Nadja's voice was pure honey, snapping Ryan back to the conversation, "I'd like you to meet

Ryan Mercury. Ryan, this is Quentin Strapp. Mister Strapp has rearranged his busy schedule to meet with you this afternoon."

Ryan took her cue. She was on full political alert, all defenses up, all polish on the surface. He smiled and stuck out his hand. "Glad to meet you. I've heard good things about you. They say if anyone can find out what happened to the President, you're the man."

Strapp took Ryan's hand, shook it precisely once, then dropped it. "Shall we go inside? These damn flowers are giving me a sinus headache."

Nadja smiled, and motioned toward the doorway, giving Ryan's hand a squeeze before letting go. "Of course. Won't you please come inside." She turned toward the entrance, and for the first time Ryan noticed Nadja's aide, Gordon Wu, standing just inside the door, watching everything with an alert intensity. The demure Asian man gave Ryan a slight nod of recognition. He was no doubt recording everything on his headcamera.

Nadja looked at Wu as she led Strapp into the house. "My study should give us adequate privacy for this conversation."

Ryan got the message. Strapp was dangerous, extremely dangerous. For Nadja to take them into the study was a sign of just how dangerous. She was trying to make him feel as comfortable as possible without giving him any control. It was a ploy she usually reserved for people of Damien Knight's caliber.

Damien Knight was CEO of Ares Macrotechnology, one of the eight transnational megacorporations. He was an extremely important individual, someone whose support was critical and whose anger could have devastating consequences. If Strapp was anywhere near as dangerous, Ryan would need to be in top form.

They entered the long main hall. Thick Persian rugs covered the shiny green and black marble floor, and an eclectic collection of art adorned the hallway. It consisted mostly of mosaics from the late Ottoman Empire period, mixed with modern sculpture from Africa. They passed the broad, curved staircase sweeping up the left-hand wall. Nadja took the lead, followed by Strapp and Ryan. Gordon Wu brought up the rear.

The air grew imperceptibly warm and humid as they passed the ornate double glass doors that led to the arboretum. The doors were dragon scale and inlaid with pewter in the pattern of huge ferns. Ryan breathed deeply and grew melancholic for a minute as he remembered the times he and Dunkelzahn had trained together inside the arboretum.

He recalled the room's massive proportions, fifteen meters high with a clear ceiling made of sheets of macroglass held up by eight huge marble pillars. The pillars were ornately carved to look like trees, and they came complete with huge stone branches and roots. Dunkelzahn grew prize orchids and tropical trees in there, but he'd also liked to use the room for training Ryan in the Silent Way.

Ryan remembered one time when the dragon had taken human form, looking exactly like Michelangelo's David. Youthful face, brown curls, perfectly proportioned body.

In the memory, the dragon's words came into Ryan's mind. *We fight now.* Then Dunkelzhan had disappeared into the forest of marble trees.

Ryan had drawn a slow breath in his black nightsuit and had taken cover himself. It was dark, and moonlight shone through the stone branches, casting skeleton shadows across the floor. In the hot, humid air Ryan wiped the sweat from his brow and tried to center himself, to gain focus so that he could hear Dunkelzahn. Could pinpoint his location by sound.

One of the keys to the Silent Way is the ability to remain absolutely quiet, and to use that silence against your adversaries. Never reveal your position, Ryanthusar. Until you are ready to strike.

Hearing nothing, Ryan began to edge around the tree. He glanced at the shadows of the tree trunks, hoping to see a bulge or a distortion that would betray Dunkelzahn's position. His own shadow was hidden by the tree at his left.

In this way, the Silent Way is like chess. A game of misdirection and cunning.

There it was, the narrow shadow of a knee and leg, jutting slightly from the silhouette of the branch overhead. Ryan made the quick calculation and rushed to Dunkelzahn's position, ready to strike.

No one was there.

A follower of the Silent Way uses the terrain to his advantage, Ryanthusar. Uses all his assets in a fight, even those that seem to be lost.

Ryan heard nothing, but felt the slight air pressure change as Dunkelzahn moved into position behind him. The shadow had been a lure. A trap.

Even in his human form, the dragon struck quickly and with enough force to send Ryan flying across the room. Pain scissored through Ryan as he landed across a stone bench. Pain was the price for failure.

Come, Ryanthusar, Dunkelzahn said in Ryan's mind, *let's try again.*

They did it again until Ryan got it right. Until he was able to fight Dunkelzahn to a standstill. He'd never beaten the wyrm, but as time went on he lost less and less often.

The memory faded. And in its place, Ryan felt anger fill him. He was furious at Strapp for interfering with his return home. Ryan quickly stifled his anger as they entered Nadja's study. Now was not the time.

The cluttered atmosphere spoke volumes about just how tight Nadja's schedule had become since Dunkelzahn's death. Sim-recorded depositions lay scattered across her huge desk while several of the room's end tables were piled neatly with hardcopy requests, all sent to the Draco Foundation. Memos from President Kyle Haeffner's office were arranged in stacks by date. No doubt these had to do with her nomination for the vacant vice-presidential spot.

Nadja's been very busy.

Ryan looked closely at her as she turned, trying to be objective, and not see her through eyes clouded by emotion. Yes, he could see the strain there, the pressure she was under. She still looked lovely, but the exhaustion was like some monster lurking just below the surface of a placid, beautiful lake. It could explode out of the water at any moment.

"Mister Strapp, you're welcome to have a seat." Nadja

gestured to one of the two high-backed leather chairs facing her desk as she walked around and sat in her own.

Ryan took a seat, but Strapp remained standing. "Thanks just the same, but this won't take long." He pulled out a small audio recorder and showed it to Nadja and Ryan. "Do you mind if I record our conversation?"

"Not at all."

Gordon Wu closed the door and stood just inside.

Strapp turned to face Ryan. "Mister Mercury, I'm sure you have some idea why I'm here."

Ryan nodded. "Of course, and I'll help in any way I can. Finding the President's assassin is of paramount importance to the country generally, as well as to myself personally." Ryan allowed himself a frown. "Dunkelzahn and I were close, and I feel guilty for not being there when it happened. I keep thinking I could have done something. I'm not sure what, but I still believe that if I'd been here, instead of out of the country, I might have been able to prevent what happened."

Strapp stood silent for a moment, his intense eyes never leaving Ryan's face. "Of course. Still, I'd like to ask you a few questions about where you were at the time of the assassination. Simply routine, you understand, but I must tell you that I'm a mage and skilled in truth detection."

Ryan met his eyes and saw nothing but cold calculation there, despite the warm tone. "Of course."

"All right, then let's get down to it. You say you were out of the country. Is that correct?"

"Yes."

"Where?"

Ryan smiled. "I was looking out for some of Dunkelzahn's business interests in Aztlan."

Strapp smiled. "Really? That's pretty dark country for a simple business trip."

Ryan nodded. "I won't try and fool you. The trip wasn't without its risks."

"Is there someone who can confirm where you were? Someone who was with you perhaps?"

Ryan frowned. "I was alone."

"I see."

"Carla Brooks can vouch for me, Mr. Strapp."

"Yes, perhaps that is so, but Ms. Brooks was in Washington at the time of the assassination."

"I spoke with her by telecom just before the explosion."

Strapp smiled, showing yellow teeth behind his thin lips. "Is this the same call the President received just prior to the assassination?"

Again, Ryan nodded. "Yes, Carla patched me through to Dunkelzahn. I had discovered what he'd sent me to find out, and I'd been given strict instructions to call him immediately. I follow orders."

Strapp's stare intensified. "What did you discover?"

Ryan shook his head. "As much as I'd like to tell you, it isn't information I have the authority to pass along."

Strapp turned abruptly, and began a casual inspection of the ancient hardcopy books that lined the study's shelves. "Mister Mercury, you disappeared for a few days following the President's death. Where were you?"

Ryan smiled, letting his exhaustion show through. "Well, my pride would like to say I was in hiding after reporting in, but I guess I'm not quite as good at covert operations as I'd like to be. I was caught just after sending the message. I was detained for several days before being rescued."

Strapp turned back slowly, open disbelief on his face. "You were caught? Why do I find that just a bit too convenient?"

Ryan let some anger show through. "You wouldn't have found it so convenient if you'd been in my place, Mr. Strapp. It was no party."

"Perhaps not, but is there a record of your incarceration? Is there someone who can corroborate your story?"

Ryan felt the anger well inside him. He remembered waking up in Roxborough's delta clinic. Not knowing who he was, trusting the face on the screen. The boyish face of Thomas Roxborough. Ryan had believed he was Roxborough. He had wanted to help free Roxborough from his vat; he had felt sorry for the man.

Roxborough had used the drug laés to erase Ryan's memory. And his scientists had implanted gengineered retroviruses to encode Roxborough's memories and personality onto Ryan's mind. All as part of a plan to transfer

Roxborough's spirit out of his disintegrating body and into Ryan's.

The image of Roxborough's vat body came to Ryan's mind, the tendrils of brain matter floating in the thick saline like dreadlocks. Wires and cybernetics shone among the translucent pink, connected to the heavy black cords that led out of his tank to his Matrix interface. Bits of re-differentiated tissue scattered throughout his amorphous flesh. Bone and muscle and organ.

That man's ruthless personality had almost overcome Ryan, and it had been Nadja's love that had brought back his own memories. And later, it had been Nadja's love again, combined with Dunkelzahn's teachings, that had helped Ryan battle Roxborough's evil desire inside him. Desire to keep the Dragon Heart and all the power that came with it.

Now, Ryan shook off the memory and glared at Strapp. "No," he said, grinding his teeth. "I was held in custody alone, and I doubt you'll find records of my stay."

Strapp nodded and perhaps he sensed how edgy Ryan was getting because he changed tactics. "All right, let's take this from a different angle. Do you suppose that what you found down there could have prompted the Azzies to take action against the President."

Ryan shrugged. He'd mentioned nothing specific about the Aztlan government or Aztechnology thus far, but there was no point in playing games with Strapp. He was just as anxious to see Dunkelzahn's killer apprehended. "I see where you're heading, but I don't think so. Make no mistake, the Azzies never liked Dunkelzahn and may have wanted him dead. But they would have needed weeks of planning and, as I understand things, the assassination happened only minutes after I called in. Unless they had planned on doing it anyway, my being discovered couldn't have had anything to do with the assassination."

Strapp scratched at the stubble on his chin. "My thoughts exactly, but I had to ask. What else did you talk to the President about during the phone conversation?"

"Nothing."

Strapp nodded and paced back around behind Ryan.

"All right, next question. How well do you know Damien Knight?"

For the first time, Ryan was actually taken by surprise. "Knight? Not well at all. I've met him once, but it was brief and informal."

"What do you think of Dunkelzahn's and Damien Knight's relationship."

Ryan chuckled. "Not much. Dunkelzahn respected Knight, I think. They played chess, which means Knight must be a slotting good master of the board. Other than that, I didn't pay it much attention. Why?"

"I'm just checking out all leads. As CEO of Ares, Knight certainly had the resources to pull off the assassination, as would any high-level megacorp executive. But Knight seems to have been closer to the President than most others. Dunkelzahn's will has been difficult to sort through, but I noticed Knight received a chess set—a much more personal item than nuyen, and indicating a long-term relationship. Anyone who could play chess with a great dragon might be able to kill him."

"You suspect him?"

Strapp gave Ryan a hard stare. "Not anymore than I suspect you, Mr. Mercury. Aren't you the 'Ryanthusar' to whom Dunkelzahn willed his Heart?"

Ryan took a step back. "Yes, but—"

"And what is this Heart? Is it an ancient magical artifact? Is it a small personal item? It doesn't matter either way, Mr. Mercury, because it incriminates you regardless. It gives you motive."

"But I—"

Strapp interrupted, scanning from Ryan to Nadja. "You both have motive, inheriting billions of nuyen, and perhaps powerful magic. You were both personally close to the President, and you, Mr. Mercury"—Strapp pointed at Ryan—"you had the resources to pull it off. You have an alibi, but it's far from airtight. You could have made that telecom call from Aztlan or from around the corner, you have no one to vouch for your being captured, and perhaps you were just lying low until you could eliminate the evidence."

Ryan clapped. "Wonderful story, Mr. Strapp, but it

would hardly hold up." But he was thinking, *This man might be able to pin the assassination on Nadja and me, even though we had nothing to do with it.*

Strapp lost the hard-line stare. "Perhaps not yet, but more digging will tell." Abruptly, he turned to Nadja. "Thank you for being so understanding, I know your schedule made this meeting a bit difficult." Then he turned back to Ryan. "You've been very cooperative, and I thank you for that."

Lying right through his teeth, thought Ryan.

"I trust you'll inform my office if you decide to make any travel plans."

Ryan stood, forced himself to maintain the appearance of civility, and stretched out his hand. "Of course. If there's anything else, give me a call. As I said before, I'm more than happy to help in any way possible."

Strapp didn't bother taking Ryan's hand, but simply looked at them both as if from far away. "I will figure out who killed the president," he said. "And I just hope for your sakes, you had nothing to do with it, because if you did, I will bury you."

Ryan ignored the threat. "Whoever killed Dunkelzahn," he said, "is strong and cunning enough to have assassinated one of the most powerful creatures to ever have existed. Even if you do figure it out without getting yourself killed, how do you propose to bring the culprits to justice?"

Strapp smiled. "I have the UCAS military. And I suppose you and the Draco Foundation as well as about two hundred million angry UCAS citizens would also like to help?"

"You got it, chummer," Ryan said. "Count me in."

8

Alice was bored. Moody.

Tall buildings of concrete and mirrored glass reached up into a night sky around her, but there was no traffic on the street as she walked through Wonderland City. Street lamps illuminated the sidewalk, reflected in silver streaks that rose up the chrome windows of the buildings. But there were no people.

Only Alice, a gentle breeze, and the absolute silence of the vacant city. Wonderland City was her private little ultraviolet electronic universe. A personal section of the interconnected computer systems that spanned the world.

To herself, Alice appeared the way she had when she'd had a physical body. When her consciousness had inhabited a natural neural network called a human brain. Now her consciousness lived in . . . well, it spanned the Matrix really. Alice looked like a young woman, human, about twenty-five years old with shoulder-length blonde hair, fair skin, and blue eyes. She wore black jeans and a plain white halter top.

She took a drag on her cigarette and folded a section of Matrix space into her. The man in her mind's eye was standing naked in a grove of trees, his obese, naked body seemed to ripple and shake with the passing wind. Next to him, in a small clearing, a mad tea party was underway. The Mad Hatter and the March Hare sat at opposite ends of a large table.

Oh, the plans she had for Thomas Roxborough. Just thinking of them sent a delicious little shiver through her. Ryan Mercury had given her the access codes to Rox's system in Panama. It had tipped the balance so she could trap his consciousness in her virtual reality. A place where she made the rules.

Rox had designed the system in which she had been flatlined so many years ago. This was her revenge. She laughed, and the sound of her good humor rang through the dark city around her like a chuckle in the wind.

Roxborough looked around at the glen, and his sneer changed to a look of mild admiration. "Well, well. This certainly is impressive." He stretched out his hand and touched it to the March Hare's fur.

"I say! Keep your mitts to yourself, old man. Would you like some tea? Well, you can't have any." With that, the Hatter and the Hare quickly gathered up everything from the table and went into the small shack.

"Alice? I don't know where you are, but my compliments. This is the most solid code I've ever come across."

"Welcome to Wonderland, Rox."

Roxborough looked around the grove, trying to pin down the location of Alice's voice. Suddenly, he looked directly at Alice as she first made her wide grin, then her head, then her tail appear on the table top. She left everything in between transparent.

Roxborough smiled, showing wide, flat buck teeth. "Alice?"

"Yesss."

"I thought there might be more to it, Cat. The city up above is well done, but this . . . this, however, is simply delightful."

Alice's Cheshire grin widened into a vicious, predatory leer. "The city above is for the sane. You, Rox, are the most deluded case of megalomania it has ever been my displeasure to encounter. I thought you might feel right at home. However, you might be interested in knowing something. Lewis Carroll's Alice was very lucky. Wonderland is full of dangerous, deadly little surprises, and even a full-blown homicidal sociopath such as yourself could get into trouble very quickly."

Roxborough gave his toothy grin again. "Homicidal sociopath? My dear Alice, you're not still going on about that bygone Crash virus are you? You really should get some help for your obsessive behavior. Why don't you program yourself a nice little Freudian psychoanalyst? It would do wonders for your state of mind."

The disembodied tail began to twitch. "Rox, you are in a very precarious position at this moment. I suggest you cooperate."

Roxborough sat in the chair recently vacated by the Mad Hatter. "Cooperation is a wonderful thing, Cat. Makes the world go 'round, don't you know? But you've given me nothing to cooperate with. You make accusations and veiled threats, but you've failed to tell me just what you want."

Alice let the rest of her icon slowly take shape. "An admission of guilt would be a start."

Roxborough crossed his arms over his naked chest. "An admission of guilt for what? I've done nothing."

Alice pulled the Wonderland universe closer to her, jerking Roxborough out of the chair. "Don't toy with me, Rox. I know your system came to the aid of the Crash entity the day it flatlined my meat body, so an admission of attempted murder would be a good place to begin. We'll go from there."

Roxborough looked up at her, a glint in his rabbit-brown eyes. "My dear, you are tragically mistaken. I had nothing to do with the viral attack, and if you believe my system came to its aid, then I'm guessing there isn't anything I can say to dissuade you. However, it simply isn't true."

Alice smiled. "Okay, you won't confess. Still, you might be interested to know that the Crash entity was never destroyed by the Echo Mirage team. It was damaged and chased away. But it could still be out there, hiding somewhere. Learning and growing with each passing cycle. Getting smarter, faster, more deadly. I don't know where it is, but I intend to locate and destroy it."

Roxborough's knee suddenly gave out and he fell to the ground with a cry of anguish. "Alice!"

"It is beginning," she said. "You are reliving your disease." Several years ago, Roxborough had been struck with systemic lupus—a degenerative disease that had eventually forced him to live out the remainder of his life in a vat, connected to tubes and the Matrix. Ever since then, Roxborough had been obsessed with getting out of his vat and into a real body.

"Alice, I swear I had nothing to do with the Crash."

"I've pinned the origin of the virus to three possible hosts. Your system at Acquisition Technologies, Gossamer Threads, or the old NASA mainframes. Both Dunkelzahn, who owned Gossamer Threads before his death, and NASA lost a great many assets during the crash. You, however, only lost data pertaining to one corporation. That in itself points a lot of blame in your direction."

"Luck," said Roxborough, with a laugh. "Simple blind luck."

"That kind of luck doesn't exist."

Roxborough sobered, and for a second his eyes lit up. "For the most part, I would agree with you. And maybe even in this case as well. You want an admission? All right. I'll tell you what I know."

In the cityscape, Alice took a drag from her cigarette and waited.

Roxborough sat on the grass and rubbed his knee. "A long time back, I was attempting a buyout of a corporation that belonged to Dunkelzahn, though I didn't realize he owned it at the time. It looked like a ripe salvage project, dabbled a bit in code research and some minor hardware production. I saw what I thought was a lot of untapped potential. So I checked it out."

"Checked it out?"

"Yeah, I hired someone to hack into his system. Old terminology, I know, but this was before cyberdecks and ASIST technology. I wanted to see if I could find any tidbits of leverage when I presented the offer. The hacker went too deep and found something that scared me. Her system got fried, but she managed to salvage some of the downloaded data."

"Who was it?"

"The hacker?"

"Yes?"

"Her name was Eva Thorinson," Roxborough said. "But I think she died a few years back."

"Convenient for you," Alice said with a grin. "What did the data show?"

"The file contained only a bit of code, but its implications were staggering. I firmly believe that what burned her computer was a precursor of the Crash virus. That's all the information I have, and the only admission you'll get."

In the grove of trees, Alice's cat tail twitched again. "That doesn't scan," she said. "Dunkelzahn lost billions of nuyen in the Crash of '29. Why would he sponsor something that would cause so much damage to nearly every company he owned? Dragons aren't in the habit of tossing away fortunes like that."

Roxborough sighed. "For such a smart little cat, you're hopelessly stupid. Two plausible possibilities present themselves. One, that whoever was doing the programming lost control of it, allowing the Crash virus to escape. It *could* have been inadvertent."

Alice mused on that for a second. "That doesn't absolve you of responsibility. What's the second possibility?"

"Just that you're dealing with a dragon."

"What's that supposed to mean?"

"Simple, my dear. Dragons don't throw anything away without a reason, but you're talking about the most intelligent, far-thinking, Machiavellian bastards on the face of the Earth. Who can ever say why they do what they do? Maybe the Crash was just part of an enormously complex plot on the wyrm's part. A plan with rewards great enough to be worth the losses."

Alice had to admit that Roxborough had a point, even though it galled her to think he might be innocent. "I'm going to check out your story. I hope for your sake you've told me the truth."

Roxborough nodded at the disappearing cat icon. Then Alice pushed that section of the Matrix away from her, back to run its course while she contemplated what Roxborough had told her.

A light drizzle drifted down, making the streets of Wonderland City shine and glow. Reflecting Alice's inner mood. Dark gray sky above mirrored in the buildings.

If Dunkelzahn had engineered the computer entity that had caused both the infamous Crash of 2029 and the death of Alice's meat body, she was going to make sure everyone knew about it. That news would affect the entire world, most of whom loved the old dragon. If it was true, Dunkelzahn's image and everything associated with him would suffer greatly.

She hoped, with everything human left in her, that Roxborough was lying.

9

Ryan breathed a sigh of relief after Quentin Strapp left Nadja's study. He hated being so high-profile. He didn't want *anyone* knowing where he was and what he was up to.

Nadja stood and looked at Gordon Wu. "I'll be indisposed for a little while," she told her aide.

Gordon nodded, then turned and walked silently out the door into the adjacent office.

Nadja looked up at Ryan, a mischievous smile forming on her lovely face. "Come on," she said, taking his hand. She led him to the dining room, a spacious chamber with marble floors covered by Indonesian throw rugs and furnished sparingly with antiques of polished rosewood.

The table was a huge marble slab upon which was laid a sumptuous meal. As Nadja indicated for him to take a seat, he suddenly realized that he was very hungry. They ate in silence for a few minutes, Ryan enjoying the rich taste of his real steak.

As he ate, Ryan remembered the scene at Hells Canyon when he had been under the influence of Roxborough's personality. When he had been drunk with the power of the newly acquired Dragon Heart.

Nadja had arrived at the airstrip in her jet. She had come to try to persuade him to give up the Dragon Heart, to continue with Dunkelzahn's mission. He had run, trying to get to the helicopter. Trying to escape so he didn't have to talk to her. Didn't have to justify his actions.

She had come between him and his escape, standing with her guards. Blocking his way to the helo.

Possessed by Roxborough's personality, he had yelled

at her, spitting obscenities. Roxborough's voice ringing through his own. The evil voice inside that had become a part of him since the memory transfer in Aztlan. The dark part of him wanted to keep the Dragon Heart, use it himself instead of giving it up as Dunkelzahn had asked.

Lost to Roxborough, Ryan had surprised Nadja's security force, moving faster than any of them could track, slipping past them to grab Nadja and hold his gun to her head. He had threatened to kill her if they didn't let him leave.

And all the while she had spoken to him, soothed him. She had kept her calm under the threat of instant death.

Until finally, Ryan had remembered himself and collapsed, begging for her forgiveness. And she had held him close, whispering her support.

Now, he pushed his empty plate away and looked up at Nadja. "I'm so sorry," he said. "I'm sorry about everything. How could I have done that? How could I have let Roxborough's personality get control and threaten you?"

She held his gaze in silence.

"I want us to stay close," he said. "I want . . . I want to get past this."

"And now?" she asked. "Are you still in control?"

"Yes," he said. "Firmly. There are occasional flashes of Roxborough's memory, but I no longer act on his impulses."

"You've changed," she said. And there was something like sadness in her expression.

Ryan nodded. "Yes, I don't think I'll ever be the same as before." He sipped his red wine. "I'm not the blind soldier I once was. I think about the big picture too much now. I think too much period. In fact, I'm plagued with indecision."

Ryan looked up at her, his gaze a soft caress. "But my essential core is the same."

"I know," she said. "The part I care about is still there."

"You think so?"

She smiled and gave him a slow nod. Ryan felt a surge of affection. He loved her. On impulse he leaned close and tried to kiss her.

She pulled back and laughed.

"What?"

Between laughs, she said, "I'm sorry, Ryan. You need a shower and perhaps a shave. You're in civilization now." She leaned over and pecked him on the cheek.

Ryan stood. "All right, a bath then. Join me in the big tub?"

Nadja threw her head back in joy. "Sure."

They went into the master bathroom and drew a hot bubble bath and turned on the jets. The tub was huge and very deep, big enough for three trolls to use without crowding. Ryan stripped and settled into the hot water, leaning back to let the jets massage his aching and exhausted muscles.

Nadja joined him a minute later, stepping through the door in her white terry cloth robe. She looked into his eyes as she disrobed, purposely holding his gaze on her face. He was tempted to look lower, to follow the curves of her elven body down past her waist to her toes. But he resisted. There was time enough for that later.

She entered the water and slipped in next to him. He ducked his head under to wet his hair, to wash his face. *Spirits, it feels good to focus on getting clean.* As he lifted his head from the water, she was on him, her arms wrapped around his neck, her body pressed close.

She moved her mouth up toward his.

A soft knock on the door made her pull away. She tensed and sat up, straightening her hair. "What is it?" she said.

Gordon Wu's voice sifted through. "Sorry to bother you, Ms. Daviar," he said. "But Damien Knight is on line one. He said it was urgent."

Nadja whispered, "Frag it." Then she raised her voice, giving Ryan an apologetic look. "Thank you, Gordon. I'll take it in here."

She sighed and reached over to the telecom on the small marble table next to the tub. She killed the tub's jets as well as the soft music that was playing, gave Ryan a "shh" gesture, then keyed line one, presumably with the video blanked.

Ryan leaned back into the hot suds. To wait. Such an interruption was inevitable, he supposed, given Nadja's position as Chairman of the Draco Foundation and current nominee for vice president of the United Canadian and American States. It was fragging annoying, though.

"Damien, my good friend," Nadja said.

Ryan knew that Nadja despised Damien Knight, who was a hardball corporate shark. He was one of the most powerful people in the world, and no matter what her personal feelings, not a person to be ignored.

"Nadja," came Damien's voice, "what, no video? I hope I'm not interrupting anything."

The only time Ryan had met Knight was in Dunkelzahn's Lake Louise lair, at a birthday party the dragon had given for Nadja. Ryan remembered Knight as he greeted Nadja with a birthday kiss. He stood just shorter than Nadja's two meters, and he was broadly built, with salt and pepper hair and a rugged face. He also had hazel eyes and a platinum-plated datajack that gleamed discreetly on his temple, almost hidden under his perfectly coifed hair. He was very smooth and carried himself with the air of a man who was used to having his way. A man in control of his environment.

Nadja steeled herself, making her face a mask even though the video was blanked. "What do you want, Knight?"

"I was hoping you'd consider letting me vote your Gavilan shares."

Nadja smiled. "Ah, so you'd have control of thirty-four percent of Ares."

Ryan knew that Knight held twenty-two percent of Ares stock, the same as the Chairman of the Board, Leonard Aurelius. The two had been battling over control of the corporation for years. Since Nadja had just inherited Gavilan Ventures from Dunkelzahn, which included twelve percent of Ares stock, she was a prime target for internal corporate politics.

Nadja continued, "And what do I get out of it?"

"My blessing with the Scott commission and my influence in Congress to help get approval of your appointment as vice president."

"You have some influence there?" Nadja asked.

"There are those who appreciate my opinion."

Ryan didn't doubt it. Knight most likely had a third of
the UCAS Congress in his pocket, and held substantial
pull over most of the rest. Ares Macrotechnology was the
single largest employer in all of UCAS and the nation's
only "home" megacorp. Ares was based out of Detroit,
while the headquarters of the other megas were located
either in Japan, Germany, or Aztlan.

Nadja laughed. "What else?"

"Nadja, you drive a hard bargain." Knight's voice was
a deep, smooth baritone. "I like that."

"If there's nothing else, Damien, my answer is no."

"Perhaps you need some time to think about it."

"Frankly, Damien, I can't see how twelve percent of
Ares is equivalent to some political clout in FDC. I have
no concerns here."

"Are you certain the Scott Commission will clear your
name?" Knight asked. "It would be a shame for you to be
indicted on conspiracy to assassinate the President. Something like that could be viewed in the media as equivalent
to guilt."

Nadja didn't flinch at the implied threat. "I can handle
the bureaucrats, Damien. Can you?"

Knight's deep laughter resonated from the telecom.
"We should play chess sometime, Nadja. I think you'd be
quite an opponent."

Nadja's smile showed teeth. "Yes, I think I might like
that. As soon as I've beaten Mr. Aurelius, I'd be glad to
start up a match with you."

"You've been in contact with Leonard?"

"Think about it, Damien."

Ryan didn't know if Nadja had been speaking with
Aurelius or not, but even the possibility would make
Knight nervous. Aurelius and Knight owned approxi-
mately equal shares of Ares. If Aurelius got control of
Nadja's Gavilan shares, Knight's control of Ares would
slip. He would undoubtedly be ousted as CEO.

Knight's voice was harsh. "You're playing in a very
complex game of corporate politics, Nadja. A very dangerous game. If you give Leonard the proxy rights to your
shares, Ares would splinter. The other megacorps would

respond. The effects would be felt globally and the Draco Foundation would suffer. And so would UCAS."

Nadja's voice oozed sarcasm. "But you would prevent all that?"

Knight ignored her tone. "Dunkelzahn was informed, and he voted for the benefit of the corporation. Ninety percent of the time, his votes were the same as mine, you can check the data. But more than that, Nadja, he and I were friends. He trusted me. He would want you to trust me."

Ryan slipped further into the hot water. Knight might be right and he might be lying, probably a bit of both. *I don't envy her,* he thought looking at the lines of doubt now evident on Nadja's face. *She has a tougher job than I'd ever want.*

Nadja breathed an inaudible sigh. "I don't know what Dunkelzahn would have wanted, and neither do you. I have control of Gavilan now, for better or for worse, and the decision rests with me and me alone."

"Of course, I—"

"Now, I appreciate any support you can give as far as Congress and my vice-presidential nomination," she said. "And also with the Scott Commission—"

"Done."

"But I need to gather more information before I sign away the voting rights for Gavilan. You can understand the need to move cautiously, can't you?"

Knight gave a harsh laugh. "Certainly. We will talk again soon." The line went dead.

Nadja looked up and let out a long sigh. "I hate that man," she said.

Ryan keyed the jets, bringing bubbles and motion back into the water. "You were awesome," he said. "Knight doesn't know what hit him."

Nadja leaned back in the water, closed her eyes and let the fluid pummel her. Letting the tension drain from her body.

Ryan floated over beside her, drawing her into his arms. He poured some aromatic oil into his palm and massaged her shoulders with it. The sharp scent of ananya filled the room.

She responded with a smile, not opening her eyes.

Eventually, he worked all the tension from her muscles. She leaned back against him as he sank deeper into the water. The jets drove fists into his tight back as he kissed her neck. And as he worked his way up to her delicately pointed ear, he realized very slowly that she had fallen asleep.

Wonderful, he thought, resting her head against his shoulder. *Now, how do I get out without waking her up?*

10

In the depot's control house, Lethe's scream seared across Burnout's mind, almost causing him to freeze up. Like the howl of a trapped ghost, and it turned his circuits to ice.

The guard fired, and the massive pistol jerked from the recoil.

Burnout recovered barely in time to sidestep the shot with all his speed. Then he swept his foot upward, impossibly high, and shot his heel spike through the soft flesh of the man's exposed throat. With a downward jerk, the spike ripped the side of the guard's neck open in a spray of blood and cartilage.

The guard flopped to the pavement, clutching at his protruding wind pipe. He drowned in his own blood.

Burnout was already moving. The bored-looking attendants didn't look bored anymore. They were moving in Burnout's direction, pulling weapons from inside their coveralls.

These were no attendants, these were professionals, mercenaries. For a moment, Burnout wondered if Ryan had anticipated him, had lain a trap, but then instinct rode supreme, and the rotor-barreled M107, mounted on his articulate arm, was roaring above his head. Two short, controlled bursts, and the mercs blew backward as fist-sized holes appeared in their stomachs and chests.

That's that, thought Burnout.

The night was silent, but he knew it wouldn't stay that way much longer. He'd hoped to handle this situation with minimal noise, but even at this sparsely populated end of town, the sound of the M107 would make people sit up and take notice. In the sprawl, that was all right. So much drek went down that locals rarely got involved. In a little burg like this, Burnout guessed that the switchboard at the local law office was lighting up like a fire fight on a moonless night.

He moved swiftly into the control house, rounding the front counter and stepping back into the office. A schedule for the automated truck-trains was on the rear wall. The one currently fueling was due to depart in three minutes.

Perfect, thought Burnout.

"Was it necessary to kill them?"

Burnout had almost forgotten Lethe's interference. He left the office and ran to the depot's main electricity hook-up. "Let's get one thing straight here. Don't frag with me like that. You nearly got us geeked with that scream."

Lethe sounded genuinely sorry. "My apologies."

Burnout pulled the cables from the hook-up and looked them over. The power lines were big, and that meant the juice would flow fast. He'd have to watch it so he didn't short-circuit. He tore off the remains of his shirt and found the two power studs on his lower abdomen. He attached the cables and let the generator rip.

As the charge flowed fast and free, he spoke, "Why did you panic?"

There was a long pause, during which he checked his internal display, which told him his energy levels had reached maximum. He shut the generator down.

"Burnout, I did not intend to endanger you. I merely find unnecessary killing abhorrent."

Burnout snorted as he ran to the body of the nearest attendant and quickly traded clothes. "Unnecessary? Did you see the size of the barrel on that Predator? Big enough to drive a tank into. It was put-up-or-shut-up time."

Burnout tore the long duster from the dead guard. The clothing had blood on it, but it was better than what he'd been wearing. It fit too tight in the shoulders, so Burnout ripped the arms off. As he was putting the duster on, two sounds hit him. The first was the deep thrum of the automated truck-train as it powered up to head out.

The second sound was the high whine of distant sirens.

Burnout moved quickly to the tractor—a low-slung, gleaming snake in bright fluorescent. Its front scoop grill hung low, and its body profile was sleek and long. The bullet-shaped front engine was ten meters long, with two sets of triple-axled wheels. A sharp, black spoiler swept up from the rear of the engine compartment.

Each of the cargo trailers was a smooth-edged wedge shape, fitting so close to the one behind that if Burnout looked at the truck-train from an angle, it seemed like one long continuous body. The trailers also had spoilers to keep the vehicle from throwing itself off the road when it reached a cruising speed of more than two hundred kilometers per hour.

"Our taxi's waiting," he said, but Lethe didn't respond. Burnout didn't think the spirit had much sense of humor, and actually, now that he thought about it, he couldn't remember ever having much of one either. That is, before Lethe had come along.

He thought about that as he scoured the office for the records. He found a heads-up display that showed routes, fuel consumption, and final destinations. The rig was on its way to Billings, and wasn't scheduled for another stop till then.

As he looked at the side of the trailer truck out in the lot, and found the ID number on the side, he wondered at the change that had taken place in him since snapping awake on the banks of the Snake River. He felt so much more focused, so much more aware of everything. At first, he'd assumed it was the Heart that had brought the fresh clarity, the keener insights. But now he was unsure. Since discovering Lethe, things had been clicking into place for him.

Before, he had been in a constant internal war. When he wasn't in motion, acting out terrible violence, his anger boiled constantly inside. He couldn't stand still without becoming filled with hatred for anyone and anything. The automatic drug dispenser that numbed his nervous system when he was about to explode into violence hadn't triggered since before the fall.

Before, his superiors had even locked him out of certain weapons like his articulate arm and its mounted gun because they were afraid he might explode into sudden violence and use it against them.

Before, his IMS would spark memories for him. Keeping him from forgetting he was alive, which he sometimes did. But now the IMS only kicked in when Lethe spoke to him. Burnout felt more solidly alive, more centered than since before his cybermancy.

He didn't know how that could be possible, but whatever the reason, he was thankful. He was no longer spending all his waking hours in a haze.

With a high whine, the rig started to pull forward, just as Burnout had hoped it would. He dashed out the door, pausing only to scoop up the Predator as the rig began to pick up speed. Burnout jumped aboard, just as the tail end of the truck accelerated out of the last pool of light on the depot's tarmac.

He held tightly to the ladder, then climbed up behind the shield of the wide rear spoiler. He used his third arm to hook around one of the spoiler's struts and settled in. The ride wasn't going to take very long.

The sound of the sirens, which had been getting steadily louder, began to quickly fade again. That was good. With the ruin of the main terminal, the law boys would probably assume he had hightailed it for open country. Only a fool would try to ride one of these trains. A fool, or someone strong enough to hang on through the incredibly rough ride. Because the truck-trains were automated, they traveled at ferocious speeds, and their wide, low body-line made it possible for them to take curves at a pace fast enough to create a couple gees. No trip for the weak.

It would also take the law a while to replay the action on the depot's surveillance cams. By that time, Burnout would be off the rig and out of their jurisdiction. No doubt he'd have to worry about Ryan Mercury closing in, or those Azzie choppers, but by the time either of them managed to pick up his trail and track him, he would be prepared.

The wind began to howl in his ears as the truck-train reached its cruising speed. Burnout felt good, and it was the first time he remembered feeling that way in a long, long time.

"Do you mind if I ask where we are going?"

Burnout liked the spirit more and more with each passing day. He could feel the changes taking place within him. Before Lethe, he'd spent his time enraged or drugged. Always on the edge, never solid. Never in control of himself.

Now, with all the magic around him, inside him, he had grown aware. Where before he merely acted, now he understood. He knew the price of his cybermancy. Of his life beyond the pale. And he dreamed of regaining his magic.

He was reminded of old man Getty, the first mage he'd found who was willing to unteach all the shamanistic mumbo-jumbo the Kodiak had taught. Old man Getty had started young Billy Madson on the right road to his magic. It was Getty who had taught him to focus on method, not emotion, who had rapped his wrists with a long thin stick every time he slipped up. Getty had taught him to put the past behind him, to reach toward the future and everything it held.

Burnout touched his side, where the Heart rested under the duster. Pressed close to his side. He could taste the power that lay dormant there. *Mana!*

Burnout smiled. "I'll tell you where we're going, Lethe," he said. "We're going back to the time of old masters and new magic.

"Back to the beginning."

11

The moon hung just a sliver below full, shining in horizontal lines through the slats of the venetian blinds. Sending ripples of light across the blankets. Ryan lay awake in the huge bed. He had slept only a few hours, awakened by dreams of Dunkelzahn's death.

He edged out of the bed and stood, naked in the moonlight. He looked down on the sleeping form of Nadja. Her dark hair spilled over the white pillowcase, and there was a slack, unbecoming expression on her face.

He smiled. *Such innocence in sleep,* he thought. *If only I could forget for long enough to get that kind of rest.*

Ryan turned away and walked to the wide French doors that opened onto the private balcony. He stepped out into the cool air and looked down on Nadja's personal courtyard, letting the cold marble caress his feet.

The wind blew gently across his skin, soothing his body, but leaving his mind in turmoil. He knew he needed sleep, but that elusive beast refused to let itself be trapped, and his mind refused to quit working. The meeting with Strapp still bothered him. As long as Ryan was a target of the investigation, the Secret Service was spending valuable manpower looking in the wrong direction.

Strapp was right in one thing. Ryan wanted to help with the investigation. Not only did he have resources the Secret Service didn't, he worried that even if they did discover who was behind the murder, they might not have the muscle to take the assassins down. Ryan could help them with that.

Strapp was a fool to think that one man could have pulled off the assassination, though it was possible that one person might have masterminded the whole thing. The way the assassination went down, it had to be a planned and coordinated effort. Vast resources would have been required, and perhaps inside help.

Ryan curled his left hand into a fist. It was so frustrating to watch others plod along on so important a task when he knew he could get the job done faster. He could organize a team before morning, be on the killer's trail before the week was out. Now that he felt as if his brain was clicking on all cylinders, he knew he could discover the killer if he just had a week to fully concentrate on it.

Some intensive digging, a little undercover time, and he'd come up with something concrete to give Strapp. An operation this big could never stay concealed forever, no matter how good the assassin proved to be.

He loosened his fist, and laughed. *Who's the fool now?* There were hundreds of people looking into finding Dunkelzahn's killer, and he was having a hard time tracking down a dead cyborg.

His thoughts were interrupted when his wristphone beeped. He punched the connect, and all of Jane's womanly charms filled the small screen. "Jane, talk to me."

Jane smiled, somehow still managing a slight pout on her full lips. "Rather abrupt way to greet a messenger bearing good tidings."

The muscles along Ryan's back tensed up. "You've found him." It was a statement, not a question. "And he's not dead."

Jane nodded, throwing blonde tangles everywhere. "Seems General Dentado and his Azzie cronies warned the area truck-train fuel depots that they were likely targets for our cyberzombie. The depot's security open-contracted some pro-level heavies to work the place undercover. I've checked the stats on these chummers, and they were hot. Desert War mercs with years of experience. Yet Burnout sliced and diced them like they were newbie runners."

Ryan felt the skin on his back crawl. "You get trid on it?"

Jane smiled again. "In glorious color. He looks like something right out of an old horror vid, Ryan. You did quite a number on him. Unfortunately, the damage seems mostly cosmetic. He moved so damn fast, I had to replay the trid three times just to see what the hell he did."

Ryan cursed. He'd come to grips with the fact that Burnout was still alive, but he'd hoped the cyberzombie would at least have been hurt.

"Ryan, forgive me saying this, but there's a drekload of bad juju about this chummer."

Roxborough's self-doubt crept from hiding, but Ryan squashed it. "You're right, Jane. He's one bad son of a slitch. But he's got something of mine and I plan to get it back. If I play this right, he'll go down fast and hard, and we'll have this bit of business out of the way quickly."

Jane's frown deepened. "And if you play it wrong?"

Ryan smiled. "Then you'll be the new owner of Assets."

Jane shook her head. "I'll pass."

"Okay, Jane. Can you prep Axler and the team? And arrange for something inconspicuous in the way of air travel for me?"

"On it."

He cut the connection, then punched in Carla Brooks' private line. She answered immediately, her white hair rumpled, and her eyes tired. "Well, Quicksilver, I see I'm not the only one who's having a hard time sleeping."

"Black Angel, I need some official transport out of the mansion. Not too flashy, maybe as part of some guard detail. I also need you to cover for me with the Secret Service."

Brooks' eyes widened. "This have to do with your mission?"

Ryan shook his head and ran his fingers through his hair, conscious for the first time that he was naked. "Yes, and we've got a hot trail to follow."

Brooks nodded. "Consider it arranged. Be ready to roll in less than an hour. I'll coordinate with Jane. I'm not sure what I'm going to tell Strapp, but I'll think of something."

"Thanks, Black Angel. I knew I could count on you." He cut the connection, and stood still for a moment, before becoming aware of the presence at his back. He smiled as Nadja's arms circled his bare waist.

Ryan turned in her grasp. She'd wrapped the sheet around herself and looked like a goddess standing on the marble balcony in the moonlight. He put his hand under her chin, tilting her face up to his. He was surprised to find tears on her cheeks.

"Going so soon?" she said.

Ryan nodded. "I wish I didn't have to."

Nadja pulled her face from his hand, and looked at the floor of the balcony. "I reserved an island beach in Georgia," she said. "Thought maybe we could spend a few days there. You know, after Congress votes on my VP nomination." Her eyes turned upward from under moist lashes.

Ryan looked at her face. The monster of exhaustion that he'd noticed earlier was closer to the surface than he'd ever seen before. "I won't be long," he said.

Nadja shook her head, sending small drops of sadness flying from her cheeks. "I don't believe that."

Ryan stepped up to her as she turned away from him. He put his big arms around her delicate shoulders. Leaned his head into the nape of her neck. Her scent was nearly overwhelming.

Her voice was small, tired. "I feel like I'm swimming in a rushing river, and no matter how hard I try, the current keeps pulling me down. The meetings, the schedules, the appointments. People demanding things from me, making accusations."

Ryan held her tightly, kissed her neck.

"When I saw you get out of the limo today, it felt like I'd caught ahold of a life raft. Like for the first time, I didn't have to do it all by myself. That there was someone who understood how I felt. Someone who was here to support me."

She turned to look up at him, and her cheeks were soaked with tears. "And now you're leaving again. I'm not sure I can handle all this by myself."

Ryan felt his love for her like a blow to the chest. She was so strong, so dedicated, and for her to admit that she might not be strong enough took a lot. He turned her around to face him, kissed her forehead, her velvet cheeks, the soft flush of her mouth.

"You are the strongest person I've ever known, Nadja. You will make it, I know you will. There's nothing I'd rather do than stay in Washington to be with you and run down some leads on Dunkelzahn's assassin." Ryan sighed. "But you know I should do this. It's what Dunkelzahn wanted me to do . . . I have to see this thing through." There was no conviction in his voice and he knew it.

She didn't seem to notice. She nodded, and smiled through her tears. "I know, Ryan. I know. You're right, of course. You always knew how to make the tough decisions; it's no wonder you were the old dragon's favorite."

Ryan laughed, and inside he was thinking. *I feel more like the decisions are making me.*

"No, Nadja, you're the tough one. I always thought you didn't need anyone."

"I don't."

Ryan's laughter grew, and he wiped the moisture from her cheeks. "Spirits, I love you."

Her smile became more seductive. "How long until you have to leave?"

Ryan looked at the time display on his wristphone. "Just under an hour."

Nadja stepped back, and let her sheet fall to the floor. Her full breasts swayed, her brown nipples standing rigid in the breeze. She turned toward the door, and Ryan admired the graceful curves of her naked body as she moved back inside. "That's not much time. I guess we'll just have to make the best of it."

He grinned and followed her inside.

12

Blood and music on the metaplanes.

Music, the sweet hurting light, growing dim.

Blood, the dank whispering darkness, spreading fast.

Lucero stood in her astral form. Just at the edge of the dark circle of black blood and basked in the painful beauty of the music and the light.

Alone.

She longed to take that final step. That ultimate plunge into brightness. *Purity.*

She edged closer. Closer. Until . . .

Without warning, Señor Oscuro appeared next to her. He collapsed down on one knee as if he were being crushed by a tremendous weight. Sweat prickled on his forehead, and the muscles in his face tensed in agony.

He gritted his teeth and stood. It seemed to take all his effort to touch her, though when he did, that touch was gentle. He pulled her back toward the center of the dark circle.

Where the blood was deepest.

"You . . . you are . . . holding up . . . well," he said.

Lucero almost screamed at the sound of that voice, but she forced herself to be calm. "If it please you, Master."

"It . . . pleases me."

The smell of blood filled her nostrils as the sound and the light from outside waned. Lucero felt the desire swell inside her again, but she resisted. She focused on the blinding light, on the terrible purity of the wondrous song.

So dull now. So distant.

A young boy appeared in the space next to Oscuro—a small boy of no more than thirteen with a rash of acne across his cheeks. The vacant look seemed to leave the child's eyes for a moment as Oscuro laid him down on an altar he'd constructed from the bodies of the first ten victims.

Oscuro grabbed a handful of the boy's hair, and pulled back viciously, exposing the soft young throat.

This one actually had time to emit a short, high-pitched whine before Oscuro's hand fell. The blood-covered knife cleaved the sound from the child's mouth, letting it end in a shrill whistle coming from the gaping windpipe.

Oscuro slapped his rough hand over the wound, slowing the flow of blood, and lifted the boy by the neck. Ignoring the twitches, he carried the body to the edge of the outer circle.

The strain was evident in the corded muscles of Oscuro's gore-drenched arms. Everything he did seemed to be a tremendous effort now, as if he had to fight the music just to keep moving. When Oscuro reached the edge of the outer circle, he removed his hand from the child's throat and let the blood flow. He traced the final meters of the circle in the thick gurgle of young life. When the circle was closed, the bright music faded even more.

Lucero did not know how much time passed as more and more sacrifices piled up along the edge of the ever-widening circle. All she knew was that in her heart she longed to leave this place. She wished to be given the strength to throw herself clear of the blood stain. Through the wall of darkness that stretched up at the edge of the stain. She yearned to plunge herself into the light.

Finally, Oscuro walked over to her as she crouched among the corpses. She was stunned and nearly catatonic from the shock of all the death, but as she looked at the dark human, she saw that he was worse.

Oscuro was in incredible pain, his face wracked with strain. As the dark part of her lightened, his struggle became harder. "Back at the *teocalli*, the Gestalt is weakening again," he said. "Too much . . . drain will kill them. They need to . . . rest."

Lucero nodded.

"You will . . . stay. I'll return when . . . when the Gestalt is stronger."

Then he was gone again.

More time passed around her. She knew not how much as she crawled her way gently over the strewn bodies, reaching the outer circle. She stopped at the edge, unable to move farther. She spoke to the light. "He is wrong," she said. "I am not strong. You have given me a strength far better than any blood magic. You have shown me that things can work for a greater good than I have ever known."

The music washed over her again, and she knew the dark spot inside her had lightened again. She heard the song and for a moment, she understood. The words were muffled, indistinct, but she knew that the song was holding back forces of horror and terrible evil. The song told her that the outcropping must never be made into a bridge.

The song reached into her mind and revealed that the dark circle threatened the light. The dark circle must be destroyed. Lucero must accept the stain on her soul and forgive herself.

She had passed the first challenge, had not let the bearded man seduce her. As she tried to hear more of the song, she knelt over the corpse at the edge of the bloody circle and reached out a hand to touch the outer barrier. She longed to stand and step from the circle, drown herself in that light, the music.

Lucero shook her head, and pulled back her hand. She knew that would accomplish nothing but alert Oscuro to her intent. "I will not fail you," she told the music. "I will stop this evil no matter what the cost."

21 August 2057

13

[11 August 2037]

13

In the early morning shadows, deep in the heart of Hells Canyon, Ryan felt an edge of annoyance as Dhin made another pass over the landing site. The monstrous rock shelf that housed the Assets, Inc. compound three-quarters of the way up the sheer cliff face was torn by heavy winds that ripped through the canyon and played havoc with the plane's vertical touch-down.

The aircraft was an Embraer-Dassault Mistral—a fat-bellied cargo shuttle. The wind pushed her around like a cat toying with a mouse. In the cockpit, Ryan watched as the ground came close. Wind hammered at the fat body of the Mistral, threatening to push the heavy commuter craft off the landing mark and out into the canyon.

"Touch-down," said Dhin.

Ryan had to give the big ork credit. He barely seemed to feel the impact. He turned as he unbuckled his safety straps. "You're a steady chummer," Ryan said. "One second I thought we were going to take a big plunge, the next you got us down on the tarmac, safe and solid."

Dhin pulled the jack from his neck and sat upright. "You don't know how close we came to chewing rocks. Next time you want to head out in the middle of the night, scan me first. I'd have told Jane this old boat was too tight a fit for the landing pad here. This slitch handles like a street sam with too much liquor in him."

Ryan nodded. "Deal."

The ork finally grinned. "Let's get inside."

As they climbed from the seats, Ryan caught sight of Axler standing just outside the doorway to the main building. Wind tugged at her blonde hair and made the tail of her black trench coat flap. But no wind could mess with the impression of cool self-confidence she radiated.

Ryan gave her a grin she didn't return. All biz.

Ryan wasn't really looking forward to the next couple of hours. The runners still didn't completely trust his leadership, and were obviously annoyed that their only decent night's sleep in a week had been cut short by his telecom call.

Dhin had been more than a little upset about being rousted in the middle of the night, and his female ork companion hadn't seemed too thrilled either.

Secret Service agent Phelps had looked even more impressive naked than she had in her body armor, and Ryan couldn't help but wonder just where she'd hidden the Ingram SMG. But there she was, just behind the door when he'd entered. She hadn't bothered to lower the Ingram until Dhin, sitting up and rubbing his eyes, told her to knock it off.

On their way to the airport yesterday, the big ork had said something about going back to the alley to help Phelps with the decimated Eurocar. One thing had led to another, and another, and then another.

Ryan had been angry, not really at Dhin, but more at himself. Now that Phelps knew he was leaving the country, the Secret Service would be alerted. That meant Strapp would be all over Carla Brooks' hoop in a matter of hours. Still, it couldn't be helped.

Ryan followed Dhin down onto the hard tarmac, and walked across to meet Axler, who stood by the newly constructed entrance to the underground facilities.

Axler came forward to meet them. "Ryan, were you serious when you said Burnout survived the fall into the canyon?"

"Jane got vid of him a good hundred klicks from here."

"Frag," she said. "I never would've thought."

"Me neither, chummer. Me neither."

"You got details?"

"A few," Ryan said. "But I've got some things to say first. What's the status here?"

She talked as they headed back to the building, her tone formal. The modifications Ryan had ordered to the compound were far from complete. It would take the mining crew at least another week to finish cutting the medical facility out, and then about two days until all the equipment arrived. The crew was on leave until the following day, and they were being bunked in Dhin's workshop.

Ryan nodded his approval. When Dunkelzahn had left Assets to Ryan in his will, it was only a ramshackle collection of buildings on the narrow ledge. Some improvements had been made by Axler, but Ryan had decided to go a few steps further.

Once the search for Burnout was in full swing, Ryan had ordered a discreet mining company to cut into the canyon with the ultimate goal of enlarging the compound to four times its original size. His plans included provisions for a cybersurgery lab, a mage library, and a training facility that would be the envy of Knight Errant.

In the back of Ryan's mind, he'd started planning again. If this mission didn't kill him, he had to think to the future. His intention for Assets was to make it the most effective, far reaching organization of shadowrunners the world had ever known.

If Dunkelzahn wasn't here to put together an army, Ryan would do it for him. At least part of it. The voice of the spirit that had carried Dunkelzahn's instructions came back to him. After Axler and company had freed him from Roxborough's clinic in Panama, Ryan had met with Nadja in Dunkelzahn's Lake Louise lair in the Canadian Rocky Mountains, in what used to be British Colombia.

Nadja had taken Ryan to a sealed chamber deep inside the lair where he would be protected from any ritual-magic assassination attempts. A spirit spoke to him in Dunkelzahn's voice, like a ghost of the old wyrm, telling Ryan of his mission, of taking the Dragon Heart to the metaplanar spike created by the Great Ghost Dance.

There will be no hiding this time, the spirit had said. *There will only be war. We must build up our defenses; we must gain the time we need to build up our technology so that we have the ability to fight the Enemy when it can cross.*

The Dragon Heart would give them the time, but now Ryan figured he'd help prepare for the war by making

Assets the covert-operations arm of the Draco Foundation. And the plan was going smoothly so far.

As they stepped inside, he brushed the hair out of his eyes, silently thanking the spirits that at least something was going smoothly. He turned to Axler. "Is there power in the command room yet?"

Axler nodded. "It's all set up, and we're on-line with Jane. Grind and I finished the equipment installation last night after the wind made further recon of the canyon impossible."

"How's the new mage?"

Axler snorted. "Miranda's still got too much of a corporate attitude, left over from her days at Fuchi. But otherwise, she's chill and she knows her biz."

Dhin came in, bringing dust and wind with him, and dropped Ryan's bag to the floor. "What's the schedule?"

Ryan looked from Dhin to Axler. "I want the whole team assembled in the command room in five minutes. We're on a tight schedule."

Axler turned away. "On it."

Dhin nodded and headed over to the command room.

Ryan picked up his own bag and moved deeper into the rock face of the canyon. The miners had strung crude lights down the hall, but when he stepped into his private quarters, he was pleasantly surprised.

Still spare in the furnishings department, the large room consisted of a single bed, a small bathroom, and a desk with a Fuchi Cyber-6 cyberdeck and a telecom set up and ready to roll. Ryan never cruised the Matrix himself, but he did run tactical simulations and made use of some of Jane's smartframes from time to time.

After splashing some water over his face, he stepped back out into the corridor and turned left, going even further into the rock. He came to the massive double doors. They were heat-shielded and made from twenty centimeters of duracrete, backed by another twenty of plexan. They could take a direct hit by anything short of an antitank missile and not even scratch.

Ryan hit the palm lock, and the doors slid silently open.

The command room was a cavernous circle, dominated by a huge oval table. The table itself contained a powerful holographic generator that could either display a main presentation to the whole table or act as a heads up display for each individual seat.

It was a testimony to Ryan's far-reaching plan that the table could easily seat fifty.

The runners were scattered around the large area, and Ryan picked up the immediate clue by how they were seated. *They're tired of the boring search.*

Nearer the door, Axler and the dwarf Grind sat together. They glanced up as Ryan entered, but continued to talk in low tones. Dhin sat opposite them, and he gave a grin and a shrug.

The new mage, Miranda, was seated by herself at the far end of the room. She was a small human with a broad oval face and a shock of jet black hair streaming down her back. She cradled a steaming cup of coffee in her hands and looked as though she was barely awake.

Ryan stepped into the room. "Miranda?"

She looked up, startled. "Travis? Travis, is it really you?"

Ryan smiled. "You look good, Miranda," he said. "But my name's not Travis. It's Quicksilver or Ryan. And I lead this team of shadowrunners."

"And at Fuchi . . ."

"I was working undercover."

Miranda scowled. "You left so suddenly. They said you'd been transferred to Kyoto, but I couldn't get word to you."

"No," Ryan said. "It was just a temporary assignment so that I'd have a solid identity when Aztechnology stole me away. It's a lot harder to infiltrate the Azzies."

Miranda sighed and took a sip of her coffee. "You went to Aztechnology? That's heavy drek," she said. Then with a glowing, intimate smile, she said, "I'm glad you made it out alive."

Ryan remembered working next to her in the labs at Fuchi. She was all professional on the surface, toeing the corporate line on the outside. But he'd seen something underneath, something that had come through in the few moments when they'd had a chance to get closer. A hidden wild undercurrent.

Ryan had never let himself become intimate with her; he'd been in love with Nadja even back then. Even if he hadn't been, he never allowed himself to get too close to anyone during the time he was undercover. He and Miranda had become friends. Friends on the verge of more.

There was something alluring about her life—the corporate life. The safety and simplicity of it, protected by the huge corporation. A life of carefree happiness.

Ryan could never let himself think that such an existence would even be remotely satisfying. He'd left abruptly and without a word, regretting he couldn't say goodbye. That he couldn't give her an explanation.

"I'm going to talk about what happened," Ryan said, walking to the head of the table. "Jane, you with us?"

"In the next best thing to the flesh, Quicksilver." Jane's voice came through the room's speakers.

"Good, let's get this show rolling," Ryan said. "Time is short, and we've got a lot of ground to cover. First of all, I have something to say."

He got nods from Axler and Grind. Dhin grunted, and Miranda peered through the steamy haze rising from her coffee.

Ryan looked hard at Axler and Grind. "I want to offer an explanation for my actions over the past few days. I've taken over control of Assets and haven't given any of you much input. I've been driving you hard without a lot of explanation. I've also been acting erratically and it probably seems like I'm on the edge of losing control. I can understand if you think I'm deranged. You might even think I'm not capable of effectively leading this group."

He saw Axler nod her assent.

"There is an explanation for my strange behavior, and I'm going give it to you. I know I couldn't work with anyone I thought was a liability."

Axler's look softened. "We don't think you're a liability, Ryan. But you haven't been yourself, not since we scooped you up from the Azzies. You've made some bad choices, decisions you wouldn't have made three months ago. It's got us worried."

Ryan took a deep breath. "When I was at the delta

clinic in Panama, they tried to erase my mind and remap it with another personality. Ever heard of Thomas Roxborough—the vatcase megalomaniac who owns a big hunk of Aztechnology? It was his mind they tried to map over mine. You saved my hoop just in time, but they'd nearly erased my memory, and there was a period of adjustment that was very confusing. It was like I had no control over what I was doing, even though I knew it was wrong. Can you understand that?"

Miranda gave a low whistle. "Aztechnology is one of the bloodier corps, and Roxborough has a reputation for utter ruthlessness. That's some serious drek."

Ryan's smile was tight. "To put it mildly. But things are different now. Roxborough is still with me, but Quicksilver's on top."

Axler frowned. "How do we know that? You've taken leadership away from me and Jane; that's not something the old Ryan would do. Assets was running smoothly before you made your 'improvements.' "

Jane came on over the speakers. "I have to agree with Axler, Quicksilver. I especially resent my current role in the scheme of things. I'm not officially part of Assets, but I've always been in control of any runs I do decide to make. From here in my box, with my virtual re-creation of all the data, it's much easier for me to form a complete picture of what's going down than it is for anyone on-site."

"Jane, I—"

"I take inputs from each runner, plus Matrix data. I can make better-informed decisions, and I can make them quicker."

"Jane, I value your expertise and I'm going to need it more than ever. Especially during the next few runs. But I'm going to be leading the team. I've got combat training that you don't, and I refuse to shirk that responsibility." Ryan turned to Axler. "I want you to be my lieutenant, and I'll need your advice. I know it's going to be hard to adjust, but I think it will improve things in the long run."

Silence engulfed the room in the wake of Ryan's speech.

"Okay," Ryan went on, "I don't want anyone to stay

who isn't satisfied with the arrangement. Now's your chance to bail out of Assets if you want to. Anyone who thinks I'm going to get him or her killed can walk. There's twenty thousand nuyen in a numbered account for each of you. I'll give you the code, and you go with my blessing."

Dhin shook his head slowly, but no one spoke.

"You all know that Roxborough would never have given you walking papers," Ryan said finally.

Axler nodded.

Ryan looked around the room, pausing when he got to Dhin. "So, do I have any takers? 'Cause if you decide to stay on board, you're on all the way. I've got some serious plans for this organization, plans that are going to ask shadowrunners to play a serious part in protecting the future of the world."

Axler sat up. "I know a lot of runners who want to make a difference," she said. "But in our line of work runners don't have much to say about whether we're on the right side or the wrong side. Shadowrunners have to do whatever the Johnsons want, and a lot of times don't even know *whose* side they're on. How can you change that?"

Ryan smiled. "We don't have to please anyone but ourselves. We've got independent funding and the means to make a difference."

"Under your leadership?" Axler asked.

"That's right," said Ryan. "You're going to have to trust me." He looked around the room, challenging any of them to get up and walk out.

Dhin answered first. "You got me, Bossman. I'm not going anywhere."

Miranda had a feral smile on her face, beaming at Ryan in that way he remembered from back at Fuchi when she was excited about an upcoming project. "Me too."

Grind looked at Axler, then laughed. "I'm in," he said.

Ryan gave Axler a hard stare. "I need you, chummer. You're my fragging lieutenant."

Axler smiled. "I'm here, Ryan. Slot it, I'll be here to the end. Let's get on with this run."

Ryan's eyes flicked toward the speakers. "How about you Jane?"

A sweet, chiming laugh filled the room. "You have to ask?"

"For the record, yes."

"Well, then, for the record, I'm with you. We may have some disagreements, but we'll work those out after this run."

Ryan nodded, and an invisible weight fell from his shoulders. "Good. Now that we're all on-line, let's get back to business. As I said, Burnout survived. Not only did he come through the fall in one piece, he managed to outmaneuver us."

Grind nodded. "That's one tough piece of tech."

Ryan nodded. "Jane, roll the trid."

The hologenerator in the table hummed quietly to life, and suddenly, there in the center of the table, the scene from the depot played itself out in slow motion. When it was over, Ryan looked around the room. "Any comments?" he asked.

Axler nodded. "This not only gives us a clue to Burnout's location, but it also shows us just how tough he is. Despite the apparent damage to his good looks, he took that fall into the canyon like a pleasure cruise."

"Yes," said Ryan. "We're going to have to assume that Burnout is still fully functional. He's fast, he's mean, and he's well armed."

Dhin cleared his throat. "How long ago was this?"

"About eight hours, give or take."

Dhin shook his wide head. "That's a lot of time for a chummer like that. He could be almost anywhere."

Ryan smiled. "That's true, but thankfully unimportant. Burnout leaves a trail through astral space, kind of like a polluted scent. I've smelled it."

Axler scanned from Miranda to Ryan, her voice cool. "So you can pick up his spoor and track him in astral space?"

"Exactly. After that, it's just a matter of time until we run him to ground."

Grind leered. "And then? You better have an army on hand to take that boy down."

Ryan smiled. "I don't need an army. I have you guys. We're not going to go head to head with him. I really don't care what happens to him, though my preference would be to throw his metal hoop into a waste compactor. No, the important thing is the Dragon Heart."

Axler cleared her throat. "You've fought him twice. What's the best way to take him down?"

Ryan shook his head. "There is no best way. But the fact is he was built to kill. He's tactically sharp, but his thinking seems to be a bit linear. I think we can use that to our advantage."

Axler nodded. "He's also out of options. Our kind visitor, General Dentado, indicated that Burnout has gone rogue. He can't count on any backup from the Azzies. He's solo."

"That's good," said Grind. "Five on one is my kind of odds."

Ryan smiled. "I must emphasize that the Dragon Heart is our goal, killing Burnout is gravy. Once we have the Heart, we can hunt him down at our leisure."

"Right," said Dhin, "I can take him out from nine hundred meters up."

"Yes," Ryan said, "but unfortunately, we can't fire a missile at him until after we've taken the Dragon Heart away. I don't now how much destructive force it can tolerate, and we absolutely cannot risk destroying it."

Around the room, four heads seemed to nod in unison.

"All right, we go wheels up in forty-five minutes. Full combat gear. Now let's head out."

The room cleared, all except for Dhin. He approached slowly and put his callused hand on Ryan's shoulder. "I've been rigging for most of fifteen years. Rigged more kinds of drek than I can remember. For the first time, your story about Roxborough has got me wondering just what it would be like to have somebody else rigging me. Welcome back, Bossman."

Dhin turned and left.

Ryan stood alone in the command room. "Jane?" he said.

There was a moment of solemn silence, then Jane's voice came on grave. "I'm sorry about what happened, Quicksilver. I don't think you're totally clean of Roxborough yet, but I'm committed to this run, and I'm going to see it through."

"Good, I need your expertise and your support."

Jane's voice held more conviction now. "You've got it, let's take this fragger out."

"Thanks." Ryan made his way quickly back to his quarters, and opened the door to find that someone had already laid out his gear. Within minutes, his body was encased in his armored nightsuit, form-fitting plycra with Kevlar III panels intercalated to maintain flexibility and absolute freedom of movement. Ryan needed to maintain silence and stealth even in heavy combat situations.

He checked his vest for his grenade pistol and narcotic throwing darts. The darts were habit; he brought them even knowing they wouldn't be much use against the cyberzombie. The clips of explosive and armor-piercing bullets for his Ingram should more than make up for it.

When he was ready and had achieved focus, Ryan pressed the earpiece for the Phillips tacticom into his right ear and attached the adhesive wire microphone to his throat. When it was all connected, he triggered the unit on his belt. "Everyone ready to roll?"

Axler's voice was full of droll humor. "Everyone except you, Quicksilver. We're suited up and boarded already."

Ryan chuckled. "Be right there."

The wind whistled in his ears as he made his way to the LAV. The Saeder-Krupp Phoenix II was a huge low-altitude vehicle, sitting where the Mistral had been an hour before. Ryan stepped under the Phoenix's wedge-shaped nose and walked back toward its tiny stub wings, to the ramp. Inside, the rest of his team was outfitted in matte-black Esprit full battle armor, including helmet and integral commlink.

Miranda was the exception. She was wearing camo T-shirt and pants and combat boots. On closer inspection, Ryan could see the yellow smiley faces on her socks where they stuck out just above the boot tops. She carried a small jeweled cane, and her wrists and neck seemed overloaded with charms and foci. The matte-black headset looked out of place on the small woman's head.

Miranda looked up and noticed Ryan's inspection. She shrugged. "You said full combat gear."

Axler hefted a Panther assault cannon and checked its clip. "We're ready to go wheels up on your mark," she said.

Behind Ryan, the ramp started to close, and he turned toward the cockpit. Dhin wore his armor, minus the helmet, and he was jacked in—slumped low in the cushioned seat.

"Jane give you the locale grid?"

Dhin's lax body didn't respond, but his voice came over Ryan's headset. "Copy. But I hope this is a fast trip. The sat-feed says we got God's own thunderstorm heading this way. It's going to cover the whole area just around noon."

Ryan nodded. "Wheels up."

The Phoenix roared to life, and Ryan barely had time to find his seat before the vehicle screamed into the air.

14

In the pre-dawn gray, the bulky Ford Canada Bison's off-road tires caught the loose gravel at the edge of the pavement, kicking up rock and dust. Burnout leaned into the turn, swiveled to the left and lashed out with his foot.

The driver's-side door, which had refused to latch after Burnout's forced entry, sailed into the chill air, landing with a crash as the Bison accelerated down the cracked asphalt of old Highway 83. Wind swept through the big cargo truck's interior, sending candy wrappers and bits of refuse through the cab.

In the hours since he'd bailed from the truck-train, Burnout's mood had grown foul. The constant presence of Lethe inside made him think too much about everything, and it was starting to slot him off something fierce.

"She was a pig," Burnout muttered to himself, not really expecting Lethe to have any comment. The spirit was still angry over the way Burnout had geeked the Bison's driver.

"She was an innocent." Lethe's voice dropped into his head like Burnout's long-forgotten conscience.

Burnout grunted. "Innocent, my hoop. You think that old slitch was out for a pleasure cruise at oh-four-hundred? Ten-to-one we jacked ourselves a drekload of red-hot BTL chips headed for Seattle or Spokane. If it makes you feel any better, we probably just saved the lives of fifty chipheads." Burnout didn't give a frag for anyone addicted to Better Than Life simsense, but he wasn't sure if Lethe would know that or not.

There was a long pause, then, "No, it does not make me feel any better."

Burnout laughed. "That's what I love about you.

Everything's so black and white. Well, here's a reality check for you, chummer. The world doesn't work that way. There's no such thing as good and evil, just different shades of gray."

"Explain yourself."

Burnout sighed and pushed the Bison up another twenty klicks an hour. According to his GPS, they should reach the abandoned mail road in less than forty minutes, provided he could keep this tub on the roadway. "There are always reasons for apparently evil acts."

"Justifiable homicide?"

"Yes."

"No such thing."

Burnout slammed his fist into the dash, trying to contain his anger. "All right, let's just forget for a minute that our little old lady was a piece of trash who has made the world a better place with her hasty departure."

Lethe chuckled, a low soft thing that Burnout found oddly comforting. "All right, it is forgotten."

Burnout nodded. "That's better. Let's say she was a granny out for a joyride to visit her brat's brats. I chose this vehicle for a reason. It's been years since I've been along this route. I don't know just how the terrain has changed. I passed up two Jackrabbits and a Westwind before this ride came along."

"You have lost me again."

"Then listen, slot it! Granny comes along in the perfect vehicle for our purposes. Now, it doesn't matter that she hadn't been doing anything wrong, that she'd led an innocent life. We needed this truck, right?"

Lethe chuckled again. "Well, at least I am still following you."

Burnout slowed to take a long, winding curve, then punched it in the short straight-away. "Now suppose we left Granny alive. What's the first thing she's going to do when the next car comes by?"

Lethe's voice took on the cautious tone Burnout had noticed him using whenever he was beginning to fall behind Burnout's logic. "She would signal the car to pick her up?"

Burnout laughed. "Fragging right. And when that car stopped, what's the next thing she would have done?"

"I think I begin to see your reasoning. She would have notified the authorities of our activities."

"Score one for the spirit. I think you're getting it. You see, even if she hadn't been a smuggler, I'd still have had to geek her to keep Mercury from picking up our trail."

Another long pause. "That is, of course, where your reasoning goes astray."

Burnout grunted and slowed the Bison to maneuver around some deep potholes. "Astray? And what do you mean? My logic is rock-solid. I had to do what I had to do."

"Maybe I'm being a bit presumptive, and forgive me if I've not followed everything exactly, but if she was a smuggler, then . . ."

Burnout's supply of patience finally dried up. "Then what? Spit it out!"

"If the woman was a smuggler, then, if I judge things correctly, the last people she would want to contact would be the authorities. So, by your reasoning, you could have left her alive and in no way jeopardized your agenda."

Burnout sat in the howling wind, realization drifting into his mind. He nearly missed the tight arc in the road way. He fought the Bison back into the curve, hearing the sound of branches snapping as the big tires caught and shredded some of the shrubs in the ditch.

In the long moments that followed, Burnout replayed everything in his mind. The squeal of the Bison's tires as it screeched to a halt in front of him, the stench of burned rubber and tar. The woman's shout, the feel of the door rending under his chrome fingers, the sight of the Predator as she pulled it from beneath the seat, and finally the sound of her neck snapping, dull and wet, her body going limp under him.

Now, Burnout had regained control of the big truck. He spoke in a soft voice, barely audible under the roar of the wind whipping in the open door. A normal person couldn't have heard him say, "You know, I hate it when you do that."

Lethe's voice was contrite. "My apologies. I did not

mean to anger you. It is simply that I dislike death in all forms, and unnecessary death—"

"I've heard the speech. Frag, I hate this."

"Again, I apologize."

They came to a long stretch of straight road, just as the sun started to poke its head over the top of the eastern range. Burnout floored the accelerator, causing the big rig to jump forward like a live thing. "Well, I don't. I don't think I was wrong to nix her, even knowing that I could have left her alive. Even if she was a smuggler, Ryan has a pretty long arm. It might have taken him a bit longer, but he still would have found out what happened. But that's not the point, I guess. The point is that I made a split-second decision. When she pulled the Predator, I had two choices."

"Yes," Lethe said. "You have made your reasons clear. Even though, in hindsight, they may not have been as sound as you would have liked them to be, I understand that you did not make your decision lightly. I underestimated you, and you deserve better. Please accept the apology."

A feeling ran through Burnout then, something he hadn't felt in years. In all his previous time under Slaver's command, he'd been treated as nothing more than a killing machine. Something to be pointed at the enemy and let go, and when there was no enemy present, Slaver had treated him as if he didn't exist, as if he was less than nothing.

He recognized the feeling. *Respect.* It felt better than any killing rush, or drug high. It was almost intoxicating.

He smiled. "Apology accepted."

They traveled for another twenty minutes in silence, because the road had deteriorated to such a level it took every ounce of Burnout's skill just to maintain speed. Finally, Burnout's GPS indicated that this was the spot, and he pulled the Bison to the edge of the road.

In the early sunlight, a wide glen stretched off to either side of the highway. To his right, Burnout could see the charred remains of an old church in a far corner of the field. Across the narrow dirt road, an even older log cabin slumped toward the ground, years of neglect having finally taken their toll.

"This is it," said Burnout.

"This is what?"

"This is where the turn-off is supposed to be. That burnt building was still a little white church when I was a kid. The Kodiak once told me that old cabin belonged to his great-grandfather, way back before the Awakening."

Burnout turned his head to the left, and let the Bison roll slowly forward. "The old mail route used to be right here." On the left of the vehicle, there was nothing but dry, yellow wheat grass, stretching up to the tree line.

"There!" Burnout pointed to a break in the trees, which had been invisible from any angle but dead on. He turned the truck off the highway and coaxed it over the grassland. As they entered the forest, the overgrown road could only be made out as two separate ruts, too narrow for the Bison's big tires.

Burnout pushed the speed up as high as he dared, and for the next hour, they climbed. Higher and higher, taking switchbacks with deft, fishtail cranks of the wheel. The air grew thinner, and the soft breeze pushing in the doorway grew warmer as the sun heated up the afternoon.

The road, which had started out as a minimal thing, turned slowly worse, until even the Bison couldn't navigate the narrow, slippery track anymore. Finally, Burnout halted the vehicle.

"This is as far as the boat will go," he said as he shut off the engine. Actually he was surprised that they had made it this far up into the Montana Rocky Mountains. In the early morning sunlight, he could see the majestic, jagged rock face of Swan Mountain off to his right, and above, the rounded, pine-covered dome of Pony Mountain loomed. The scent of honeysuckle and huckleberries filled the air as a starling broke from cover and shot into the sky.

Burnout collected what remained of his gear. In the rear storage compartment, he found extra rounds for the twin Predators he now carried. Something about the rear space seemed wrong to him, the dimensions off by almost a meter.

He leaned forward, grabbed the carpeting off the rear wall of the compartment, and found the locked, hidden compartment. One swing of his fist and the heavy lock shattered.

Hundreds of BTL chips flew everywhere. Better-Than-Life were highly addictive simsense chips with sensory limits well beyond legal. Harder than drugs, and more addictive, these silicon babies burned users out, and many of them died.

Burnout shook his head. "Told you she was low-life. Now are you happy?"

"Luck."

It was a simple word, but it lodged deep inside Burnout's psyche and refused to be pushed away. He didn't respond, trying to concentrate on the tasks at hand. He shut the rear compartment, stuffed the extra clips into the duster's pockets. Checked the Heart to make sure it was secure at his side, then strode into the brush.

They climbed fast, Burnout's legs pistoning, his hands snatching for a hold on anything. Rocks and trees flashed by as he moved, his entire focus bent on covering ground. He disregarded the path they crossed after about ten minutes of climbing. "That's the way I went when I was a child. I'm pleased to see it's still in good shape, that means the Kodiak has been using it regularly."

The IMS kicked in. "What if it is being used by someone other than your friend? It is possible he has died and that someone a bit less helpful has taken up residence on the mountain top."

Burnout grunted and caught the lower limb of a tree to pull himself up a sharp incline. "Possible, but not likely. Besides, we'll know when we get there, and that shouldn't be much longer."

Despite his glib response, Burnout found that Lethe's comment brought more than a bit of doubt with it. If the Kodiak wasn't there, then Burnout's list of options dwindled considerably.

As he ran, he realized that he was nervous. Something he hadn't experienced since the day he discovered the full extent of his power at age seventeen.

He wasn't so much nervous that the Kodiak would be

dead, but more that the old man might just as well decide against helping them, or even worse, might tell Burnout that he was unable to help. That the Heart would remain forever just beyond his grasp.

What's happening to me? he wondered. Before Lethe, this kind of self-doubt was a dim feeling easily quashed or alleviated by action. Now, with an expanding awareness of the world around him came a deeper understanding of how dangerous this whole situation had become.

Lethe's comments about the smuggler still bothered him, but he didn't know why. Her death had been more than warranted. Maybe it was remorse. Maybe it was that he hadn't thought it through completely. That Lethe was right; Burnout had gotten *lucky*. In this game, against these odds, and with such high stakes, luck just didn't cut it.

He'd have to be more careful in the future, maybe even talk to Lethe when he made a plan.

The very idea of consulting someone before making a move caused an itch in a place he just couldn't scratch. But the truth of it was that the spirit looked at things from a whole different angle. And it was a viewpoint that could prove valuable.

Burnout was still considering this when they crested a nearly vertical rise and then stepped out onto the edge of a small lake. Almost four hundred meters across and ringed on three sides by dense forest, the placid green waters looked cool and clean. Just off shore, Burnout saw a fish jump, a huge salmon that he suspected had fought its way back up the streams to the lake to spawn and die.

"This is Cat Lake," he said. "The Kodiak ice-fishes here when the lean season makes hunting hard."

"It is beautiful."

Burnout said nothing, but simply circled the lake to where the rocky ground sloped up gently from the shore. As he scrambled up the rise, he looked out over the vast valley that fell away to his side, and for just an instant, he was a boy again, clinging to his mother's hand, frightened, tired, but filled with awe as he looked out into the vast wilderness.

His whole childhood had been spent within the confines of thc sprawl, and even though he'd been told such wild places still existed, he'd never really been able to imagine just how awe-inspiring they could be. He had gripped his mother's hand tightly, laughing with a giddy, intoxicated humor.

His mother had just kept pulling him onward.

Now, his nervousness increased as they crested the small rise, and Burnout stopped.

Just a hundred meters ahead, across smooth granite, the tower rose into the sky, its rough-timber skeleton frame topped with a circular turret. At the base of the tower, a cabin had been built using the huge main struts as a support base.

From the small smokestack on the cabin's roof, a pale gray cloud puffed skyward until it was caught by the breeze and dispelled. Burnout's cybernetic sense of smell caught the scent, and for the first time since beginning his journey, a tremendous weight fell from his shoulders. He knew that musky scent, and it brought with it many memories, flooding him and leaving him with one feeling.

It smelled like home.

Suddenly, he heard a sound echo from deep within the tree line. Burnout readied himself and within a minute, a huge shambling form bearing an impossibly huge armload of firewood pushed through the trees, heading for the cabin. The form was that of a man, taller even than Burnout, though the cyberzombie remembered him as being much bigger.

The man wore loose-fitting linens and a dark fur coat. The clothing only added to the impression of vast size and power, though the man's clothing did nothing to hide the bulging gut. A snow-white beard rolled down his chest, joining in a glorious snarl with the salt and pepper locks coming from the man's head.

The man took two more steps before stopping. He tilted his head high. Wide nostrils flared, sniffing.

Then, with a move so fast it seemed impossible for so much mass to move so swiftly, the man dropped the wood and turned in Burnout's direction. The large double-headed axe, which had been hanging from the man's belt, seemed to materialize in his huge paws.

He sniffed again, his tiny eyes closed. Then, in a deep growl, the old man spoke. "I don't know your scent, and you don't belong here. Leave the way you came."

Burnout felt a strange tremor run though his body, something that told him not to disobey. He laughed.

"Old Kodiak, it's me. Burn . . . Billy Madson. It's been a long time since you first taught me the beginning ways of the path. My mother brought me, remember?"

The old man's defensive posture didn't falter. "I remember my own, creature. Billy Madson was very gifted, headstrong, and impatient. You are not him. Leave now."

Burnout took a step forward. "Old Kodiak, things have changed, more than I'd like to admit. But it *is* me, Billy Madson. I've returned to you because I need your help, and you are the last option I have. Please, you must help me."

The old man's eyes finally focused on Burnout. They seemed to grow bright, and Burnout knew he was looking into the astral. The Kodiak stared for a minute, then stepped back. "Billy, my son, what has been done to you?" The deep growl took on the slightest quail of despair. "There is so little of you left, and even that fractured bit of spirit is completely overwhelmed by something golden that is trapped inside you."

The old man stepped forward. "Have you come for me to free your spirit from this abomination? To set things right with you again?"

Burnout shook his head sadly, abruptly aware of his chrome body, suddenly more than a bit ashamed of what he'd become. "No, Kodiak. I've laid my bets, and I don't doubt that the end will come soon. But first I must talk to you."

The old man frowned. "My son, what could one who has forsaken everything the fates meant him to be have to say?"

Burnout felt those words like a blow, but still a smile came to his lips as his hands dipped into the cloth at his waist.

"What I have to say can wait. First, it's what I have to show you." Burnout held the Heart out toward the old man, the sunlight catching the perfection of its creation, sending out a dazzling wash of golden light that made the sun seem pale.

Under the sparkle of the Heart's light, the old man sank to his knees. "Oh, my son. I fear for you, for you hold the beginning, or possibly the end, of the world in your hands."

15

Ryan sank into the bottom of his seat as the Phoenix II LAV accelerated into the air. The wind had little effect on the heavy vehicle, and the ride was solid, if a little jerky as Dhin tried to keep them below local radar.

Dhin's voice came over the tacticom. "ETA forty-three minutes."

Ryan nodded. "Copy," he said. "Jane, you on-line?"

"I'm in my virtual steel box and ready to integrate everybody's feed," came her digital voice.

"Excellent, you'll be my clairvoyance for the others. What's the situation on site?"

"Well, Quicksilver, you're not going to like this. The whole place is crawling with local law. They're still freaked over Burnout, and they've got traffic closed off from all directions. Some local shaman is doing a lot of mumbo-jumbo, but he doesn't seem to be getting anywhere. If anything, that's spooking the local cops even more. You roll in there the wrong way and things could get ugly."

Axler cut in. "Ready for plan beta, Quicksilver?"

Plan Beta was a simple diversionary tactic, which would call for Dhin setting down somewhere outside the perimeter, then both he and Jane arranging for a distraction while the primary team got in and got out.

Ryan thought about it, then laughed. "No. Dhin, fly straight in. Land on an open stretch of pavement by the depot building."

Axler laughed. "What, you planning on just buzzing in and pushing all the law kids around like you were Daniel Howling Coyote jumped up from the burial ground?"

Ryan nodded. "That's exactly what I plan on doing. Jane, can you get mc Nadja on a private channel?"

"Sure, Quicksilver. Connecting now."

Ryan waited in silence for a moment. Then Nadja's sleepy, concerned voice filled his ears. "Ryan? Is everything all right?"

A dull, empty ache filled Ryan's chest. "Yes, everything's fine. I need a favor."

"Name it."

"We're headed into a hot situation near Kooskia in the Salish-Shidhe Council lands. We need some big official pull, because were short on time and long on jurisdiction. I don't want some second-rate cop telling us that we can't inspect the site. Think you can help us out?"

Nadja's voice was no longer concerned, it was all business now. "What's the time frame?"

"Twenty minutes, give or take."

Nadja sighed. "The Native American Nations loved Dunkelzahn, and Salish-Shidhe is no exception. You'll have the full cooperation of their entire government."

"Thanks. It'll save us valuable time."

"You're welcome," Nadja said. "And Ryan?" The concern was back in her voice.

"Yes?"

"Do you know what you're doing?"

Ryan smiled. "I'm taking care of business as fast as I can so I can get back to you."

Nadja laughed. "Good answer."

The line went dead.

Grind's voice filled his ears. "Frag, Ryan. You have to keep teaching us the basic rules of shadowrunning?"

Miranda looked across the small cabin of the Phoenix. "What basic rule?"

Axler's voice held a note of impatience. "Use *all* your talents, even if some of them *are* legal."

The rest of the trip went quickly, and as the team checked their equipment one last time, the LAV howled into hover position and descended. With a soft thump, they were down, and Dhin cut the engines. The doors hissed open, and the team hit dirt to find themselves staring into the barrels of more than twenty assault rifles.

A big man stepped forward into the still-blowing jet wash from the Phoenix. The dark skin of his face declared his Amerind heritage, and his tusked mouth showed his ork metatype. "Name and business, or we open fire."

Ryan didn't even slow his advance. "Check with your superiors. I have clearance to take charge of this crime scene." Ryan's magically enhanced senses were at full alert, and he felt confident. "I don't need you getting in the way. Now get these guns out of my face, or I'll have your badge."

On the tacticom, Ryan heard Grind whisper, "*Cojones* of pure titanium."

The big ork didn't back down. "I said, name and business, or we—"

Ryan cut him off with a wave of his hand. "I heard you the first time. Get on the horn to your commanding officer, then get out of our way. I'll give you one minute."

Ryan could see the hesitation in the ork's eyes.

The cop stared at Ryan as if to judge his sincerity. "Frag!" he said finally, then turned away. "Get me Captain Novak on the line. Now!"

The ork walked to his vehicle, and spoke quickly through his commlink for a few moments. The conversation seemed heated. Within a minute he returned, his back stiff, his face flushed. "My apologies for your reception, sir. My entire force is at your disposal, of course."

Ryan signaled for the rest of his team to move out. "Just tell your boys to stay out of our way. We'll be gone in a few minutes."

He didn't wait for the man's response, but signaled Miranda to take the far end of the compound, then shifted his sight to the astral as he walked toward the station. It only took a minute for Ryan to see that Burnout had been here. The whole area was polluted. But as he searched, he could not see any trails leading away from the depot.

"Miranda, you see anything?"

Miranda's voice came over the tacticom. "This is odd . . . I see a lot of background, but no definite trail. If a cyberzombie was here, the evidence should be plain."

Just then, Jane cut in. "Quicksilver," she said, "I've picked up buzz of a murder at the junction of I-200 and

Old Route 83. It's got Burnout written all over it. Local law also found the door to a Ford Canada Bison just a few minutes up 83."

"Just the door?"

"Yeah, mangled pretty good, too. Ripped right off the hinges. Looks like our metal monster ditched the truck-train and carjacked himself some wheels."

Ryan turned, whirling his arm above his head in the signal to rally up and return to the Phoenix. "Let's roll," he said, running toward it. "Thanks, Jane. Pipe the coordinates to Dhin. We're on our way."

Then he was through the doors of the LAV, and they were firing into the air. Through the small window, Ryan looked down at the upturned faces of the local law boys. Their confusion was so apparent, he couldn't help but laugh as the Phoenix II shot into the morning sky.

A few minutes later, Dhin's voice came over the tacticom. "Approaching location."

Ryan peered out the thick macroglass side window. He could make out a few cop cars and a lot of backed up traffic, but there wasn't much to see. He pushed his vision into the astral, looking around for the telltale signs of Burnout's passage.

The trail was subtle, like a shimmering wave, heat interference outlined with a green sparkle. It was much less visible than it should be, which answered the questions of why Ryan couldn't pick it up back at the depot. It was only because the astral background was a lot dimmer out here that Ryan could perceive it at all.

Burnout is somehow masking his aura, Ryan thought. *Perhaps it's an accidental effect of the Dragon Heart.*

"I think I've picked up the trail," Miranda said. "But it's nothing like the slime path of a cyberzombie."

Ryan refocused on the physical and turned toward her. "Can you follow it?"

"I think so," Miranda said. "Let me see." Then her body slumped as she went astral. Miranda was projecting her consciousness into the astral plane and following the trail left by Burnout. It was something Ryan couldn't do. As a physical adept, he could see into the astral plane, but he couldn't separate his consciousness from his physical being.

Axler and Grind sat ready, their eyes riveted to Miranda's slumped form. Suddenly Miranda's eyes opened. "The trail is straight. He's headed north."

Ryan's fists unclenched. He'd worried that Burnout might have doubled back on them, which would have meant he knew he was being pursued. As it was, the cyberzombie was making a buzz line for his destination, and unless he had a very big card left to play, in the form of some heavy friends to help him out, he was unaware of how close the team had gotten.

All the better. If Burnout had time to prepare, their reception could get hot, but if they managed to take him by surprise, they might just smoke him out before he knew what hit him.

Ryan looked at Miranda. "Track him in the astral. Let's pin him down."

Miranda nodded and closed her eyes again.

"Dhin," said Ryan.

"Yes?"

"North, until I tell you differently."

"Copy."

In the cabin, the roar of rockets thundered as the Phoenix II leapt forward. They traveled like that for another five minutes, until Miranda opened her eyes again. "Frag, that boy travels well."

Ryan took the seat facing the mage. "You got him locked?"

Miranda nodded. "Yes, but there's something you should know."

"What?"

"There's a shaman and some kind of spirit with him."

Ryan, who had been lost in his own thoughts for a moment, was snatched back to reality. "What spirit?" He had a sinking feeling inside.

"Don't know," Miranda said. "But it's the most powerful one I've ever seen, and it's inside our cyberzombie."

Lethe, Ryan thought. *Who else could it be?*

16

In the heavy morning air, the smoke from the small campfire sent dim, gray smoke into the canopy of pines. Off to
the east, Burnout saw the dark mass of clouds, growing
larger. A storm was coming, he could feel its tension in
the muggy stillness.

It's nearly upon us, he thought.

On the other side of the campfire, the Kodiak knelt on a
gigantic bearskin, which just fit inside the large circle of
talismana he had laid out on the rocky soil. His medicine
lodge. Next to the Kodiak sat the Heart, gleaming yellow
in a giant bear's claw. The Heart seemed to glow dully in
the darkening morning.

Burnout glanced up at the Kodiak. The old man had
started his spiritual journey almost an hour ago, beginning
with soft chants accompanied by the rhythmic rattle of a
bone shaker. Now, his painted face was streaked with
sweat, and he didn't speak; instead, he simply swayed to
some internal beat only he could hear.

Just like old times, thought Burnout.

Since the start of the ceremony, Lethe had said nothing,
though Burnout could almost sense the spirit communing
outside his perception. The longer they stayed together,
the more attuned he and the Lethe seemed to be.

Burnout watched the approaching storm, and a feeling
of apprehension grew in him. It felt like . . . like . . .

Mercury comes.

Burnout looked down at his ravaged body, the skin of
his hands flayed to the chrome, the dermal sheathing
poking through a ragged hole in his coveralls. The telescoping fingers that had served him so well were mangled

and twisted, severed in places and unable to effectively retract.

Burnout knew he was the most efficient killing machine tech and magic could produce. Both times he'd gone up against Ryan, the simple human—with no chrome Burnout could discern—had proven tougher than anything Burnout could have imagined. Each time, the man had scarred Burnout and come through alive.

Questions plagued Burnout with their unanswerable intensity. Why had this man been chosen by Dunkelzahn? What lay hidden beneath Mercury's human exterior that made him a match for the best that science and the dark arts could produce?

In his peripheral vision, he saw that the Kodiak had stopped swaying and had opened his eyes. The Heart had darkened, and it lay quiet. The Kodiak heaved a heavy sigh and sat upright on the bearskin. Exhaustion lined his face as he spoke. "I have talked with Bear, my son. He has shown me the truth of things, both seen and unseen."

Burnout leaned forward hungrily. "Yes, what did Bear tell you about the Heart?"

The Kodiak's narrow eyes looked sad. "Of the artifact you call the Heart, Bear said simply that it follows its own destiny. It isn't for you or any man to possess and control. It has a place in the sacred dance, and though it might be useful to you for now, it will fulfill its destiny."

Burnout sat back, unsure of how to take what the old man had said. "Does that mean I can tap into it? That I can—"

The old man waved him off. "Your relationship to the . . . Heart is nebulous at best. You can do with it what you can. It cannot give you back the gift you have thrown away."

Burnout nodded. He had longed to feel the power of the magic arts he had once wielded with pleasure. Now that yearning faded with a grim sigh.

"As the Heart makes its moves according to the sacred dance, you might be able to connect with it. That's all I can tell you."

Burnout knew it was all he could have hoped for and more than he deserved. He was about to stand, when the

Kodiak spoke again. "The Bear has spoken to me of the spirit that travels with you."

Once again, Burnout found himself leaning forward.

"The one you call Lethe is directly tied to the Heart and its sacred dance. Though now, through methods unspeakable, it is also tied to you. Bear does not think the two of you can be separated at this time. And even if it were possible, it would most likely kill one, if not both, of you."

Burnout wondered how Lethe felt about being a prisoner inside him.

The Kodiak chuckled. "So I suggest you get used to him, son. It looks as if this Lethe is going to be with you for some time."

Burnout nodded. "I don't want to get rid of Lethe, Kodiak. He's proven himself, and I trust him."

The old man closed his eyes and gave a tired smile. "That's good, my son, because the spirit's presence is the only thing that makes you human. The abomination you've become is tempered by the proximity of Lethe. With him near, you become more than the sum of your parts. Without him, any chance you might have of contacting the essence of the Heart will disappear."

Again Burnout nodded, though this time more to himself. It was just as he'd thought. Lethe was the one responsible for his heightened awareness, his increased memory retention.

The old man's face became grave. "Bear also told me of another who is tied to you and the Heart."

"Another?"

"One who tracks you."

Ryan. So my gut hunch was right.

Burnout stood, suddenly anxious. "Yes, the one called Ryan Mercury."

"Bear told me that the one you call Mercury is even now in pursuit of the Heart that you carry."

So Mercury is coming, for sure. Burnout felt the familiar anticipation roll through him. *I will be ready for you, Mercury. You may be the best I've met, but I will destroy you like I have the others.*

"This one stalking you, this Mercury, you are aware how powerful he is?"

Burnout nodded. "He is the most formidable opponent I have ever faced, and each time we meet he gets better. He learns more and more of my capabilities, but always seems to be able to surprise me."

The old man stroked his thick beard. "Bear has told me that he is even more powerful than you can imagine."

Burnout gave him a hard look. "In what way?"

The Kodiak frowned. "Bear did not reveal specifics, saying only that the being named Mercury is powerful enough that you, even as . . . altered as you've become, are no match for him. There is one thing that can be used to your advantage, however."

Burnout looked down at the ruin of his body. "Give it to me. I can use all the help I can get."

"Mercury has no idea just how powerful he is."

Burnout looked up sharply. "What?"

"Mercury has come nowhere close to realizing his full potential."

Burnout grinned. "He can't use what he doesn't know about. He is only as strong as he thinks he is."

"He will be here soon," the Kodiak said. "And he comes ready for battle."

Burnout stood. "Then I better prepare. I think Mercury is in for a few surprises when he arrives."

The old man rose as well. "My son, he comes in force. No matter how well prepared you are, there is no way you will stand against his onslaught alone."

Burnout shrugged. "Thanks for the advice, Kodiak. But I'm tired of running, and I don't have anywhere to go even if I had the stomach for it."

The old man's voice grew compassionate. "I said you could not stand up to him alone. But this is my mountain, my home. No matter what dark paths you have chosen to follow, you were once my student, and that makes you as much of a son to me as any blood tie. No one harms my children in my home. I am not as young as I once was, but my powers have not waned. I am far more powerful today than when you came to me all those years ago. You will not stand alone when Mercury arrives."

Burnout looked at the old man. "Thank you," he said. "For everything."

Into Burnout's mind came Lethe's voice filled with fierce determination. "No. You will not stand alone. The Kodiak and I will be here with you. Ryan has already tried once to take the Heart for his own. He abandoned his devotion to his ancient master, and it was only by your intervention that the Dragon Heart was torn from his selfish hands. He must never be allowed to take it back."

17

Ryan sat in the Phoenix II's cabin, cruising above Old Route 83, listening to the roar of the engines. Outside, the winds of the approaching thunderstorm howled like a banshee. The hole in his gut grew hollow as he listened to Miranda.

"It's like Burnout is possessed, but not quite. His aura looks nothing like what I've seen in other cyberzombies. It's as though there's another spirit hovering in and around him, and one big fragger too. Never seen a presence like that."

Axler turned to Ryan. "You thinking what I'm thinking?"

Ryan nodded. "Lethe."

Axler's fine eyebrows drew tight. "Never did trust that astral piece of drek."

Ryan sighed. "That also explains why Burnout's aura is masked and his trail is hard to follow. Where are they?"

"He's on a mountain top, not far from here."

Ryan stood and looked down at Miranda. "You said there was a shaman with him?"

"I think so. I've gotten good at identifying them. He was certainly a gifted old man, but he could have been a mage."

"Did the shaman tag you when you made your pass?"

Miranda smiled, showing white teeth. "Null chance. I was very discreet."

"I'm counting on it," Ryan said. "If Burnout has any idea we're coming, he'll be prepared. Or gone." Ryan turned and spoke into the tacticom. "Dhin?"

"Yes?"

"Give me the status on that storm you've been promising me."

"Look out the window, Bossman. One picture is worth a thousand lines of code."

Ryan ducked to the macroglass porthole. Massive black clouds were spreading rapidly, lit with flashes of lightning. The LAV was headed for the heart of the darkness.

All right, thought Ryan. The tactician in him took over. The storm should hit in the next hour, and his team would follow it in, by-the-book assault.

He turned, "Jane?"

Her voice sounded in his earphone. "Here, Quicksilver."

"You got satellite imagery of Pony Mountain?"

"I just decked into the weather feeds, courtesy of Ares Macrotechnology," Jane said. "They're not military-grade, but should do for our assault. And they come in glorious full-color, three-D topographical."

"Thanks," Ryan said. In the rear of the cabin, the small holographic display lit up with a three-dimensional terrain map of the surrounding area.

Ryan turned to Miranda. "Can you pinpoint him?"

Miranda's almond eyes fixed on Ryan, and she smiled. "Of course."

Ryan stepped back to the holo display. "Show me."

Miranda pointed to the display. "This ridge line here. Pony Mountain. There's a tower of some sort right at the southeast edge."

Ryan nodded, studying the terrain of the mountain top, which was shaped like an upside-down triangle.

Grind whistled. "That's a rough piece of ground there, Ryan. Sheer cliff faces on two sides, dense forest and open ground on the others."

Axler stepped up to the display. "The only landing zone is this spot of barren ground just up from this tiny lake. Unless we want to hike in?"

Miranda was shaking her head. "Not if we can help it."

Axler went on. "The ground practically funnels us straight toward the tower. If he's ready for us or if the noise of this bird alerts him too soon, he could take us out with a few missiles before we get three hundred meters."

Ryan looked at the map for a moment, then the plan came to him. "Okay, this is how it's going down."

Grind edged in next to him. "You're going in? I know you're a good tactician, Quicksilver, but this is prime ground for an ambush. Standard strategy would suggest forcing his hand, forcing him off the mountain and into a position of our choosing, not his."

Ryan looked at the dwarf. "You spooked by our cyberzombie?"

"He's a killing machine, Ryan."

"Yes, but I've got a plan."

Axler spoke. "Spill it, Ryan. We're with you."

Ryan smiled and turned back to the holo display. "Twice I've almost died because I underestimated Burnout. I'm not going to make that mistake a third time."

The rest of the team gathered around him and the display.

"All right," said Ryan "Here's how this goes down."

He looked at the rest of them. "Axler, you and Miranda are Alpha team. Grind and I will be Beta." He turned back to the map. "Grind was right. The terrain works against us here. We have to assume that Burnout chose this spot to minimize the risk of being outflanked."

Axler nodded. "Taking the only avenue to the tower is like walking down a dragon's throat. He'll chew us up and spit us right back out."

Ryan smiled. "Yes, except we won't be taking that avenue."

Axler looked at Ryan coldly. "How else?"

Ryan pointed to the cliff face on the far side of the clearing. "Here."

"Pretty fragging dangerous," Axler said.

"Hear me out," Ryan said. "This plan has its drawbacks, but at least listen to it before you pick it apart. Burnout is smart, and he's tough. It's going to take all of us working together to make sure this comes off without any of us getting iced."

Axler waited. "Go ahead."

Ryan nodded and turned back to the map. "Burnout's

got incredible hearing and will most likely notice the Phoenix before we clear a thousand meters. Even with the storm. Now, this craft has all the aerodynamics of a large rock when you cut the engines. She falls, and she falls fast. I'm going to have Dhin take her up to her max altitude—about two thousand meters, if I'm correct. Situate us above the cliff edge, here."

He pointed again to the sheer rock face.

"Dhin will then cut the engines. We'll freefall to just below the cliff's edge, and he'll hit the engines. Given the amount of thrust needed to bank our fall, it should sound just like a thunderclap rolling through the valley."

Ryan looked around at them. Both Axler and Grind were nodding, smiling. Only Miranda looked apprehensive. "In the few seconds following, Alpha and Beta teams will debark on the cliff's edge. Then Dhin will take the Phoenix up and over, landing at the LZ here, in the clearing just where Burnout would expect us to be."

Ryan pointed to the south edge of the ridge. "Alpha team will skirt the cliff here, while Beta team moves along this slope." He pointed to the north side, facing the lake.

"During this, Dhin will land and send out the two drones; one air, one ground, to head toward the cabin. Making just enough noise so Burnout will think we're prime targets for the ambush."

Grind's face pulled into a snarled grin. "Simple cut and sweep. Very nice."

"Thanks. The first team to tag Burnout calls it. Hopefully, it will be the drones, but if not, whichever team tags him does nothing until the other team is in position. Got it?"

Miranda's apprehension came to the surface. "What if Burnout makes contact first?"

Ryan nodded. "Good question. If unavoidable contact happens, Dhin will use the drones to keep him occupied until reinforcements arrive. Any questions?"

Axler brushed a stray strand of hair back from her face. "Yeah. What about the shaman? He could have some pretty nasty surprises in store for us."

Miranda laughed. "Leave the old man to me. Ain't no backwoods piece of drek gonna spoil our play. I'll eat him for lunch."

Ryan winced. Miranda was an excellent mage, especially in theory and experimental spell design, but could she slice and dice in the non-corporate world? He didn't know. "I sure hope you're right, Miranda. 'Cause if not, this whole mission is going to turn to drek."

Miranda fingered the large ruby pendant that hung from her neck. "Trust me. The old man is going to find out the hard way just how well I know what I'm doing."

Ryan stared at her, searching for clues to what lay under the arrogance. "You got something against shamans?"

Miranda shook her head. "Undisciplined slots," she snarled, giving Ryan a sly smile. "No, got nothing against them. I'm just juiced up for a fight. It's been a long time since I felt the pleasure of raging mana."

Ryan smiled. "Just don't burn it all too soon."

Her smile faded. "You handle the tactics, I'll deal with the arcana."

Her attitude bothered him, but he really didn't have much choice but to give her the benefit of the doubt. "Okay," he said, looking around at the others. "Any further questions?"

They all shook their heads.

"Dhin?"

"Yes?"

"You ready for action?"

There was laughter over Ryan's earpiece. "I'm already into position for the power dive. The storm is really starting to kick things around down there. Better strap yourselves in. This is going to be a hell of a ride."

Ryan shut off the topographical display. "Jane?"

"Ready to coordinate tacticom and vid from here, Quicksilver."

"All right, everybody strap in."

In the next few seconds, the team strapped themselves in to their crash harnesses and made one last check of their weapons and ammunition. When they were all ready, Ryan said, "Dhin. Take us down."

The steady rocket roar, a constant background noise until now, went silent. Ryan's stomach shot into his throat as the Phoenix II began to fall, picking up speed as it dropped from the sky.

18

On the far edge of the Matrix, in a deep pocket of pure ultraviolet information, the world of Wonderland stretched tendrils out into cyberspace. Alice rarely traveled through the Matrix to find what she wanted. Instead, Wonderland pulled that information into itself.

Alice and Wonderland were one and the same. Two facets of the same gem. Two manifestations of the same code. In this case, she was checking out Rox's story about Dunkelzahn's role in the Crash of '29.

The shining city stretched up into a glossy black sky around her as she walked. Moody and smoking more cigarettes than she should. Virtual smokes didn't have the drawbacks of the real thing, but the narcotic effects were programmed in. The city street felt like a canyon of mirrored blue glass, a trench of glistening mist over an empty urban landscape. No people, only buildings. This was her city and she rarely shared it.

Guess I'll have to deal with Rox sooner or later. Wonderland had checked out his story, but had turned up a few inconsistencies. Anomalies. Alice didn't like anomalies.

She opened a window and peered through into the land programmed to run like Lewis Carroll's Wonderland. She faded herself into that reality as the Cheshire cat, noticing that Rox had survived to reach a carefully sculptured garden of white roses, some of which seemed to have been painted red.

On the far side of the garden, a game of croquet was in progress. Man-sized playing cards, each with swords at their flat sides, leaned on each other to form crude bridges.

A huge woman, dressed in an ornate red frock and

wearing a crystal tiara in her high-piled hair, was screaming at the top of her lungs. " 'Off with his head!' I said, 'Off with his head!' "

The guards, who had tumbled to the ground when she began screaming, rushed about in a frenzy, trying to find the offending party. Unfortunately, the Queen of Hearts seemed to be pointing in all directions, one right after the other. She even pointed to a rose bush that an over-zealous guard had lopped to the ground.

The Queen looked at the bush and wailed, "Now, off with *his* head." This time she had finally settled on the guard who had chopped down the roses.

The other two grabbed the third and hauled him away.

Alice looked around for Roxborough, finally spotting him near the garden entrance. Tucked under his arm, a great pink flamingo struggled to get free while Roxborough tried to get the small hedgehog at his feet to stay still long enough for him to use the flamingo to hit the poor creature.

Roxborough looked years older than he had the last time, and he had covered his fat body with a table cloth, wrapped around like a towel and tucked to stay up under his arms. He winced in pain as he moved, bending down slowly.

Alice knew the lupus was extremely painful, and would continue to worsen if her program was allowed to run its course.

Roxborough grimaced and dropped the flamingo, which jumped away from him in an explosion of pink feathers. He screamed suddenly and collapsed to the ground in a heap. The small hedgehog unrolled from its protective ball and scampered after the flamingo.

Roxborough spotted Alice's Cheshire cat icon and glared at her. "Damn it, Alice! I've told you everything I know."

"Oh, I hardly believe that, Rox. In fact, you've been very naughty."

"Naughty? Get bent, Alice."

Alice settled in the tree above him. "You seemed to have left out a pulse or two of data regarding the story of your alleged attempt to purchase Gossamer Threads."

Roxborough looked at her, then shook his head. He was in obvious pain, though he was trying to pretend otherwise. "It's a pity you had to show up just now. I'd finally gotten the hang of this game. I think I could have actually beaten the Queen this round. That damn flamingo was a dud, though. Wouldn't even keep his neck stiff. Every time his head hit the hedgehog, the little bugger rolled less than a meter."

Alice's tone was soft. "Rox, stick to the subject, or you'll be the next one to lose your head here."

"Did I hear someone say lose your head?"

The Queen waddled up to the tree, breathing hard. "Hello, Cat. You want me to take this little bastard's head?"

Alice grinned at Roxborough.

"It would be my pleasure, you understand. We haven't had a good beheading in quite a while."

Roxborough snorted. "You just took the guardsman's head a few moments ago."

The Queen looked baffled. "Isn't that what I said? We haven't had a beheading in quite a while."

Roxborough gave Alice a pleading look. "All right, Cat. As you said, back to the subject. Just what are you accusing me of?"

"Lying for one. You told me you were trying to buy Gossamer Threads. What you left out was how that was being done. And last, if not the most damning, is that you kind of changed the order of how things went down."

Roxborough raised an eyebrow. "Oh?"

Rage filled Alice. "You told me that you had your hacker hit the place after you had already decided to buy it out. I just double checked that. Eva Thorinson was working for Acquisition Technologies, doing routine runs against a number of small companies. It wasn't until after Thorinson's equipment got fried that you attempted to acquire Gossamer Threads. And you didn't try to buy it. There was no bargaining table for you to go to. You tried a hostile take-over."

"Whatever protection they had was good enough to keep Eva out, and I wanted it," Rox said with a nervous glance at the Queen of Hearts, who was watching the conversation with detached fascination.

Alice grinned. "However, you forgot that most important rule. Don't deal with a dragon, and better yet, never try to frag one over. Dunkelzahn burned you good on that deal."

Roxborough looked up at her, wincing. "Look, Alice. Let's take this step by step. All right, I wasn't completely honest, but that doesn't matter. Dunkelzahn was the one with the code. Not me."

"I don't believe you. I think it's just as likely that you created the Crash entity and used it to try to get a hold on a number of companies. Maybe it just backfired on you."

"You don't believe me? Why don't you check with your old friend Damien Knight. He was so sure the Big D was behind that whole mess that he's been working on a way to kill the old lizard for years." Roxborough let out a harsh laugh. "And he might just have been the one to succeed."

Alice felt as if she had just been punched in the gut. "Knight?"

"Why not? Look at their entire relationship. Deadly moves on a chessboard that uses human pawns. Damien profited a good deal from the dragon's death. His lackey, Kyle Haeffner, is now in the White House."

Alice was stunned. Damien was a close friend of hers, he'd kept her alive after the Crash virus had flatlined her. Damien had saved her, kept her sane for a while. And the mention of Kyle's name brought memories crashing in. Memories of her young, human body. Of love and marriage, of a life so far removed from the here and now that it felt alien to her. Twenty-eight years ago she had been married to Kyle Haeffner.

The queen spoke, "This one!" She pointed to Roxborough. "Off with his head!"

"No! Alice, think about it. Damien had the money, the time, the access, and more than enough motive. Like I said, Knight always thought Dunkelzahn was responsible for the Crash. Knight lost a lot more than money."

Alice stood stunned for a moment. She didn't believe

Roxborough, but without checking, things seemed to fit together too well for her to disregard his information.

Guards surrounded Roxborough and carried him off with great effort. The queen was smiling, her flushed face aglow with delight. "Finally, a beheading to remember."

"Alice!" Roxborough yelled. "Alice, at least give me a chance here."

But Alice had faded out again. She stood in the hissing rain, the glossy street lamps reflecting off the looking-glass surfaces all around. The black ice streets, the mirror buildings that spiked into the sky.

She walked, letting the rain soak her through. Until she was chilled and miserable. Wonderland would search the Matrix for confirmation of Roxborough's claims, and in the meantime, she walked. Alone except for the empty city and the static of rain.

19

As the Phoenix II fell through the stormy black sky, Grind and Axler howled, grins of delight on their faces. Miranda's eyes were closed, and she looked relaxed for the first time since Ryan had outlined the assault plan.

As they plummeted, the boom of thunder grew deafening until it seemed as if they were under attack. Ryan could see white flashes all around the LAV as they fell through the growing darkness.

"Everybody brace yourselves! This is going to be a quick stop." Dhin sounded calm.

There was an explosion, bigger than the rest, and serious gee forces slammed the runners deep into their cushioned seats. Ryan felt as though all the breath had been knocked out of him.

"Cliff's edge!" shouted Dhin. "Go, go, go!"

Ryan was the first out of his restraints. He jumped to the door and triggered it.

Cold rain slashed at his face as the door swung out, and a devil's fork of lightning lit up the black sky outside. The LAV hovered just at the cliff's edge, and the world was a dim gray in the torrential rain.

"Great job, Dhin," Ryan yelled into the tacticom. "We won't need to rappel." He jumped, landing on a wet outcropping of rock. Miranda was next, then Axler and Grind leapt simultaneously, landing with weapons drawn.

"Everyone's down," said Ryan.

The Phoenix II's doors closed themselves as Dhin pulsed the jets and maneuvered the big machine upward. He shot over their heads, going east.

As Axler and Miranda headed south and Ryan and Grind started north, they could hear the sound of the LAV burning brush in an attack landing. Hopefully, Burnout would believe that the runners were still aboard and react accordingly.

"Deploying drones," said Dhin.

Then there was nothing but the sound of thunder, the flash of electricity, and the chill of rain.

Ryan and Grind moved quickly over the rocky terrain. Just to their right, far below, they could see the black mirror surface of Cat Lake, rippled with the pounding water of the storm.

Miranda's voice came nervously through the comm. "I can't see drek in this rain," she said. "And I've lost the old man."

Axler came on. "Stay chill," she said. "Focus on the objective. The shaman will show."

Ryan nodded silently to her advice. Axler was right on. A good leader, and the one who would be in charge if he weren't here. Grind and Ryan had made it a hundred meters, and were just getting into position to make their sweep at the tower.

Suddenly, through the hissing rainstorm came a crash and a rumble that wasn't thunder.

"Frag, Miranda! Watch it!"

Axler's voice.

There was a short scream, which was cut off mid-breath.

"We have contact. Miranda's down!"

"We're coming," Ryan said, breaking into a fast run. Grind came just behind him. As they ran, they could hear the sound of Dhin's drones opening fire.

"Jane, did you get a feed from one of them? What happened?"

Jane's voice sounded angry over the tacticom. "A log jam fell on Axler and Miranda," she said. "Axler dove out just in time, but Miranda is still down. Don't know how bad it is, but I don't think she's gone yet."

"I hope she's all right," Ryan said. "We need her."

Jane interrupted. "Axler's engaging some huge creature I can't quite make out. Looks like a bear or something. She might need help taking it down."

Ryan concentrated on his magic and increased his

speed. Like wind through the trees he moved. Barely touching the ground, weaving through the trunks of the pines. He pulled out in front of Grind and was ten meters ahead when the ground erupted at his feet.

Like an explosion from the earth, a creature of roots and dirt and humus popped to the surface before him. Ryan threw himself to the left just before the thing's metal blades sliced the air where he had been.

He tumbled and fired his Ingram. In front of him was something out a nightmare. Burnout, naked to the waist, his body covered in mud, like some undead creature crawling from the grave, leapt out of the hole in the earth.

"Ambush!" yelled Grind, then he opened fire.

But Burnout was no longer where he had been. With reflexes so swift Ryan could barely follow him, the cyber-zombie sprang almost three meters straight up. While Burnout was still in the air, and in a flash of lightning, Ryan could see the mechanical third arm sweep upward, its mounted weapon sighting in on Grind.

Grind was on the move, the mounted weapon chewing up the ground where the dwarf had just been.

Ryan kept rolling as the cyberzombie flew. He looked into the astral, trying to see the Dragon Heart. *Did Burnout still have it?*

Ryan found what he was looking for instantly. The Dragon Heart glowed amid the bright astral flares that made up Burnout's aura. And Miranda had been right, Lethe was here as well—like a stabilizing energy that served to anchor the cyberzombie's spirit. *Is the spirit trapped inside,* Ryan wondered, *or a willing possessor? Or perhaps he has taken control?*

A split second passed before Ryan brought himself back. "Target engaged!"

Jane came on. "Dhin's Stealth Sniper is coming your way, Quicksilver."

"Copy, Jane."

Grind came up behind Ryan, laying down a sheet of lead at the airborne body of Burnout, trying not to give the cyberzombie any clear shots.

As Ryan rolled to his feet, he saw Grind take a burst to the chest. The dwarf was thrown to the ground. Ryan didn't hesitate. He knew he had to engage Burnout hand to hand; the weapon mounted on his third arm packed too much punch for open-ground combat.

Ryan moved, lightning-quick, and was on Burnout before he could react. A round from one of the twin Predators Burnout held took meat off Ryan's shoulder, but he ignored it, channeling the pain away as he tackled the bigger man.

He grabbed Burnout's third arm and twisted with all his strength. The twist, combined with the momentum of the cyberzombie landing, wrenched the weapon upward, its servos straining. Metal bent, hydraulics screamed, and the big gun went dead.

Ryan felt a stabbing pain in his side, and shifted just fast enough to avoid the entire length of a sharp metal spike jutting from the heel of Burnout's foot. The weapon penetrated through his ribs, but not far enough to puncture any internal organs.

Too fragging close! Ryan ignored the pain and brought his Ingram up, triggering it as he raised his arm toward the cyberzombie's torso.

Burnout twisted violently out of Ryan's grasp, dodging the shots. Then he struck at the gun hand, making Ryan jerk it out of aim. The pain in his gut faded slowly as he concentrated with his magic. Ryan jumped for Burnout, a flying kick to the head. He connected, just as the cyberzombie's hands clasped Ryan's knee.

Pain exploded in Ryan's calf muscles, but the kick knocked Burnout backward. The cyberzombie somersaulted and landed on his feet, then rushed Ryan, who was on the ground.

Ryan rose to one knee, covered in mud and blood, bringing the Ingram up. He knew he wouldn't make it.

He reached out with his magic, trying to touch the Dragon Heart, trying to draw strength from it. He could sense its presence like a small mana sun, but he couldn't tap into the power. His telekinetic strike barely made Burnout flinch.

The cyberzombie crashed into Ryan, monoblades snapping out of his forearms and targeting Ryan's head.

Ryan planted his feet on the man's metal torso and

rolled with the impact, then pushed off and sent him flying through the air behind him. One of the blades left a deep cut in his Kevlar. Then the air around him was lit up with muzzle flash, and he became aware of the whine of Dhin's air drone as it peppered Burnout with light rounds.

That seemed to slow him down, but he dodged and grabbed the flying drone in a move so fast Ryan almost didn't catch it. Burnout jammed his hand into the whirling blades and destroyed the drone.

Ryan struggled up, bringing the Ingram up again, this time with the grenade gun in his other hand. He let loose with the armor-piercing clip and caught Burnout full in the shoulder. A clean hit that obviously hurt the cyborg.

Burnout gave Ryan a pained look, then faded from sight. *What the frag?* Ryan looked into the astral and saw the trail left by the cyberzombie, barely visible as it stretched away into the darkness. *How did he pull off that disappearing act?*

Ryan knew it wasn't mimetic or camouflage technology. Nothing like that existed. *Must be magic,* he thought. *Which means Lethe.* That made sense; he knew Lethe could hide himself in the astral, but Ryan also knew how to see him. It took a little more concentration and attention to detail, but Ryan had seen the spirit before and he could find Burnout now, regardless.

Behind Ryan, Grind stood, his body armor in tattered ruins all the way down to the thin trickles of blood cascading down his chest. It was quickly washed clean by the falling rain.

Ryan went to him. "You look like soggy drek."

"I'm solid. Saved again by Esprit combat armor. It hurts, though."

Ryan put a hand on his shoulder. "Let's go."

There was a short scream through the tacticom.

"We're getting battered here," came Axler's panting voice. "Miranda banished two nature spirits before this thing that looked like a bear-man burst past me and mauled her. If we don't get help soon, there's not going to be much left to take home."

Jane's voice cut in. "Miranda's lost her tacticom, and from Axler's visual, I'd say they need help, pronto."

"On it," said Ryan, breaking into a run. "Spell out the situation."

"Axler tried to draw the bear-thing and the nature spirits back to the clearing where she and Miranda would have some open ground to finish them. Looks like she got a bit more than she bargained for. You better hurry, Quicksilver. I'm worried about Miranda."

Ryan ran in disbelief. How bad could it be? Axler was combat supreme. Hand to hand, one of the best fighters he'd ever seen. And what happened to Miranda's confidence?

Ryan hit the grassy knoll that led up to the rocky clearing. Two hundred meters up, the Phoenix II sat like a monstrous bug cowering from the rain. Its running lights glared, but couldn't match the almost continual lightning that danced around them. Thunderclaps split the night sky with searing booms.

As Ryan moved forward, a huge tongue of flame shot from off to his left. In the afterglow, he saw the fire engulf Miranda.

He angled toward her, running.

Ahead, the rigid, flaming form of Miranda was hedged in by two shapes that blocked Ryan's view. Both looked like huge masses of fur and plant material. They were manifesting nature spirits, obviously summoned by the shaman.

Suddenly, Axler flashed into his line of sight, coming around from behind a tree a hundred meters ahead. In front of her were two more spirits—tall, tree-looking spirits, moving faster than should be possible for such large plant-based creatures. Axler backed away from them as Dhin's Steel Lynx drone peppered the spirits with rounds from its minigun.

"Dhin!" Ryan yelled. "The drone will have null effect on the spirits. Find the shaman and concentrate fire there."

Axler broke in, panting her words. "The shaman looks like a bear," she said. "Maybe some sort of shapechange spell."

Something about Axler looked wrong, then Ryan realized she was missing part of her left arm. Chrome glistened, and Ryan could see sparks flash from the hole in her elbow socket. Ryan was still twenty meters away when Axler moved suddenly, striking at a huge form that Ryan had thought was part of the trees.

The bear-man.

In the flashes of lightning, Ryan's infrared vision couldn't keep up, but once the bear-man moved, he could see the faint signature under the heavy cloak. The bear-man bled from many tiny cuts and bullet holes, though he seemed unaffected by them.

He roared, going berserk and striking hard with a huge paw. The attack caught Axler mid-jump and sent her flying.

Axler sailed twelve meters in the air and slammed into the trunk of a huge pine. Her limp body slid down to the ground.

Ryan heard Miranda scream. The two tree spirits who fought her shredded into wood pulp. She staggered then, the flames flickering out on her body, and collapsed from the drain of using so much magic. It was just a momentary pause, but it was enough.

"No!" Ryan screamed.

The bear-man crossed the distance in three steps, insanely fast. One huge paw grabbed Miranda's right thigh, the other clawed her neck.

The thing held her above its head, and a dull whoofing roar sounded in the clearing.

Miranda thrashed in the shaman's grip, struggling, battering the creature with her free arm. To no avail.

Ryan brought his Ingram on target and opened fire. The first few rounds hit home, but then a nature spirit manifested, blocking his line of sight. Ryan adjusted immediately; he drew up and circled to gain a clear shot. He fired another short burst, then moved again as the spirit manifested again.

The bear-man was hit, dropping to one knee. He held Miranda raised over his head.

Struggling.

The creature roared again, and in that second, Ryan knew what it was going to do. He dove for a shot around the spirit. Aimed higher, the burst taking the bear-man's right arm off at the elbow.

It was already too late.

Ryan watched helplessly as the bear-man slammed Miranda down.

20

Against the flowing blood, the music refused to dim. The song sounded strong and bright, beating against the ever-widening circle of blood and sacrifices.

Lucero stood at the edge of the dark patch, oblivious to the limbs of the dead that lay slippery under her feet. Her heart strained toward the music, toward the light, even as her need struggled backward, behind her to the familiar form of Señor Oscuro as he spilled more blood.

Something was different this time. Even with the Gestalt, even with the tapped power of the Locus, his work was far more difficult than before. He grimaced in pain as he worked, wincing in the struggle just to move around.

Lucero turned to watch him, with a feeling of fear and pity. He could never understand the music, could never know its beauty, because unlike Lucero, his entire soul was a wasteland of silence and darkness.

Oscuro had given up on single sacrifices, and had brought several acolytes with him. He was killing them two at a time. His muscular forearm rippled as he made the slash, and the two girls lying side by side on the flesh altar sprayed blood.

Oscuro's face was a mask of pain as he used the skull of one of the dead as a crude *Chac-Mool,* catching the blood of the sacrifices in the hollowed-out cavity. Once the *Chac-Mool* was filled, Oscuro staggered to the edge of the circle just meters from Lucero.

Pulling his hand from the skull's empty eye sockets, he let blood splash out, completing the circle.

Suddenly, the air grew darker, and the music dimmed.

I'm sorry, she prayed to the light. *Please forgive me for what is being done to you.*

With that thought, she felt the gray spot in her soul grow lighter, and with it, the music raised in volume just a notch.

Oscuro fell to one knee, and his panting breath could be heard over the sound of the singing. He looked up at Lucero and smiled, the look in his eyes chilling her gut.

"That was a close one, my child. I thought the slitch would take me before I finished the barrier."

His tone was ragged, as if he had just run a long distance, and he wiped dark liquid away from his forehead.

He's sweating blood, realized Lucero. She had thought he was just covered in the blood of his sacrifices, but where he'd wiped the blood away, she could see fresh blood bead up on the pale, sickly looking skin.

He looked her in the eye, studying her for a moment, and Lucero was filled with panic. *He knows!* she thought. *How could he not know? I'm the reason he has to struggle so hard. Now, he's looked into my eyes and seen my love for the music, my desire for the light.*

He sees the graying of my soul.

Oscuro smiled. "Help me to stand, child. I know you cannot help the sacrifices because of the delicate balance you have to maintain, but that does not mean you can't give your master a hand to his feet."

Lucero swallowed the lump of fear in her throat, and stepped forward to the bearded man.

He stretched forward a bloody hand, and with a shudder, she grabbed it in her own and pulled.

Oscuro stood, keeping her hand in his. Eye to eye, Lucero became acutely aware of the stench of blood, the sweet aroma of her addiction. She licked her lips nervously as her hunger grew.

Suddenly, a smile formed on Oscuro's face—a smile full of gentleness and concern. Lucero's fear faded, and she couldn't understand how she had ever felt pity for the amazing man.

"Little one, you have withstood so much, and have accomplished so much for me. You are truly a remarkable servant."

She bowed her head. "Thank you, Master."

His bloody hand slipped under her chin, and raised her head to look him in the eyes.

To her, he took on the look of something dangerously beautiful. The blood that covered him beckoned to her, and she found herself wishing she could kiss him, could lick the blood from his face, from his hands.

The music rose.

No! she thought. *I will resist the blood temptation.*

Pain flashed across Oscuro's face and he took a step away from her.

Lucero looked down at herself, and she could see the dull glow coming from inside. She was lightening the circle!

The dull glow filtered outward from her, forcing Oscuro away. His expression went from pain to determination. "I must go now."

She stood in awe of what was happening to her. The music grew louder and louder to her, until Oscuro had to yell to be heard.

"You will come with me."

Her voice cracked as she said, "Why?"

He forced a smile. "Your spirit is strong, but the balance is upset. You will not be allowed to go into the light. It will destroy you." He had backed away almost to the piled corpses at the edge of the dark circle.

Then, just as Lucero's dim light reached the brittle edge of the dark circle, Oscuro waved his hand in the air. A casual gesture that made a funnel of the world. The funnel sucked her down into a river of darkness.

Behind her, the music and the light plowed over the dark circle, purifying it. Bathing out its filth with beauty and perfect harmony. Brilliant and pure white.

But she was too far away to touch it, to hear it. She rushed down the flow of dark current and screamed. And she was still screaming as her spirit slammed into her meat body.

21

In the cold rain, Ryan watched Miranda fall. The bear-man brought her down across his knee, and the crack of her back as she landed ripped through the clearing.

Miranda's scream held a note of agony, and for a moment, the gray world around Ryan went still. He felt rain on his face, pain in his shoulder and gut, but it all seemed so distant.

Focus returned with Miranda's second scream, snapping Ryan back to reality. He clicked into full alert, senses heightened, reflexes as taut as monowire. He ran at the bear-man, easily ducking inside the nature spirit.

Once close, Ryan fired his Ingram and prepared to close the final meters.

No spirits manifested to block the barrage of bullets, and the man came apart, erupting in a spray of crimson that painted the trees. The bear-man began to turn, but only made it halfway around when Ryan's burst took out his knees and he crumpled into a heap. Freed, the spirits vanished into astral space.

Dead.

Then Ryan was on him, pushing around him to get to Miranda.

She lay like a broken doll, her legs jutting away from the rest of her torso in an impossible position. Her face was streaked with blood and grime; her hair, where it hadn't been burned off, was plastered to her head, like a dirty helmet.

Blood came from her mouth, and she was missing several teeth.

Ryan almost couldn't bear the sight. There was a sharp pain in his heart, and he accepted responsibility. "Dhin,

I'm bringing Miranda in. Get ready to take her for emergency medical treatment."

"On it."

"Axler?"

"I'm here, Quicksilver," came Axler's voice. "Chewed up but not spit out."

"You going to make it?"

Axler chuckled. "It's nothing a few hundred kay nuyen won't fix."

"Glad to hear it," Ryan said. "Sit tight and keep your Nikons peeled for Burnout. He's still out there."

Miranda opened her eyes and looked at him. Her voice was like that of a child, soft and breathless. "Ryan."

Ryan knelt. "I'm here, Miranda."

"No . . . invasive treatment."

Ryan nodded. For a mage, putting metal into the body, any kind of invasive treatment, meant losing power.

She swallowed, and more blood escaped her lips. "Fragger dead?"

Ryan turned and rolled the huge form over, and stared in surprise. Huge, the destroyed face was still ringed by dirty white whiskers. The top of the man's head was completely gone. "He's dead," Ryan said.

Miranda smiled and closed her eyes.

Ryan's vision shifted to the astral. She still lived, but her grasp on this world was becoming more tenuous by the moment.

"Jane, contact DocWagon and give me an estimate on how soon we can rendezvous with one of their paramedical teams."

"Already on it, Quicksilver. There's a small branch clinic in Polson. Ten minutes away in the Phoenix."

"Let's do it," he said. "And get me an on-line first-aid program, one of those virtual doctors."

"You want me to talk you through patching her up?"

"Yeah, she's not gonna make ten minutes like this."

Grind came limping over.

Ryan looked up at him. "You okay?"

Grind nodded.

"Tend to Axler," Ryan said. "Help her to the LAV."

"On it."

"Dhin, bring the stretcher. I'm pretty sure her back is broken."

"Coming, Bossman."

First, stop the bleeding, Ryan thought. He pulled a huge combat knife from his boot and cut several strips from his nightsuit. He used them to tie over her wounds.

Dhin returned with the stretcher and helped Ryan slide it under Miranda. They carried her the fifty meters to the Phoenix II and laid her gently on the floor. Ryan gritted his teeth and continued patching the wounds, following instructions from Jane.

Grind and Axler hobbled in, the dwarf supporting Axler's weight since her right leg seemed to be broken just below the knee. Her bad arm hung strangely askew, broken off at the elbow. She was a mess, but seemed to be in minimal pain.

"Ryan." It was Miranda again, her voice even more faint.

"I'm still here, Miranda."

She looked at him, her eyes going in and out of focus. "You get the cyborg?"

Ryan looked at her for a moment, and considered lying. Then he shook his head. "Sorry. But we will."

She tried to speak again, but clenched up as pain from her back shot through her.

Dhin shot her full of Syndorphin.

Her body went slack and she passed out.

"All right, Dhin. You go wheels up. Now."

"What about you, Bossman?"

"I'm staying to finish it with Burnout," he said.

Grind made an effort to stand. "If you're staying, then I'm staying."

From the corner of his eye, Ryan caught movement. So fast it was a blur, streaked by rain. He turned, pulling his Ingram, but even as he raised the weapon, he knew it was too late.

A hulking form disappeared into the darkness. Burnout, but he was carrying something. The shaman. Burnout had stole the shaman's body out from under their noses.

Grind was already down the ramp, running.

"Dhin! Get Miranda and Axler to the clinic." Then Ryan was running as well.

He and Grind came barreling around the grove of pines, and found themselves running along the second cliff face. A steep slope of loose shale. Utterly impossible to traverse because the rock was so slippery, and small landslides of shale sheets continued to slip down the mountain.

They careened around an outcropping of rock to find Burnout in front of them. The cyberzombie had jammed his now useless third arm around the dead man's waist, and was using him as a shield of sorts. He fired his Predators at Grind, catching the dwarf in the shoulder. Knocking Grind back.

Lightning flashed, close. The thunderclap completely drowned out the barrage of fire from Ryan's Ingram as he opened up.

The shaman's body absorbed the bulk of the burst, but Burnout took two rounds to the thigh and staggered backward.

Then Burnout's Predator barked again, and Ryan dodged to the side. He hit the ground, and came to a rolling crouch, his Ingram spraying the space where Burnout had stood a moment before.

The cyberzombie was gone. Disappeared again, and for a moment Ryan wondered if Lethe had hidden him. But after the crash of thunder faded from Ryan's ears, he heard the distinct sound of a rock slide. Burnout thrashing as he plummeted down the cliff face.

Ryan jumped to his feet and ran the few meters to the cliff's edge. When he looked down, there was nothing but a steep shale cliff, reaching all the way down to a small dark lake, hundreds of meters below. A wash of stones fell all across the face of the mountain, but the thick rain made it hard to see Burnout, if he was even down there.

Frag, he thought. *Not again.*

22

Inside Burnout's body, Lethe fell. The slippery flat shale was like a jagged slide beneath them as they plummeted. The rain-slick stones formed an avalanche wave in front of them, rippling out on either side to bring down tons of rock.

Burnout used the Kodiak's body as a cushion of sorts, trying to maintain an edge of control as they fell. The cold brittle air was chilling and wet around them. The wind like a wall of ice needles. Lethe felt everything Burnout felt with absolute clarity. His spirit was ensconced now. Irretrievably tied to Burnout.

For now, it is perhaps for the best, he thought.

Burnout's mind was full of anger, hate toward Ryan Mercury for the death of the Kodiak. Lethe could taste the emotion like a palpable scent. He could feel Burnout's thoughts and emotions almost like they were his own. In fact, he found them harder and harder to ignore.

The anger filled him, and brought with it an image. An elf with a painted face, lounging in a French garden. Walls of ancient masonry surrounded the courtyard. Salt air and the dull roar of the sea. Blue sky and water of cobalt.

Anger and frustration boiled inside, overwhelming.

The elf smiled, but his eyes glared. "This is an unexpected visit," he said.

Angry, heated words were exchanged. A conversation that blended into an emotional collage.

Then the scene faded from Lethe's mind, and he could not recall anymore.

"What was that?" Burnout asked, digging his heels as he tried to slow their fall.

"You saw that, too?"

"Yes."

"I don't know," Lethe said. "I think it was a memory."

"A memory of what?"

"I don't know. Maybe it's one of mine."

Burnout said nothing.

The lake came up like a black wall, like an impenetrable slab of the darkest asphalt. But Burnout had dug in with his heels and his claws in an effort to slow them down. The dark water slammed into them. Shaking their body to the metal core. Then the chill came as they drifted to the bottom, swallowed whole by the icy liquid.

23

Ryan stood in the pouring rain, looking down at the black-hole surface of the lake three hundred meters below. *Burnout planned this escape,* he thought. *He left himself a way out.*

Ryan knew that spoke volumes about the cyber-zombie's psyche. It meant Burnout valued his own life, and that was unusual.

Cyberzombies held a fragile and tenuous grip on life. Sometimes the cybermantic blood magic that tricked the spirit into staying with the body simply failed. Many early attempts had died spontaneously. For Burnout to have developed a sense of self-preservation meant he was thinking as an individual. *It must be the influence of the Dragon Heart,* Ryan thought. *Or perhaps Lethe.*

Ryan spoke into the tacticom mike attached to his throat. "Dhin, you airborne yet?"

"Firing up now."

"Wait ten seconds. Grind and I are coming with you."

Grind was standing three meters away, and he looked over. "You don't want to search for him?"

"I want to see this thing through," Ryan said. "But everything in due time. Right now, we need to take care of Miranda and Axler." He turned and ran back to the clearing and climbed into the Phoenix II.

Grind was just behind him. "I'm in," the dwarf said. "Go! Go!"

The jets screamed, and the LAV lifted into the boiling black sky. "I've contacted DocWagon in Polson," came Jane's voice. "They'll rendezvous with you in five minutes."

"Excellent," said Ryan, kneeling beside Miranda. He held the scarred flesh of her burned arm.

She woke then, her eyes defocused from the drug-induced sleep. Her voice was a whisper. "I was . . . dreaming."

Ryan's voice dried in the back of his throat.

"I dreamed that you . . . that you got to me in time, Travis. I mean Quicksilver."

Ryan squeezed her hand gently.

Miranda smiled. "You get him?"

Again, Ryan wanted to lie, wanted to tell her that Burnout was a twisted mass of charred chrome. He looked into her eyes, saw the agony and couldn't deceive her. He shook his head. "We lost him. He used the shale rock slide to escape."

Miranda laid her head back into the folded tarp that Dhin had given her for a pillow.

"But we'll get him," Ryan said. "You and me. We'll get him together, and we'll make him pay for this."

Miranda smiled, making her cracked lips bleed. "No lies, Quicksilver, not . . . for you and me. I'm not gonna make it." A wracking cough got hold of her then, and blood came out of her mouth in a fine mist.

Ryan stroked her head gently, feeling the blistered skin under his hand. "You rest now. Save your strength. You've come this far, and we're going to patch you up better than new."

"Even if I . . . stay alive. I'm not gonna be . . . in any condition to . . ."—Miranda's breath came in hacking gasps—"fight Burnout," she finished.

"Shh," Ryan said. "Burnout and I are tied together by the Dragon Heart; we'll meet again."

Her eyes clouded. "Travis," she said. She was becoming delirious. "Travis, thanks for . . . helping me get out."

"Ssh, Miranda."

"It was because of you that I . . . left Fuchi. I have you to . . . thank."

Miranda smiled again, and the blood from her mouth ran down her cheeks. "It's been quite a ride period." She laughed, a choking rattling sound that started another coughing fit.

"Try not to talk." Ryan felt cold anger swelling inside him.

She sighed, the sound bubbling in her chest. "Promise me . . . one . . . thing."

Ryan's vision blurred from his anger. "Anything."

She motioned him closer, and as he leaned in, she whispered, "Promise that it won't . . . have been for nothing." Miranda collapsed into unconsciousness.

Ryan clenched his fists, gritted his teeth. "I promise," he said, his voice flat, cold. "Burnout will pay, and the Dragon Heart will reach its resting place. I promise you that, Miranda."

Ryan wiped his eyes as Dhin landed the Phoenix II. As the DocWagon parameds swarmed in to take her. It was going to be close, they said. She was in a coma now; brain-death imminent.

Ryan concentrated with his astral sight, looking for her aura as the parameds worked on her, but it was faint and growing weaker.

The anger clawed inside him like a trapped beast, and his whisper was a harsh, barren sound in his throat. "If she dies, Burnout will pay."

24

In blackness, deep below the surface of Cat Lake's still waters, Burnout clung to a huge rock, waiting patiently in the lake's icy womb. Several times during the afternoon, he'd resurfaced to fill his air tank, careful not to be seen.

Ryan Mercury and his team seemed to have left, but Burnout didn't want to take any chances. Lethe didn't either, and he touched the Heart and used its power to mask Burnout's presence.

Finally, after six hours had passed, Burnout decided the danger had passed. Ryan and his team weren't coming back right away. He released his hold on the rock, and pulled the limp form of the shaman from its resting place under two large rocks. Together, they drifted to the surface.

Burnout broke the water's mirror like some technological nightmare leviathan, a robotic grim reaper. He looked nothing like a human anymore. Any remaining flesh had been ripped and soaked to gray, wrinkled patches that clung to small portions of his metal frame. To his banded synthetic muscles.

As he reached out to grab the shaman's body, he caught sight of his forearm in the morning light. He'd had the name Burnout scarred into the flesh as a reminder to himself of everything he'd lost, but even that was mostly gone. Now the "out" had been scraped away, and all that remained of his name was the "Burn." It seemed fitting.

The Kodiak's body bobbled up beside him, and he quietly pulled it ashore. He stopped on the rocky shale bank in the shadow of a large boulder, all senses alert. The evening air hung chill and gray over the surface of Cat Lake.

The taint of cordite was fading, but still clung to the trees and rocks. A subtle reminder of death and destruction.

There might still be danger, and Burnout was taking no chances. Ryan had come at him like the pro Burnout knew him to be. If the Kodiak hadn't stood by him, Ryan would have beaten Burnout, and this small lake would probably have been his grave.

Burnout reached behind his back and grabbed hold of the dysfunctional cyberarm that hung, bent and twisted, just over his head. His estimation of Ryan's physical strength went up another few notches. Even accounting for the centrifugal force involved, no mere human would have been able to bend the titanium struts.

With a grunt, Burnout finished Ryan's work, and ripped the arm off at the base, leaving a jagged stump. Without looking at it, he tossed it over his shoulder to land in the lake with a quiet splash.

Without a word, Burnout hoisted the Kodiak's body onto his shoulder and fought his way back up the slope. Lethe was silent during the two-hour climb, and Burnout was glad for it. He was thinking about the Kodiak's sacrifice. He was no criminal like the old lady, and though Burnout hadn't actually pulled the trigger that had caused his death, he felt no less responsible.

"The Kodiak chose his own fate," Lethe said.

Reading my mind?

No response.

"I know," Burnout said. "But I drew Ryan here. He came for the Heart."

"You did not ask for the Kodiak's help. He gave it willingly. You are not to blame."

"I don't blame myself," Burnout said, his words acid with vehemence. "I blame Ryan Mercury." He reached the top and stood. "But I am not without responsibility in the matter."

Standing on the rim of the cliff, the dead man's body at his feet, Burnout looked around. The trees were bent and broken, trunks chewed from heavy gunfire. The once peaceful place looked like a war zone.

He walked to the tower and stepped inside the cabin resting under the tower's protection. With a minimum of excess movement, Burnout gathered all of the Kodiak's magical trinkets and supplies, the deerskin cloak the old man had worn, and took them all outside.

He walked to the long, rickety ladder that led to the top of the tower and hauled everything up the hundred meters to the open platform at the top. A small perch, the tower top was a simple platform empty except for the swivel chair someone had bolted to the wooden planks centuries before.

The chair was rusted into a position facing eastward, and was covered by the skin of a cougar. Burnout remembered the Kodiak killing that cougar so many years before. This had been the Kodiak's favorite place in the world. He had told Burnout that there Bear often showed him mysteries that ground-bound followers could never hope to see.

From this height, Burnout looked far into the next valley, seeing the sunset peeking its fiery eye just below the last tatters of the storm clouds. Brilliant streaks of blazing red burned the sky, like tongues of fire.

Very fitting.

Burnout went back down the ladder, pulled the shaman's body over his shoulder, and then returned to the top. He set the dead man in the chair, propping the soggy body upright so his faceless head looked into the heart of the setting sun. Then Burnout laid all of the shaman's possessions around him, and finally covered the old man with the deerskin.

He climbed back down the ladder, went into the cabin, and began a fire in the old shack's potbelly stove. When he had a nice blaze going, he took some kindling and ignited the shaman's bedding. Then he stepped back out into the morning air just as the roof of the shack caught fire.

He retreated to a safe distance and watched the tower burn.

"My friend, you gave your life for me, and now I commend your soul to Bear. May he tend to you."

It only took minutes for the ancient wood of the tower to catch, and suddenly, it seemed as if the structure was a pillar of pure flame. Smoke rocketed skyward, seeming to ignore the slight breeze that had begun to blow.

After a half-hour, the huge structure collapsed to the ground with a rumbling crash like rolling thunder. Burning rubble flew up and gouts of flame shot into the sky.

"A fitting pyre," Lethe said.

Burnout nodded and continued to watch the remains of the tower burn. Because of the recent rain, the fire refused to spread to the surrounding vegetation. It confined itself to the tower, and as that structure was consumed, it slowly dwindled. It was almost as if the blaze knew its purpose.

"I've been thinking," Lethe said.

Burnout watched the trails of smoke strain for the sky, and thought about those last few hours before the attack. "Well, that makes one of us."

"Perhaps all this death could have been averted. Perhaps if I had killed Ryan Mercury when I had the chance. When I first realized that he wanted the Heart for his selfish purposes."

Burnout shook his head. "In this game, everybody makes their own choices. I chose to steal the Heart, Mercury chose to track me to take it back. Ryan Mercury and I are to blame for the death. No one else."

Burnout turned away from the smoking wreckage and scrambled to the shallow hunting blind he'd made yesterday afternoon. The one he'd waited in to surprise Mercury. It had been a surprise, all right. For both of them. Mercury had run true to form . . . his tactical ability besting Burnout's fighting prowess by enough to keep them at a stalemate.

Burnout had expected Mercury to come down the funnel and land in the clearing. Then he and the Kodiak would have crushed the enemy between them. Instead of catching their prey in a vice, they'd found themselves in a much wider pincer. Still, their positioning had caught Ryan by surprise.

He gathered up the small amount of supplies he'd stashed in the hole, the spare ammo, and the extra Predator. Then he began his trek down the mountain side.

Mercury would be back before long, his desire for the Heart fueled by the losses he'd suffered. Burnout intended to be long gone when Mercury showed up with reinforcements.

"Ryan Mercury is the key," Lethe said. "He is the only obstacle to—"

"What the frag are you going on about? Of course Mercury is the key."

"Did I say that aloud?"

"I heard it."

Lethe was silent for minute. Then, "I'd like to help you kill Ryan Mercury."

25

Back at Assets, Inc. Ryan's fogged mind responded to the needle shower's stinging jets the way a blind beggar would respond to the scent of a hearty meal. He turned his body so the steaming water could hit every part of him, the force of the spray cleansing the blood and the scent of death from his body.

Miranda had died before reaching the clinic. Her body had given out under the strain.

Ryan had made the short flight back to Assets with Dhin and Grind in the Phoenix II. Axler remained at the clinic for an arm and a leg replacement. Transfusions of Syndorphin had taken away the physical pain, but she was just as slotted off about Miranda's death as Ryan.

Ryan had stayed for a while, trying to cheer Axler up by distracting her with cyberware catalogs, trying to get her to pick out her favorite mods on her new 'ware. It was going to cost a lot of nuyen, but Ryan didn't care. Axler was worth whatever she wanted.

Now, he rubbed soap around the wound Burnout had left in his ribs. Ryan knew that without medical attention the injury would have been fatal for any other man, but he had already felt the healing begin during the afternoon.

By the time Dhin got a chance to take a look at his injuries, the wound had already sealed over. Dhin had looked at the amount of blood on his clothing and raised an inquisitive eyebrow, making his brutish face seem somehow refined.

"I've always been a fast healer," Ryan replied to the unspoken question.

Now, as he rubbed at the quickly forming scar tissue,

he wondered about that. He knew that magic had something to do with it, something to do with his speed, his
strength, but that didn't seem to explain it anymore.

Ryan knew plenty of others like himself. Physical
adepts who mastered their bodies magically and pushed
past limits no norm could hope to match. He'd even
known one other person who followed the Invisible Way,
which was similar to the Silent Way that Dunkelzahn had
taught him. She was extremely advanced in her technique,
and he had learned some valuable things from her.

Still, she couldn't compete with him in combat. Not
even close. He would always fall back on his lessons
in the arboretum, the battles with Dunkelzahn in the
darkness and stillness of the spectral shadows. Those
lessons and his innate magic gave him the edge in every
fight.

It had taken every effort of machine and magic to make
a viable opponent for him.

How can that be possible?

Ryan shook his head, sending a spray of water against
the wall. Dunkelzahn had always told him that even
among his own kind, he was special. It was for that reason
that the dragon had rescued him the day his parents died,
because of his special gift.

Ryan felt a wave of self-disgust. *And like a good little
soldier, I didn't ask questions. Now it's too late to ask
them, and I don't seem to have any answers.*

He was about to shut off the shower, when his wristphone beeped. Ryan looked at the screen to see Jane's
code. He didn't care if Jane saw him in the shower. After
all, she'd seen him in worse places.

Ryan thumbed the receiver, "Hello, Jane, I was—"

He stopped short. The face that filled the screen wasn't
Jane's. For just a moment, his breath caught in his throat.
It was the face of a woman he never expected to hear from
again.

Deep in his heart, the part of him that was Roxborough
felt a shiver of fear.

Ryan quelled the feeling and gave a warm smile.
"Alice, so good to see you. Sorry about the shower, but
you should be more honest when you call."

Alice's small mouth grew from a smile to a lascivious grin. "You don't know how long it's been since I've surprised a man in the shower. My, my, aren't we a big boy? And in all the right places too."

Ryan laughed, and it felt good even though it hurt. "What's biz?"

"I thought you should know that I've gone into Rox's host in Panama and wiped all the files pertaining to his spirit-transfer procedure. Everything about memory encoding and personality remapping. It's all been wiped."

"I'm grateful, Alice. Thank you."

Alice grew somber. "You're welcome," she said. "Though I didn't really do it for you. Now I have a question."

"Yes?"

"How's your Rox?"

Ryan grunted. "Still there, but with each day, he seems a bit dimmer in my head, and lately, I can tell my thoughts from his."

"That's good." Alice took a drag of her cigarette. "But you still have his memories?"

"I think so."

"Ryan, I've come into possession of some very disturbing information lately, and I'd like you to confirm or deny it, based on Rox's memories."

"What is it?"

"Remember that Roxborough is the source of this info so it's highly suspect. But so far it scans true with what I've been able to pull from the Matrix. Be forewarned, it's very disturbing."

Suddenly, Ryan was tired again. He didn't want any more disturbing information, he didn't want any more responsibility. His load was too heavy already. "Consider me forewarned," he said.

Alice smiled. "I like a man with guts," she said, and before Ryan could respond, she continued. "The information concerns Dunkelzahn's assassination. It may even be enough to get you to the person responsible."

Ryan's attention snapped into full awareness, his whole body tensed, and the hair on the back of his neck stood on end. "Spill it, and you better not be fragging with me."

Alice gave him a cool look. "I assume that threat was made in jest. Either that, or you're an idiot and I've severely overestimated you."

Ryan forced himself to take a deep breath, forced his muscles to unwind. "My apologies, Alice. Things have been a bit haywire lately."

She smiled. "Forgiven. Believe me, I've been keeping tabs on you, and I know the stress you're under. If this information was any less important, I would simply let you continue on your way and tell you later."

"I understand. Now, please, tell me what Rox told you. If I remember anything that either confirms or denies what he said, I'll let you know."

Alice nodded. "During the Crash of '29, a man named Major David Gavilan discovered information that led him to believe that a corporation called Gossamer Threads was responsible for the programming that led to the creation of the Crash virus."

Ryan was stunned. "What? Are you saying Dunkelzahn was behind the Crash?"

Alice shook her head. "No, I'm not saying anything of the sort. I'm simply saying that David discovered information that led *him* to believe that Gossamer Threads was working on the virus, just prior to the breakdown."

"David?"

"An old friend," Alice said, and there was note of sadness in her voice. "You might know him as Damien Knight."

Ryan sucked air. "Damien Knight was head of Echo Mirage?"

"His name was David Gavilan back then."

"None of this rings any bells in my Roxborough memories," Ryan said. "And I don't see how Dunkelzahn factors into the whole Crash scenario. He lost billions. Even Gossamer Threads went belly up."

Alice sighed. "I know, and frankly I'd like to believe that Dunkelzahn wouldn't have indulged in such an evil venture." She paused, forcing her voice to sound impartial, but Ryan could tell that it was difficult for her to discuss the Crash without anger. "Still," she went on, "you're missing the point, again. It doesn't matter who was actually responsible as long as you understand that David thought it was Dunkelzahn."

Ryan nodded. "I'm following."

"Good, now for a bit of history. Damien Knight rose to the head of Ares Macrotechnology in something called the Nanosecond Buyout. You've heard of it?"

Ryan nodded. "You can stop treating me like I'm mentally challenged, Alice. Everyone who's anyone knows about the instant takeover."

Alice arched her eyebrows. "Well, what everyone doesn't know is that in all likelihood it was Dunkelzahn's help that made the buyout a success."

"I believe it," Ryan said. "Knight had to have help from someone with a healthy cred-line."

"Perhaps Dunkelzahn helped him out to make up for the damage caused by the Crash."

"He felt responsible?" Ryan asked.

"Why not?"

Ryan shook his head. "Not Dunkelzahn's MO. He might've helped Knight accomplish the Nanosecond Buyout, but I doubt it was out of guilt. In my experience, guilt is not an emotion that dragons feel strongly."

"Maybe Knight knew about Dunkelzahn's connection to the Crash and was blackmailing him."

"More likely, but very dangerous for Knight."

Alice's ocean-blue eyes sparkled. "Remember that the two of them had on ongoing chess match, and Knight did not always lose. He had the dragon's respect."

Ryan nodded, and suddenly a nagging itch got him. It was the memory of Quentin Strapp standing in Nadja's office. He was so smooth, hitting Ryan with hard questions, then abruptly changing tactics, suddenly asking him about Damien Knight.

"You still with me, Ryan?"

Ryan shook off the memory, but couldn't quite stifle the rage that was beginning to fill him. "Yeah, still here. I'll tell you as soon as you're finished. Go on."

"Let me take this step by step. One: David Gavilan, head of Echo Mirage, defeats the Crash entity, but loses close friends and comes under the scrutiny of the media. His personal life is ruined, and he is forced to disappear and change identities just to keep living. This I know because I was there.

"Two: He becomes Damien Knight and uses some of the cutting-edge technology created to defeat the Crash, plus his knowledge of corporate raiding, to concoct the scheme behind the Nanosecond Buyout. He knows of Dunkelzahn's involvement with the crash, whatever it was, and he threatens to expose it unless the dragon funds his plan.

"The Nanosecond Buyout works brilliantly and David is now the major shareholder in Ares Macrotechnology, one of the top megacorporations. Only he didn't count on the fact that Dunkelzahn was better at corporate maneuvering."

"You're talking about Gavilan Ventures," Ryan said, and the story was becoming clear to him, sending chills down his spine despite the hot water.

"Yes, when the dust settled from the buyout, David owned twenty-two percent of Ares, almost the exact amount owned by the previous CEO, Leonard Aurelius. But Dunkelzahn owned Gavilan Ventures and its twelve percent of Ares. With Aurelius and Knight constantly voting their shares against one another, Dunkelzahn's twelve percent became the determining voting block. The dragon controlled a lot of the corp. In effect, the dragon held a measure of leverage over Knight."

Ryan smiled. "Someone like Knight would hate that."

"I think he did. I think he harbored a secret hatred of the wyrm for years. Damien Knight is the perhaps the only person who might have been able to hide his feelings from the dragon. After all, their chess matches went on for days, even weeks at a time."

Ryan nodded. *She's making sense.*

"So, over the years, Knight waits, plots, and comes up with the perfect plan."

Ryan snorted. "And just what plan might that be? Do you have details? Out-plotting a dragon is a little like trying to move a mountain one rock at a time. No matter how many stones you take away, there always seems to be one more."

She smiled. "Granted, but you're talking about Damien Knight here. No, I don't have details on how he did it. Not yet anyway. But I know him in a way you don't, and I can attest to just how brilliant and twisted he is. Think about how much he's gained by Dunkelzahn's death. He chose the perfect moment."

"How's that?"

"When Dunkelzahn died, Kyle Haeffner became President of the UCAS."

"And . . ."

"Kyle was my husband before I flatlined. He and David were great friends. Thick as thieves for years."

The water chilled on Ryan's skin, and he had to remember to breathe.

"After the Crash entity hit me, Kyle was devastated. David did everything in his power to keep my meat body alive. David felt responsible for my condition, and he bent over backward to make it up to Kyle."

Alice's voice grew sharp. "As a result, Kyle became David's lackey and faithful lap dog. Stayed in contact when David changed names, picked up a tidy sum in the Nanosecond Buyout, and went on to become quite the entrepreneur. Even remarried." Alice said that last with acid in her voice.

Ryan's jaw muscles clenched. "And now, Knight's lap dog is president of UCAS. In a position to pull any strings that might be helpful to Knight."

Alice shrugged. "It looks that way."

"Frag."

Alice held up a hand. "Ryan, I haven't spoken to David about this, but I'm certain he would deny any involvement with the assassination. I was hoping your recollection of what Rox knew of the events might provide some clue."

Ryan closed his eyes and tried to remember, but all that came back were some fragments. *Acquisition Technologies.* The name popped into his head. It was one of Roxborough's corporations at the time of the Crash. "I'm still having a hard time putting his past into context," Ryan said. "And frankly, I've been concerned with other things recently."

"I'm sorry about Miranda," Alice said.

Frag, is there anything you don't *know about, Alice?*

Ryan felt the anger rising inside, and his hands balled into fists. "Thanks for the info, Alice. I'll let you know if I remember anything."

"And if I learn any more about how he might have pulled it off, I'll get in touch."

Ryan nodded. "Please do."

Then she was gone. Like a ghost in the machine.

Ryan shut off the water, suddenly drained. His mind filled with blood, and rage ran through his veins. He could picture himself ripping Knight limb from limb. Revenge for destroying the creature who had shown Ryan love.

But what about Burnout?

Ryan knew he couldn't give up on finding the Dragon Heart, but he knew he had to act on this information quickly. If Knight was half as smart as Alice believed him to be, every moment lost was another moment for Knight to rewrite history so that his role in the assassination was erased.

I don't know what to do.

Even as that thought thundered through his head, he realized that it was wrong. He did know what to do. This was the break he'd been waiting for, his chance to avenge Dunkelzahn. He wasn't about to let it slide by.

He quickly punched up Jane's code.

"Quicksilver, naked again?"

"At least you still notice. Any news?"

"The satellite images showed the tower on Pony Mountain go up in flames an hour ago. Looks like our boy's on the move again."

"Jane, I need you to assemble a team."

Jane looked startled. "Who? You don't have a mage, Axler's out for a day or two, Grind is still recovering, and Dhin is dog-tired. I'd say Assets is pretty bad off. They need some down time."

Ryan shook his head violently. "I'm not talking

about Assets. It can be anyone. They just have to be mage-heavy."

Jane frowned. "What for?"

Ryan smiled. "I need them to track Burnout for a while. Dhin and Grind are going to Washington with me."

26

Burnout descended the Pony Mountain path in silence,
thinking about what Lethe had just said. He was making
his way in the ever-darkening night toward the Ford
Bison truck he'd left halfway down the mountain. Lethe's
words came back over and over.

I'd like to help you kill Ryan Mercury.

Burnout could feel the tension roll through him. A tiny
shiver of anticipation hit him then, and he laughed.

"Do you find my decision to seek someone's death as
humorous?"

"In a sick way," Burnout said. "It's ironic."

"Ironic or not, my offer should not be taken lightly.
And it does not come without a price."

"What price? I don't have anything left to give but my
life, and that would kind of defeat the purpose, don't you
think?"

"You are not entirely devoid of possessions."

For the first time since discovering the spirit, something in its voice brought a chill to Burnout's circuitry.
"Keep talking."

"Let me tell you a story."

Burnout climbed down a sharp incline, sliding in the
wet soil. "Just get to the point, Lethe. I'm not in the most
patient mood."

"Indulge me, Burnout. You are lacking information that
could make the difference between life and death for the
entire world, and I think it's time you knew the whole
truth."

Burnout stopped in his tracks. "I thought you were
always honest with me. That I could trust you. Now
you're telling me you've been holding out on me?"

Lethe's voice was stern. "Since the time our association began, I have come to respect you as a warrior and to value you in many other ways. Even as a friend. However, the information I'm about to impart to you is of such magnitude that I could not have shared it until now. Even as close as we've become, I only tell you this because the situation is desperate."

Burnout grunted, and continued his journey back down the mountain side. He hoped Ryan hadn't discovered the Ford Bison. Without the truck, traveling would be much slower and far more exhausting. "All right," he said. "You've got my attention."

"You are familiar with the Great Ghost Dance?"

Burnout snorted. "I used to be a mage, remember." From what Burnout could recall, the Great Ghost Dance was a massive sacrifice led by Daniel Howling Coyote in the early years of magic. Many shamans had sacrificed themselves in order to power the ritual magic that had wakened the Earth and caused many volcanoes to erupt.

Lethe's voice dropped through Burnout's IMS. "When magic of such magnitude is performed, it has an effect on the other planes of existence. It raises the level of mana into a spike that travels across the metaplanes."

"You're losing me, spirit."

"Let me try to show you."

Lethe was silent for a minute. An image welled into Burnout's memory. He stood on a gigantic outcropping of rock. The outcropping stretched for an unimaginable distance, spanning a bottomless abyss.

Across the abyss at the farthest reaches of his sight, he noticed the other side. And he felt revulsion as he looked. A revulsion that grew into terror. Into horror, until he knew that the distant, tiny figures that writhed around on the opposite cliff were utterly evil.

Then came a glorious sound. The beautiful song of a goddess who stood on the very tip of the outcropping. Just over the Chasm. She sang and a bright white light spread out from her, immobilizing him. In the glory of her song, he forgot who he was, he did not care. He merely was. Blissful. Content.

Basking in the perfection.

The vision faded.

"I see now," Burnout said after a minute. He ducked his head to avoid low branches, and scrambled down a grassy hill. "But what does it have to do with me?"

"Let me finish. The occurrence of the Great Ghost Dance has upset a very delicate balance in the metaplanes. As the level of magic rises, our plane and the plane of these creatures grows slowly closer. In time, the distance will be close enough that the evil will be able to cross unaided."

"How long?"

Lethe sighed. "A few thousand years, at the least."

Burnout grunted again. "So we go back to my original question. What's this got to do with me?"

"The Dance has created a bridge of sorts. It spans some of the distance to the other side. Even now, the creatures are building a bridge of their own. If they are allowed to complete the narrow gap that remains, they will invade this world in force, thousands of years too soon. Well before mankind is prepared for the upcoming war."

Burnout whistled. "Frag. How long until that happens?"

"Could be tomorrow, could be a thousand years."

Once again, Burnout stopped in his tracks. "You're telling me that at any moment our world could be overrun by a metaplanar enemy?"

A long pause followed. "Perhaps, but there is one who stands against them."

"The goddess."

"Yes. Her name is Thayla, and her song is so beautiful that it is like fire to them. Thayla's song is of perfect purity and goodness; it is a golden light of such power that normal beings are trapped in its beauty and cannot move. To the creatures from the other side, it is the most painful thing they can imagine. While she sings, they cannot move forward with the construction of their side of the bridge."

"So as long as she keeps singing, this world is safe."

"Yes."

"That still doesn't answer where I fit in."

"There are those on our side of the Chasm who are

trying to silence her song, and she is weakening. She needs the Dragon Heart to destroy the bridge."

Burnout didn't respond for a moment, he just kept moving. They were almost to the Bison. "So the Kodiak was correct when he said that the Heart was either the salvation—or the destruction—of the world."

"Yes."

Burnout grunted. "Well, frag 'em. This world hasn't done me any favors."

"I am truly sorry about that," Lethe said. "But this is important, and it means a great deal to me."

Burnout held up his hand for quiet. They had reached the Bison.

The vehicle sat exactly as they'd left it. Burnout scanned the ground with his low-light vision jacked up all the way. There were footprints all around the vehicle. He circled the Bison, but couldn't discern any booby traps. No hanging wires, no infrared detectors.

He stepped closer, and through the hole where the front door had been he could see the small note taped to the vehicle controls. Cautiously, he walked to the side of the vehicle, all his enhanced senses attuned.

"You notice any magic tricks on the vehicle?" he asked Lethe.

"No. There are no wards or magical traps of any kind."

He reached into the vehicle and gingerly pulled the note from the controls. And in the light of the just-rising moon, he read it.

"It's not over, Burnout. I've got your number. And some time, when you least expect it, I'm going to pay you a visit. You've got no cover, you've got no identity, you've got nowhere to run. Hide, if you think that will do you any good, but you've got to know I'll find you. When I do, Burnout, I promise, you'll die slowly. Circuit by circuit, synapse by synapse. You have no idea what you've done, and for that you have my pity. Still, pity won't save you, chummer.

"Until we meet again. By the way, tell Lethe hello. If I have my way, he'll burn in Hell right beside you for betraying the cause."

Burnout crumpled the note in his hand, rage boiling

through him. But this rage was different from the hot anger he was used to. This was a cold hunger that would only be sated by Ryan's lifeless body bleeding at his feet.

Burnout stood in the moonshadow of the great pines, the dappled silver playing over the ground. "All right, Lethe. You're right. The Heart is no good to me, at least not without you, and Mercury isn't going to rest until we're both history. Tell me about this deal."

"It's simple really," the spirit said. "Though I think your hatred for this man is beginning to affect me. The deal is: you promise to help me take the Dragon Heart to Thayla, and I will deliver Ryan Mercury into your hands."

Burnout laughed. "What makes you think you can do what I can't?"

"Burnout, my friend, you do not know Mercury in the way I do. I have fought alongside him, I know his strengths and his weaknesses. I was there when he succumbed to the seductive power of the Dragon Heart and claimed it for himself. I knew then that he could never be trusted to carry the Heart to Thayla. Without that his life is forfeit to my goal."

"How do we defeat him?"

"Whenever you have faced him, you have confronted his strength. As much as I dislike the idea, it's time to confront him where he is the weakest."

"And just where would that be? As far as I can tell, Ryan Mercury doesn't have any weaknesses."

"In the sprawl named Washington FDC there lives a woman named Nadja Daviar. She is Mercury's one weakness. If you have her, then you have him."

Burnout's laughter carried in the night air, and all around the Bison the woods were deathly still. "Deal!"

27

Ryan woke from a nightmare, cold sweat streaming down his face, soaking his shirt and the cushion of the Mistral's passenger seat beneath him. He straightened up, then leaned forward and put his head against his knees.

His mind refused to let go of the dream. The pouring rain back at the top of Pony Mountain. The dense forest lit by flashes of lightning, shaken by thunder. Ryan fought Burnout again, but this time, the cyberzombie had gone down before his onslaught.

In his battle rage, Ryan lifted the metal body over his head and threw it against the trunk of the tree. Instead of feeling relief, the sound of Burnout's spine cracking had brought horror, and he'd rushed to the man's side, turned him over, and screamed.

It was Miranda's face looking back up at him.

Ryan screamed, a high-pitched wail that had become the sound of the engines as his subconscious reluctantly released its hold on his mind. *Don't need an interpreter to divine the meaning behind that one,* thought Ryan.

Ryan sat up in the Mistral's dark cabin, making the déjà vu landing back into National Airport in FDC. He blinked away the tears and rubbed sleep from his eyes. Everything was set for keeping track of Burnout. Jane had put together a small group consisting of two mages and a samurai.

Ryan had left the note on the Bison as a last-second whim, a bit of psychological warfare to throw Burnout off balance.

Miranda's death was hitting him harder than it should, he knew that. Runs like this were dangerous and sometimes people died. *Maybe I'm going soft.* Regardless, he wanted out now. Dunkelzahn's mission would have to take a back seat to Ryan's persecution of Damien Knight.

Dhin's drowsy voice filtered through the cabin. "We'll be on the ground in five."

Ryan nodded. Readied his gear as they landed. The trip from the airport to the mansion was made in a haze. Ryan was dimly aware of the limo ride and of the smell of cherry blossoms, but everything else was clouded by a distant fog.

It wasn't until Nadja stood before him on the mansion steps, her hair pulled back into a loose ponytail, her soft cotton robe pulled snugly about her, that Ryan came back to reality. He tried to ask her about the meeting he had arranged with her and Carla Brooks and Jane-in-the-box.

"Shh," she said. "Tomorrow." Then she took him by the hand and led him into the house, upstairs to the bedroom and beyond into the master bath.

A huge tub full of steaming water waited for him, and as she stripped his clothes from his body, he thought of Pony Mountain in the hard wash of the rain.

Nadja dropped her robe, revealing her tightly muscled stomach, her hardening brown nipples. She gazed into his eyes and led him into the hot water.

As the heat robbed the strength from his muscles, easing the knots even as it stung his crudely bandaged wounds, Nadja kissed him softly. His forehead, his neck, his eyes, his lips.

She kissed him to hardness, and in the lazy liquid, she wrapped herself around him.

With a tenderness he'd never known, she made love to him. Carrying him to sweet oblivion. He let himself forget about Miranda, about Burnout. About Damien Knight. His cares and worries melted into the embrace with the woman he loved, giving him a measure of peace he'd seldom known.

After, he slept without dreams for the first time in his life.

22 August 2057

28

In the first gray light of the morning, Burnout belly-crawled through the boggy field at the end of the Missoula International Airport. The sound of VTOL transports screamed through the sky overhead as he moved toward the perimeter fencing.

Behind him, the abandoned Ford Bison slowly slipped beneath the surface of the swamp.

It had been a long and difficult drive from Pony Mountain in the dark. The distance was only about two hundred and fifty klicks, but the terrain was mountainous and extremely rugged. They'd come south on the eastern side of the Swan Mountains, then over the pass to the outskirts of Missoula, using abandoned and washed-out roads where people hadn't driven in over a decade.

As they'd approached civilization, Burnout had used the Bison's on-board telecom to call the airfield and get a rundown of all departing suborbitals bound for the FDC sprawl. Armed with that information, he and Lethe had managed to get to the far end of the strip, courtesy of Burnout's still functional GPS.

Now, he was moving silently toward the small guard post. The station was a crude corrugated steel structure, roughly the size of a small storage shed. It looked like an ancient outhouse, and the only thing that belied the image was the small satellite dish mounted on the roof.

The soft twang of some country singer filtered through the open windows, lilting about lost loves, dearly departed dogs, and missing money. One guard was a dwarf with a huge paunch, seated with his feet up on the desk, snoring loudly, almost in rhythm to the slide guitar. The other guard was a young human with Amerind features who took furtive drinks from a bottle inside a paper sack and kept paging through a *Playtrog* magazine.

Burnout scanned for cameras and stationary or track-mounted drones, but could find none.

"There are two watcher spirits," Lethe said. "But they won't see us."

"Good." Burnout moved up to the window in silence. He slipped inside, and with the butt of his Predator hit the human's temple, sending the body flying. The guard crashed into the metal wall, his magazine fluttering to the floor. As the man sank into unconsciousness, a small trickle of blood seeped from the side of his head.

The sleeping guard woke, but it was too late. Burnout had lifted him up by the neck and removed his Colt Man-hunter. "Help me and you won't die."

The dwarf's eyes snapped open and filled with horror. Burnout could see the wheels turning behind them. The dwarf nodded.

Holding the guard, Burnout took a quick inventory. The desk, which was cluttered with hardcopy reports and candy wrappers, also held a small cyberdeck. That would be useful. Burnout turned. Something was nagging at him, and it took him a moment to place it.

. He looked behind him, found the small radio on the big filing cabinet, just above him. Whining steel guitars and slow country vocals. With a quick swipe of his hand, the radio sailed across the room, shattering against the door frame.

The night went silent.

"Never could stomach that drek." He set the dwarf back in his chair, but didn't let go of his neck. "Now, tell me about runway security."

The guard shivered. "I can't."

Burnout just tightened his grip. "You can tell, or I can find it on the cyberdeck after you're dead."

"Ack!" the dwarf choked. "All right, I'll tell you."

"Each corp has twenty people on the tarmac, but most of them watch the baggage. We don't get much traffic here, and it's mostly tribal."

"Good, come with me, and if you make noise, you die."

A quick nod from the dwarf and Burnout was loping

across the tarmac in the lightening gray morning. He spoke under his breath to Lethe. "In less than twelve minutes, you and I will be airborne, and a few hours after that, we'll be touching down in Washington FDC."

Lethe's voice dropped into his mind. "How do you plan on bypassing FDC security? I don't know for sure, but it would seem reasonable that any of the airports there will be heavily secured. If you intend to hijack an aircraft, won't they be waiting for us when we land?"

Burnout laughed and lifted the dwarf so that movement would be quicker. "If I was going to hijack the aircraft, they'd be all over us, and this would be the shortest trip in history. Security at all the major FDC airports is definitely triple A. Even if I was planning to stow away somewhere inside the vehicle, we'd probably get nabbed within half a minute of landing."

Lethe's tone was dry. "I take it, then, that you plan to do neither of these things."

"That's right."

"What then?"

"Can't you read my mind yet, spirit?"

Lethe chuckled. "Not quite," he said. "I'm getting some of your thoughts, however."

Burnout said nothing as he came up behind a small hangar and stood in the shadow of some storage dumpsters. He peered around the corner. Across a hundred meters of runway and taxiway sat the main terminal building. Jets and suborbitals clustered around it like flies on drek. "Now, dwarf," Burnout said, "show me where the security is, and if you lie, I will know and you will die."

The dwarf gave Burnout the information he needed and was rewarded with a precise blow to the back of the head. The small man's body sagged into unconsciousness, and Burnout tucked it away inside one of the storage dumpsters.

Then he made his way toward the terminal, carefully skirting the highly secure areas. He didn't have much time; the Transworld flight he needed to board was just beginning its taxi.

"If you're not going to hijack an aircraft and you're not going to stow away, what are you planning?" Lethe said.

"The TransWorld plane is a Federated-Boeing 3800. She's got no VTOL capabilities, but she's fast. She's got the quadruple rear wheels like the old jumbo jets so the wheel wells are huge."

"You're planning to ride in with the landing gear?"

"Right."

"What happens when the pilot retracts the wheels?"

"I'll have to puncture one of the tires to make sure we aren't crushed." They were nearing the terminal now, and just ahead, the monstrous, single-wing jetcraft loomed as it began forward thrust.

"I think that this plan sounds . . . "

"Yeah? Sounds how?"

"It sounds like if you're not careful, you might just do Ryan Mercury's job for him."

Burnout laughed again. "Relax, I've done it before. Can't say as I enjoyed it, and there's no in-flight movie, but it will get us there." He accelerated, dodged under the belly of the craft, and jumped past the huge balloon tires, rapidly picking up speed. He latched onto one of the legs and climbed into the small landing gear cavity.

Within minutes he could see the ground rocketing underneath them, then pulling away. *I'm coming for you, Ryan Mercury. And now I know how to hit you where it will hurt the most.*

And her name is Nadja Daviar.

29

A sweet voice came to his ears. "Wake up, dear."

Ryan rolled in the soft silk sheets and slowly opened
one eye. The display on his wristphone read 0912 hours.
Nearly nine hours uninterrupted sleep. He couldn't
remember the last time he'd slept so deeply, or for that
duration. *No wonder my brain doesn't want to wake up,*
he thought.

Nadja's kiss fell gently on his cheek. "Gordon brought
up breakfast for us," she said. "I've already eaten, have
some early business to deal with. Also, Carla is here; we
can start the meeting as soon as you're ready."

Ryan's eyes snapped open. *The meeting!* Yes, he had
much to tell them of Damien Knight. How could he have
slept so long?

He sat up and swung his legs out of the big bed. The
smell of real eggs and fresh bacon drifted in the air. The
coffee aroma was pungent and strong.

Ryan's stomach rumbled. "We'll meet in a half-hour if
that's okay. After I eat."

Nadja smiled. "In my study," she said. "I'll notify
Jane." Then she was gone, leaving him in the room with
the breakfast.

Ryan ate and showered, wishing he could take time to
enjoy both activities. But he was anxious for this meeting.
Anxious to hear what Carla and Nadja and Jane would
have to say. He dressed quickly in comfortable pants and
a loose cotton shirt and walked down to Nadja's study.

Gordon Wu met him outside. "I'll tell her you're here,"
he said, turning to the telecom.

"Is her study secure?" Ryan asked.

The man gave him a puzzled look. "Of course, sir," he

said. "It is swept by the Secret Service once a day." Wu winked. "And after they leave, Miss Brooks' staff sweeps it again." He gestured for Ryan to enter.

"Thanks." Ryan stepped through the door and into Nadja's private workspace.

In front of her desk, which was still piled with papers and disks, Nadja had arranged three high-back leather chairs in a semi-circle around a huge tridscreen. Two of the chairs were occupied, and the trid screen showed a fourth chair, identical except for the fact that it existed only in the virtual reality of the Matrix.

Carla Brooks looked up to meet Ryan's gaze as he entered. Her white hair was cut close to her scalp, a dusting of platinum stubble over her deep black skin. She wore a sharp Zoé business suit and was carrying weapons underneath. "Hello, Quicksilver," she said. "It's good to see you back alive. I think Quentin Strapp has some more questions for you, and he'd be very upset if he had to ask them of a corpse."

Ryan laughed. "Good to see you too, Black Angel. After this meeting, I think we'll have something to tell Strapp that will make him very happy."

Jane looked out through the tridscreen, her blonde hair shining. Her puffed-out cartoon lips pouted as she spoke. "And just what is that?"

Ryan met her eyes as he walked over to take his chair with the three women. "I know who killed Dunkelzahn," he said.

Nobody said a word.

And in the silence, Ryan's magically enhanced hearing could actually pick out the individual heartbeats of two of the three people sitting around him. The only reason he couldn't pick out the third was because while the trid did Jane enough justice that Ryan could hear the minute squeak of red leather when it rubbed against red vinyl, Jane hadn't bothered programming in a pulse for herself.

It was Carla who finally broke the silence. "How?" It was a whisper.

Ryan leaned back in the comfortable chair. "Let me tell you a story," he said. "It starts way back before the Crash of '29 . . ."

Ryan spilled the whole scenario to them. Everything Alice had told him about Damien Knight's hatred for Dunkelzahn. All about the Nanosecond Buyout and the hold Knight had over Kyle Haeffner.

Jane listened with anger evident on her face. That anger growing as Ryan unraveled the story.

Carla watched him in silence, a look of astonishment dawning on her dark features.

Nadja simply gazed at him and nodded. Ryan could see her sharp mind making various connections, could see all the implications of what he'd said fall into place. "Ryan, you of course realize the vast repercussions of your accusations. What surety do you have?"

Carla broke in. "Yes, even if your information is accurate, it's all circumstantial. You've established motive. We know he had the capability and the opportunity. But that doesn't mean he did it."

"Ryan," Nadja said, "do you have any specifics on how it was pulled off? How did he plant the bomb or the magic ritual or whatever it was that killed Dunkelzahn?"

Ryan gave her a pleading look. "None. Carla's right. All the evidence is circumstantial, but with someone of Damien Knight's power and influence, I doubt any direct evidence will ever present itself. He's too smart, too savvy to ever leave any discernible link that would point to him."

Carla straightened up. "The evidence is compelling, and it should be reported to Strapp and the Scott Commission immediately. But I don't want it getting to the press."

Jane's icon looked at her. "Tell Strapp? Tell the Scott Commission? And just what do you intend to say? Hey, Quentin, one of your primary suspects just told me that someone else did it. So how about we stop investigating Ryan, and start investigating Damien Knight, someone who has a rock-solid alibi? After they threw you off the Commission, they'd lock you up in an asylum."

Carla started to respond, but Nadja cut her off. "Jane's right. We all know Ryan, and we know enough to trust him completely, but that's not going to cut it with Strapp."

Ryan smiled at her. "My gut says this is the right

direction to be looking in, but I doubt we can expect any
sort of official backup on it."

Carla gave Jane a sharp glance. "So what do you suggest instead?"

Jane's icon looked up. Her huge, pouty lips were set in
a firm line. "Covert hit."

The stunned look hit Carla again. "You out of your
fragging mind? Assassinate Damien Knight? Even with
the best team you could put together, I wouldn't attempt
that in a thousand years. There's only one person I know
who could . . . " She looked at Ryan and fell silent.

Ryan laughed, softly. "Yes, Carla, I could probably do
it. But I think you're right. An ice job just doesn't feel
right. At least not yet."

Jane shook her head. "People, think about it for a
moment. I trust Quicksilver more than any other meat
walking the planet. If he says Knight killed our beloved
dragon, then I know he's right. But I also know that no
Scott Commission, no *government* force is going to have
the balls or the muscle to bring Knight to justice. He'll
skate and leave someone else to take the fall. The only
way to make him pay is to wipe every trace of him off the
face of the earth."

There was a pause while everyone took in just what
Jane had said.

"Which, of course, is why we can't take him down,"
Nadja said, her voice like a granite gavel coming down.
Not to be denied.

Ryan turned to her. "I know that tone," he said.
"Explain."

Nadja smiled. "On one hand, Jane is completely correct. However, two things are working against us here.
One, even if we kill him, that won't solve our biggest
problem. Both Ryan and I would still be under suspicion
for murdering Dunkelzahn. Considering what we know
about Strapp's line of reasoning, he might just believe
that Ryan, Knight, and I were all working together, but
had a falling out.

"Two, Ryan said it himself. All the evidence is circumstantial. Even he's not sure just how far to trust his infor-
mant. So if we ice Knight, and we're wrong, then the

fallout will be heavy enough to bury us all. We need to be absolutely sure. If we knew for a fact that Knight was behind it, I would vote for geeking him, then digging hard into his actions prior to the assassination. With him dead, there would be no one to thwart our efforts. Still, I need more proof before I can agree to such drastic actions."

Carla leaned forward, passion flashing on her face. "You've all gone off the fragging deep end! This is a witch hunt. We have no concrete evidence that implicates *anyone*. I know what security measures were taken to protect Dunkelzahn. I've gone over and over possible weaknesses, the nature of the blast. And I'll do it again, but the real evidence is too slim to reach any kind of conclusion. You have no proof."

"Carla—"

"Quicksilver, of all people, you should know how rash and dangerous it is just to have this conversation, let alone contemplate carrying all this drek out. Killing someone of Damien Knight's station will shake the world to its very core, especially after the assassination of Dunkelzahn. We're talking widespread paranoia. Killing mid-level execs don't mean drek, but you start axing people like Knight, the corps will seize up in a panic."

Ryan help up his hands. "Easy, Carla. No one is doing anything yet. This is just a strategy meeting. You and I know that when you're trying to come up with a plan, you start at the most extreme and work down to something more manageable. Don't take it so personally. I need you calm and thinking straight. The second you decide something can't be done, then you can't do it, and that may limit your options down the line."

Carla took a deep breath, then nodded and leaned back.

Ryan turned to face the other women. "Okay, give me alternatives."

Jane arched a monofilament-thin eyebrow. "Such as? You say you can ice Knight, I say it needs to be done. What else is there to talk about?"

Ryan turned to Jane's icon. "Such as the fact that *I'm* not sure it needs to be done. I don't kill without reason, and no matter my feelings about Knight, I don't intend to start now."

"Finally, the voice of reason," said Carla, with a tired clap.

Ryan frowned. "Don't get too comfortable with that, Carla. I said I don't kill without reason. I haven't absolutely confirmed my information, and to be honest, that is the main thing keeping Damien walking and talking right now. I like Nadja's idea. We find out more, then decide on a course of action."

Nadja looked up from her desk top, where she'd been typing for the last minute. "Ryan, Damien will be at the Watergate Hotel this afternoon. At a luncheon party to garner support for my vice-presidential bid. He probably wants to pick my brain on how I'll be voting my Gavilan stock."

Ryan nodded.

Nadja went on. "I could have a private meet with him, try and force his hand. Maybe he'll toss us a bone."

Jane snorted. "Yeah, and maybe blue monkeys will fly out of my hoop."

Ryan laughed. "Jane's got it right. He'll never drop anything to you. He'll have so many personal defenses up, it'll probably take him an hour just to mentally prepare for the luncheon."

Carla shrugged. "Then what? We kidnap him and brainwash him into confessing?" Her voice indicated sarcasm, but Ryan considered the request seriously for a minute before discarding it.

Ryan stood and paced around, stopping at the window. He looked out over the immaculately sculptured grounds. Something from Roxborough's past was surfacing to haunt him.

Roxborough was in London, at a party for the CEO of Intellynx, a mid-level corp that he wanted to buy out. Ryan remembered feeling nervous, almost shaking with apprehension. But he also felt a thrill of excitement, the titillation of the hunt.

He had spent over an hour flattering the CEO's private secretary, Ryan couldn't recall her name. After a lifetime of getting her just drunk enough that she forgot who he was, and what his presence meant, Roxborough had recorded her graphic tales of the sexual orgies, fetish parties, and under-the-desk encounters she'd participated in. All at the command of her boss, a happily married CEO.

All he had to do was play the chip once, and the CEO was literally on his knees. Begging Roxborough to take what he wanted, just not to play the chip to his wife.

Ryan smiled and turned from the window. "No, Knight will never let anything show to you. However"—he turned to Nadja, where she sat at the desk—"do you have a date for this afternoon?"

Jane's eyes began to gleam, and Nadja smiled. "Why, Ryan, are you asking me on a date?"

"I still think you're all crazy." Carla was slumped in her chair, a look of defeat on her finely chiseled features.

Ryan turned to her. "Carla, I promise you this. If, and that's a very large if, Damien is foolish enough to let anything leak out today, we'll convene for another meeting before any action is taken. If we have any concrete evidence to take to Strapp or the Scott Commission, then that's the way we'll play it. If not, then we'll choose a course of action at that time. Agreed?"

After a long pause, Carla nodded her head. "No," she said. "I won't go along with it." She stood and walked to the door. "Quicksilver, if you want to proceed with this, I won't get in your way, but even by turning a blind eye, I'm sticking my neck out here. Don't frag with me. Okay?"

She was out the door before he had a chance to respond. *Well,* Ryan thought. *That's better than nothing, I suppose.*

Suddenly, Jane sat upright. "Quicksilver, gotta go too. Got some new feedback on our special project. Seems the . . . man you had them follow is on the move." Then she vanished.

Ryan turned to Nadja, who was already delving into the multitude of duties she had to accomplish before the luncheon. He went to her, putting his arms around her shoulders. He wanted to know that she was still on his side.

"Just a nano," she said, shaking him off. "Let me finish this."

She didn't mean anything by it, but it left him feeling

cold. He released her and walked to the window and looked out at the azalea bushes in full flower.

"Don't brood," Nadja said a minute later, coming up behind him and sliding her arms around his waist.

He turned in her grasp, and seeing the smile on her face, he laughed. "I'm not brooding," he said. "Just unsure if I'm doing the right thing."

She kissed him. "Don't let Carla spook you. She's got a government position now and can't afford conspiracies. She's giving you all she can."

Ryan smiled. Nadja was right, of course.

Her tone became serious. "If Damien Knight did kill Dunkelzahn, then he's more dangerous than we ever thought . . ." She let the sentence hang, knowing she didn't need to finish it.

"He's always been dangerous," Ryan said. "He's the king snake, but I'm the mongoose."

Nadja smiled. "Just be more careful than you've ever been in your life. I almost lost you once, and it will slot me off something fierce if you were to get yourself geeked this time."

Ryan laughed. "You know I would do anything to avoid facing your anger."

30

The morning sun shone like an inferno down through the open shutters and into Lucero's small room. She was in the physical world, the *teocalli* in San Marcos. It seemed like ages since she'd been physical, and she trembled from weakness.

She knelt on the stone floor by the edge of her small cot, her naked, scarred body covered in sweat. She was emaciated and malnourished, only just starting to regain her strength after her long stay in the metaplanes.

"Señor Oscuro is ready for you now," said one of the temple attendants.

Two young acolytes helped her walk. She knew she had outlived her usefulness, that she had succumbed to the light. She had embraced the beauty of the song and was now being taken to be sacrificed to Quetzalcóatl.

Oscuro knows, she thought. *He knows I've turned against him, and I'm going to be sacrificed.*

Somewhere in that thought, Lucero found a certain comfort. At least, if she were dead, she could no longer help in the dark destruction of the light.

They took her through the sanctuary and outside, up the long stairs of the step-pyramid temple that was the *teocalli* devoted to the Great Feathered Serpent, Quetzalcóatl. Lucero took one long last look at the world around her as she ascended toward the Blood Mage Gestalt at the apex.

How many times had she been part of their ritual when she was a member of the Gestalt herself? How many times had an old and burned-out member been brought as sacrifice to power a ritual sending? Too many times to remember.

Now it is my turn. It would all have been so simple before she had been touched by the light. But now, all this seemed evil to her, a perversion of magic. To use life energy for such purposes, to destroy innocent lives in order to achieve power and domination.

The landscape around the temple had changed in the days she had spent at the metaplanar spike. Far below the temple and down the hill, a huge crowd of people had gathered around the lake where the Locus had been discovered. Drawn to its power.

Lucero found herself hypnotized by the allure of the huge black stone. Its glossy surface was cut perfectly flat, like the facet of an onyx diamond, and it seemed to absorb all light around it. Like a magical black hole, it was pulling people into its vortex.

The lake itself had been drained, the water channeled away by huge pipes, and security fences had been set up. And in the dry lake bed, Lucero could make out the foundations of a new *teocalli*. They were building it right on top of the Locus.

In the distance, Lucero saw many more people coming. Thousands and thousands of people migrating to be near the Locus. They camped in huge tent cities, chanting and celebrating the end of the Aztec Fifth Sun.

Which, she knew, meant the coming of *tzitzimine*— demons who would devour the world. A shiver passed through her. Had she seen those demons across the Chasm?

Señor Oscuro met her at the temple's apex. He looked her over closely and whispered in her ear. "There has been a change in you, my child."

For a moment, Lucero was close to fainting.

"Even as your flesh grew weak, something in your spirit grew stronger. You overused your gift and burned it out. Somehow, your time at the bridge seems to have healed you to a certain extent. Today, you will take your rightful place in a blood ceremony to help speed your healing."

At first, Lucero could barely comprehend the words Oscuro spoke, but as the truth gradually dawned on her, she wept for joy. In her deepest heart of hearts, she willed a silent prayer of thanks to the light for this gift.

She had dreamed of rejoining the Gestalt.

The ten of them stood and looked at her. They were all human, their skin a mosaic of tattoos and runic scars just like hers. There were thick needle-track marks on their necks and a dark emptiness in their eyes.

They wore crimson robes and were attended by the healers and technicians who connected their veins to the blood-circulating machines, then to each Gestalt member through heavy-gauge catheters in their necks.

Oscuro motioned for her to take her place among them, and she complied, allowing herself to become part of the blood circle. But as the ceremony began, something in her changed again. As the blood coursed through her, the dark spot on her soul turned foul and rank, blacker than it had ever been. Her lust for blood consumed her, and she began to thrash on the floor, breaking the connecting tube, and circumventing the pattern of blood flow.

The rest of the gathered Gestalt looked at her, a mixture of horror and anger vying for dominance on their faces. Only Oscuro showed no reaction. Moving as if nothing were happening, Oscuro took the first of the chosen victims, and moved the girl into the circle.

Instead of placing her on the altar, Oscuro made the girl kneel at Lucero's feet. As Lucero stood, panting, wild-eyed above the sacrifice, Oscuro had used the tip of his ornamental dagger to draw the finest cut over her jugular vein.

A thin spray of blood shot out, showering Lucero's chest and stomach.

The smell of it, oh, the smell, thought Lucero.

Even as a small part of her mind rebelled, trying to maintain control over her addiction, the rest of her spirit was consumed. In her frail condition, Lucero literally ripped the little girl apart.

Her fingers were like steel claws, her teeth monofilament razors. She chewed her way through the girl's neck while her fingers ripped open the child's gut. Lucero was filled with the delicious scent of the young one's death, and she reveled in the orgy of sensations.

She lost control then, absorbing the sheer power of the girl's life energy, pulling it into herself like sweet nourishment. She came to a few minutes later to find herself rolling on the floor in a large circle of bone and blood and intestine.

Horror filled her then, and she looked around the circle of mages, her glance finally falling on Oscuro. He stood over her, his face beaming, like a proud father.

An attendant was ordered to take her back to her room while the rest of the Gestalt finished the ceremony. And as she stumbled the way to her small room, the realization of what she'd done, of what she'd become, hit her.

I am just like Oscuro. A monster.

She had betrayed the light, had let her addiction consume again. And now, there was something more. Some dark power had entered her, had taken over that secret place in her where her true self belonged.

She looked around the room that she had once found so comfortable, where she had always found solace. Now, all she saw was tainted by hatred, as if the very things she had found good about this place had turned foul.

Is this how Oscuro sees the world?

Lucero thought it might just be. Everything good seemed disgusting, everything dark and putrid seemed lovely and desirable. Her mind told her to surrender to it, accept it.

After the acolytes left her, Lucero staggered to her feet, still quivering with the power of the girl's life energy. She stumbled to the small foot locker at the base of her bed and tossed the contents on the floor. After a frantic moment of searching, Lucero held the large carved dagger aloft to the light.

It had been a gift from her teacher on the day she had been accepted to the Gestalt. The blade was edged with orichalcum, and it was virgin. The dagger had never tasted blood, and it brought a grim smile to her lips to think that its first victim would be its owner.

Lucero knelt on the floor next to the cot and positioned the blade so that the butt of the handle rested on the bed's wooden frame, the tip pointed to the ceiling. She positioned her chin against the tip, steadying the blade with her hand. All she had to do was relax her posture and the razor-sharp tip would drive straight through her throat and up into her brain.

As she knelt, fresh tears spilled down her cheeks. They weren't tears of fear or self-pity, they were tears of sorrow. "I'm sorry," she whispered to her memory of the music, to the light. "Because of me, you have suffered, and I can't bear to let it continue."

Just as she started to relax her stance, and felt the tip penetrate her skin, the heavy door at her back swung inward.

No!

She tried to throw herself on the blade, but found herself frozen in place.

Lucero waited there, her blood dripping down the knife's edge, and could see him out of the corner of her eye. His dark hand reached beneath her chin and lifted her head.

The knife fell free and dropped to the bed.

His narrow dark eyes held a glint of amusement, and with his free hand, he stroked his thin beard. "My child, you have borne so much. But it is time. You are healed enough for you to return. Body and soul."

Oscuro smiled, and suddenly her heart was glad. She couldn't understand what she'd been thinking. How could she be so selfish as to try and take her own life when there was so much work to be done?

Oscuro helped her to her feet and cleaned the blood off her scarred body with a damp towel. He smiled all the while, and never said a word about how he had found her.

She realized then that he had expected her attempt at self-sacrifice. That he had perhaps orchestrated it. Now, the foul part of her soul, which had spread to engulf her, was retreating to a small core.

"You are the balance, my child," he said. "The crux, and I hold you very dear."

She found herself admiring him even more, liking the way the dim light cast its shadow over his sharp features. He dressed her in a robe of white linen, and then stood before her holding out his hand. Beckoning for her to join him.

They walked from the room, and as they headed for the altar, Lucero wondered if perhaps Oscuro had planned the whole ordeal. She wondered if maybe he knew that the spot on her soul had become so dark during her blood orgy that she would be unable to return to the bridge. So he had planned her little attempt at redemption just to further his own designs.

She wondered just which thoughts in her head were her own and which had been placed there by Oscuro. Then there was no more time for wondering because they had entered the altar room, and it was time for her to return.

Like her master had said, there was so much work to be done.

31

Ryan sat next to Nadja in the Draco Foundation Mitsubishi Nightsky as they drove past the front of the Watergate Hotel. The area was surrounded by a huge crowd of people—tourists, mourners, media hounds, and even worshippers who considered Dunkelzahn a martyred saint. The blast crater was a massive hole in the center of the boulevard, blocked off by five-meter-tall hurricane fencing and protected by federal security agents.

Above the crater hovered a prismatic cloud that glowed with energy. It writhed and morphed, roiling like an undulating droplet of oil on water, sending out a rainbow of light that was visible even in the middle of the afternoon. Ryan knew that the fabric of physical space had been torn away here. When Dunkelzahn had died in the explosion, the barrier to astral space had been eliminated.

The limo continued its slow and arduous way, through the crowd and up the circle drive to the hotel doors. *What a mess,* thought Ryan. As gala events go, the intimate gathering at the hotel was a news coverage nightmare.

When the tridsnoops had found out that all press was barred from the gathering, they began spouting about freedom of the press. When that didn't get anywhere, they tried to infiltrate the private luncheon as everything from security personnel to wait staff.

Unfortunately for them, Carla Brooks was in rare form. She seemed to be everywhere at once, personally checking the staff and going over every detail with her hand-picked security squad. She was ruthless in weeding out anyone who didn't belong, and even snoops she'd worked with before, people who thought they might have some pull with her, found themselves shut out.

Jane-in-the-box had quashed three attempts by deckers to pirate the security-camera feed, sending some artistically nasty bits of IC back along the line to fry the runners as a warning. By one o'clock, the word was out. This party was off limits. If the news services were going to get anything, they would have to wait on the steps of the hotel like everyone else and take whatever prepared statements the party's attendants were willing to give.

Needless to say, this slotted off more than one self-important investigative news team, and the mood out in front of the hotel was getting ugly by the time Ryan and Nadja rolled up to the front door in the Draco Foundation Mitsubishi Nightsky.

Ryan stepped out first, immediately flanked by several of Carla's security personnel. Ryan caught sight of Matthews standing guard up near the double glass doors of the entrance. The old man gave him a secret grin.

Ryan never thought his disguise—complete with dark brown hair, brown eyes, and three glued-on datajacks on his temple—would fool anyone who knew him personally, but he still didn't like having his picture taken. The slight changes were enough to make a bystander pass over him without a glance, however.

To the tridsnoops lining the carpet that rolled up to the door, he was just another Draco Foundation heavy, guarding Miss Daviar. He wore a simple black tuxedo that fit him in a way that didn't let him pack any heavy hardware. The only concessions he'd made were the Walther PB-100 pistol strapped to his right calf and a miniature camera hidden in the third fake datajack. He was on a remote feed, straight to Jane, who would be monitoring him at all times.

As Ryan forcefully cleared a small space on the sidewalk, Nadja stepped out behind him. He could almost hear the collective gasp of the people back home watching. She had pulled out all the stops today. Dressed in a ruby red gown flown in from Paris, she was adorned at the neck and wrist with flowing strands of natural pearls.

The gleaming white beads tumbled between her breasts, casting a glow over her flesh that seemed almost translucent in the harsh lights of the camera crews. Her raven hair flowed down the bare part of her upper back, and as she moved, it seemed to caress her skin like a lover.

As Ryan stood amid the flashing glare of the cameras, Nadja stopped and spoke briefly with the reporters. She laughed at some questions one of them asked, and her brilliant white teeth flashed.

Oh-so-tridogenic, thought Ryan. *It's no wonder the country's in love with her.* He smiled. *It's no wonder I'm in love with her.*

"We'll just have to wait and see, won't we?" she responded to the reporter. "If my country needs my services, I'll be more than happy to accept this nomination. However, if a more suitable candidate is found, I will give my full support."

She got misty-eyed, right on cue, her voice taking on a lilting, hypnotic tone. "Dunkelzahn would have wanted the vice president to be the best person for the job, someone who could do the most good for the country. Right now, I just feel honored that the citizens, and President Haeffner, think I might be right for the job."

A din of shouts followed this last comment, but Nadja simply held up her hand, and all went quiet. "No more questions, please. I'll hold a formal press conference tomorrow, but now is not the time for making statements."

With that, she swept through the double glass doors, following closely on Ryan's heels, leaving a strangely subdued crowd behind her. As Ryan stepped past Matthews, he could hear the old man whisper, "Frag, she's good."

Ryan smiled and gave him a wink.

They entered the hotel and waited for the security detail to clear an elevator. Then they were up to the penthouse suite. Ryan dropped the bodyguard role and drew up alongside Nadja as they walked.

The penthouse suite was as beautiful as it was cozy, providing a stunning view of the downtown cluster and the Potomac. A full bar provided refreshment, and the pool sparkled with reflected sun on the patio. Small

tables, surrounded by comfortable chairs, had been carefully positioned so that intimate groups could congregate
and talk with a relative feeling of privacy.

Damien Knight was already there when Ryan and
Nadja made their entrance. As were President Haeffner
and many members of Congress, all accompanied by their
respective security entourages. One or two people in this
room had had dealings with the infamous Quicksilver in
the past, and Ryan was pleased by the sense of discomfort
he felt flutter through the room as Nadja took his arm in
intimate fashion.

She made whispering sounds in his ear, and on cue, he
laughed softly. All their moves had been worked out
beforehand, and like a veteran team, they executed them
flawlessly.

They made a beautiful couple, and Ryan was acutely
aware of the impact they had when together. In fact, he
was counting on it.

With a kiss on his cheek, Nadja excused herself and
began to mingle.

Ryan stepped up to the bar that was being tended by a
big ork. To Ryan, the gnarled face screamed Secret Service, but that was to be expected. He hoped the poor man
knew how to mix a drink, or everyone else would know
just how thorough Brooks had been.

"What can I get you, sir?"

Ryan smiled. He hadn't allowed himself a drink in over
a year. There had been too much to do, with no time for
relaxation or the risk of being caught off guard. He didn't
really enjoy the effects of alcohol, but over the years he'd
learned how to appreciate the taste. Now, the situation
demanded that he seem casual and relaxed, and he didn't
mind what he had to do.

"Double Remy, heated."

He watched the big man gracefully pour scalding water
into the crystal snifter, to warm the glass. Then he drained
the water and poured in a generous amount of the amber
liquid. Ryan took it and raised the glass to his nose, suddenly aware of someone standing directly behind him.

He didn't turn, but merely inhaled the heady scent of

his drink, savoring the rich smell. He took a sip of the hot cognac, letting it steep down his throat.

"A fine brandy, if you like that kind of thing."

Just a bit a head of schedule, Ryan thought, recognizing the voice.

He turned, feigning surprise, and noticed that Knight had left his aide, Gerrold Watkins, with the rest of the Ares contingent. *So this little conversation is going to be off the record.*

"Mr. Knight," Ryan said. "I'm sorry, you've caught me enjoying one of my secret vices." He grinned, and Damien Knight's return smile was well-practiced enough to seem genuine.

"Oh, Mister Mercury, we all have our little secrets, don't we?"

Ryan shrugged. "You appreciate a fine cognac, Mr. Knight?"

Knight's smile softened. "Actually, about a year or so back, I stumbled onto a hidden reserve of a brandy called Germain Robin. They stopped production sometime around the turn of the century. Twenty-five bottles of the closest thing to heaven on this planet. You should stop by some evening. We'll pop one."

Ryan forced a wide smile. "That would be wonderful. I happen to have some fat Honduras cigars that go so well with a good brandy."

Damien frowned. "Actually, if you have a few minutes, I'd like to talk to you."

Come to me, you little fly. Come, step into my web.

Ryan kept his face neutral, hiding his relief.

"Of course. Would you like to sit?"

It had been a calculated risk, showing up here and displaying his and Nadja's relationship so openly. However, the idea had occurred to Ryan because he knew that the only way to get anything from Knight was to make the man come to him.

Under normal circumstances, Knight would have kept half the room between himself and Ryan. A snake doesn't slither too close to the mongoose unless it wishes to do battle. Or, unless the viper thinks it's fast enough to kill the mongoose with one quick strike.

Ryan knew Knight wasn't here to kill, he was here to do a little dance, to try and hypnotize the mongoose. Knight wanted to use Ryan. *For someone so dangerous, Knight, you're refreshingly predictable.*

Damien led him to one of the small, unoccupied tables. Ryan noticed how several people shifted to get out of their way. Some of them were frightened by Knight, and the others knew just a bit too much about Ryan Mercury to feel safe without some distance.

They sat, and Ryan took another sip of his cognac. "What can I do for you, Mister Knight?"

Knight propped his elbows on the table and leaned forward. "I'm surprised to see you here, Mercury. Especially coming as Miss Daviar's escort. Don't you realize you could cost her the nomination?"

Ryan smiled. "Well, I'm not so sure she really wants it anyway. She's got so much on her hands right now, the VP would only add to a schedule that's already over-full."

Knight sat back, and his expression grew thoughtful. "You know, I've always had a difficult time reading you."

Here it comes, thought Ryan. *Draw me in, then cut me off at the knees.*

"What's to read? Nadja's busy, and might not even have the time for this whole political gig. Dunkelzahn left her to stir quite a few pots, so to speak."

Knight's smile was tight. "Yes, he did. That doesn't seem like it would leave much time for a romantic life, does it?"

Ryan shrugged. "We both have tight schedules, but that just makes the time we have together that much more special."

Knight looked as if he were going to be ill.

"Yes, I can see how it would. However, with such limited time in the day, I could see where Nadja might be unable to give her attention to some of the finer details."

Ryan gave him a questioning look. "I'm not sure I follow?"

Damien smiled like a shark. "Well, she's been left quite a few different positions to fill. Not a problem for a dragon, but somewhat overwhelming for a simple metahuman, wouldn't you agree?"

Ryan followed his lead. "Oh, yes. In fact, she and I were just talking about all the company stock she now has to vote. She's not even that familiar with the workings of quite a few of them. I mean, she's got a pretty good hang on stuff like the Gavilan stock, but other things are a bit esoteric."

And the fly lands, thought Ryan, watching Knight's eyes light up.

"Exactly," Knight said. "In fact, I have a meeting with her in about half an hour to discuss that particular stock."

"Really, I was unaware."

Knight said nothing and for just a moment Ryan thought he might have been a bit heavy-handed. Knight leaned back, and his face went still.

Knight seemed to be thinking hard, and Ryan could see when he reached a decision. "Ryan, just between you and me, I'm worried about Miss Daviar. Especially in relation to her dealings with Gavilan. There's so much political back-stabbing going on there right now that I'm afraid it might be a bit much for her."

Ryan leaned forward, doing his best impersonation of a little kid being told a secret. "Really? I guess that's not so surprising after what happened to Dunkelzahn."

Knight nodded, playing his fatherly role to the hilt. "You know, I just thought of something. In my meeting with Daviar, I'm going to suggest that she give me temporary proxy rights to Gavilan. Just until she comes to know who all the main players are and where they stand. That way, she won't do anything she might regret later."

Ryan smiled. "That's very kind of you."

Knight's face turned conspiratorial again. "However, you, better than anyone, should know how strong-willed she is. I'm just afraid she'll misinterpret my offer. I would hate for her to refuse me, then kick herself for it later."

"How can I help?"

Knight actually leaned over and patted his arm. "Just talk to her. I'm sure she trusts you, and if you give her a gentle nudge in the right direction, we might just be able to avoid a big mess."

Ryan smiled. "You got it. I'll do anything for her."

Knight smiled and stretched out his hand. "It was a pleasure talking to you."

Ryan took the offered hand, but didn't release it. He let his face turn thoughtful. "You know, I heard your name come up in conversation the other day."

Knight, realizing he wasn't going to get his hand back, sat. His smile faded, replaced by a cautious look. "Oh, really? In what context?"

Ryan grinned and turned loose of Knight's hand. "Oh, I think it was an ex-employee of yours."

Knight's grin was thin, strained. "Someone you 'helped' relocate?"

Ryan shook his head. "No, no, no. It was someone you worked with before my time."

Knight's thin smile turned positively painful. "I hope this person had good things to say."

Ryan's smile grew predatory. "Oh, good and bad. She said you had some secrets, but she also said you were good in the sack."

It was a shot in the dark—something in Alice's tone when she'd talked about "David"—and Ryan was pleased with the results.

Knight turned white. "Her name?"

Ryan tapped his forefinger on his chin. "Let me see, I think it was . . . Alice. Yes, that's it. It was Alice Haeffner. Quite a nice lady, actually."

Knight looked as if someone had kicked the wind out him. "You spoke to her?"

Ryan's smile softened. "Yes. Seems she'd been speaking to another old friend of yours, a Thomas Roxborough. They have some pretty interesting views of your relationship with my former employer."

Knight was actually shaking. "Mister Mercury, thank you for the conversation, but I do have other people to talk to. If you'll excuse me."

As he was standing, Ryan dropped the bomb. "It seems that both Alice and Roxborough think you might have blamed Dunkelzahn for the Crash. That maybe you've held a grudge for more than two decades, and that possibly, just possibly, you might have finally gotten your revenge."

It was just a simple tick of the eye, but from someone as professional as Knight it was like a signed confession. Without another word, Knight left the table.

Ryan took another sip of his cognac, which had gone lukewarm. He turned and found Nadja's eyes on him. He blinked, slowly, their prearranged signal, and stood.

It took Ryan almost twenty minutes to extract himself from the gathering and make it to the back stairwell. Then he was past security and out the fire door.

He keyed his wristphone. "Jane, you get all that?"

Jane's voice floated into the concrete doorway. "In glorious color. That was a thing of beauty, Quicksilver."

Ryan reached the ground floor, and Brooks cleared him with security. Her face was grim when she bade him goodbye. Ryan made his way to the small Eurocar he had stashed in the employee parking lot.

"Jane, can you get tabs on Knight?"

"No problem there, Quicksilver. However, even in light of how surprisingly successful your evening was, you might want to drop it for now."

"What's up?"

"That call I got earlier was from the team you had me hire to watch Burnout. You called it correctly. He's heading straight for you, and he'll be there soon."

"Jane, we're going to have to be careful. Get tabs on Knight, and get Grind and Dhin prepped. Damien hosed up, and he knows it, but the proof will be in what he does next, and when he gives me that proof, I want to be there."

"Copy," Jane said. "Grind and Dhin are ready to roll, and Knight is still at the party."

"Good. Keep me informed."

He cut the connection, and reached the dark blue Eurocar. He was just leaning over to open the door when his senses screamed danger.

Ryan spun, clicking into high gear as he scanned for escape routes.

Rows of parked cars. Pillars and low roof of gray duracrete. Not a lot of room to maneuver.

Twelve men seemed to melt from the shadows. Coming at him fast. They were heavily armored, packing Ares military weaponry, and they moved like complete pros. If it hadn't been for the small Knight Errant logo on each Kevlar III-covered chest, Ryan could have taken them for high-paid assassins.

Frag! I've underestimated Knight again.

He looked to the metal door that led to the staircase, fifteen meters away. Too far.

The twelve armored men formed a wide circle around him. One of them spoke. "If you would be so kind as to drop to your face, Mister Mercury, it would be greatly appreciated. We have orders not to kill you unless we really feel like it."

Ryan shook his head. He might get three, maybe four of them, but there were too many. By the time he got his gun out, they'd have cut out his knees. Unless. . .

Ryan held his hands up in surrender. "I don't want trouble," he said. "I'm unarmed."

"On the ground!"

Suddenly, and without warning, Ryan dove for the Eurocar, flattening himself to slide under the belly of the vehicle.

His would-be captors were caught off-guard, moving as if in slow motion. They fired, but too late. Ryan heard bullets ricochet off the car as he rolled, reaching into his calf holster for his pistol as he crossed the narrow space between the Eurocar and a Chrysler-Nissan Jackrabbit.

A plan formed in his mind as he moved. He almost had his gun and would use it to. . .

Sharp pain erupted in Ryan's chest and the side of his head as a burst of gel-pack bullets hit home.

Drek, he thought, and for a moment blackness threatened to engulf him.

Several seconds must have passed because Ryan found himself being dragged out from under the Jackrabbit. Drifting in and out of consciousness.

The man who had spoken stepped forward, quickly and decisively. "This is going to hurt you more than it hurts me," the man said with an abrupt laugh.

Pain exploded behind Ryan's right ear, and everything went black.

32

The Federated-Boeing 3800 arched down from the darkening sky, coming closer and closer to the sea of twinkling lights that seemed to stretch past the horizon. As the 3800 touched down, tires smoking on hot tarmac, Burnout rolled from the wheel well, hit the pavement in a shower of sparks, and skidded to a stop as the 3800 shot past him.

In less than a second, he was on his feet, running for the lightly wooded area just to the side of the landing strip. "So far so good."

"Yes, so far so good. Remind me not to travel with you very often." Lethe's tone was dry and sardonic.

Burnout grinned. "Hey, you made a joke. And here I thought you were hopeless."

"I was not joking."

Burnout laughed as he dashed between thin maple trees and made for the long-term parking structure. A mammoth four-story building constructed of five slabs of duracrete stacked on top of each other, the long-term parking was full of cars, but otherwise completely deserted.

Burnout skirted the building until he had the positions of all the surveillance equipment scoped out. He found the vehicle he wanted, a late-model Ford Americar. It was situated perfectly between two of the cameras' blind spots, and the third camera only covered the car once a minute.

Plenty of time, thought Burnout.

Just as the camera made its sweep, Burnout rushed from his hiding place, leapt over the low duracrete wall, and hit the Americar. It took him less than five seconds to open the door, another eight seconds to disable the car alarm, and twenty more to hot-wire the big sedan.

As the engine roared to life, Burnout swung his chrome elbow in a vicious arc, smashing it into the back of the driver's seat.

With a tortured whine, the seat snapped off at the base of the upright, allowing Burnout to sit comfortably, without being cramped against the windshield.

Burnout backed the car out of its space and pulled up to the automated gate. He found the parking stub on the dash, fed it into the machine, grinned his metal smile into the surveillance camera, and waited as the gate electronically deducted forty-six nuyen from the account of Elizabeth Farley.

As the long arm levered upward, Burnout accelerated out into the night. The streets were crowded, despite all the violence that had occurred recently, and Burnout had to keep his head down to avoid frightening the other drivers on the George Mason Bridge.

As traffic thinned out coming into the city, Burnout began to feel uneasy. It wasn't anything specific, just a vague tightening of the chrome parts where his gut should have been.

Lethe's voice dropped through his IMS. "I sense you are ill at ease. Is there a problem?"

Burnout didn't answer for a moment. It was strange how close he and Lethe had become. The spirit was becoming uncannily good at reading his moods, at sensing his thoughts. In a way, it was comforting. He shared a bond with Lethe that he'd never experienced with any other creature in his life. Still, it was spooky at times. He shrugged. "Nothing I can pin down. Maybe I'm just having a problem with there not being a problem."

Lethe sighed. "Your statement is as cryptic as usual, but I think I follow. You are wondering why Ryan hasn't been dogging your every footstep, why he hasn't been hiding behind every tree, every doorway."

Burnout nodded. "Yeah, I guess that's it. This all seems too easy, like we're walking into a trap."

Lethe chuckled. "In a manner of speaking, we are."

"What?"

"Do you think Ryan doesn't know we're here?"

Burnout's voice was bitter. "Well, I was kind of hoping. I thought maybe you were clouding my trail so he wouldn't know we're coming."

Lethe laughed. "Don't you see? We want Ryan to know we're coming. He left you that note in hopes of drawing you out. He wanted you to come for him. Every time he's tried to track you, you have defeated him, and the cost was becoming very high for him. He needs to get you on his home ground, in a place where he controls all the elements. He wants you to come for him."

Burnout frowned. "Why doesn't that make me feel any better? I've been letting you call the shots since Pony Mountain, and suddenly, I have a feeling I'm fragged."

"Not by any stretch of the imagination. I thought the logic here would be self-evident."

"Well, it's not," Burnout snarled.

"All right, my friend. Let me explain. You are walking into a trap. Mercury thinks he's got you. I'm sure we've been under astral surveillance since we left the mountain. That's how he works. However, he's failed to take a few things into account."

"Like?"

"Like the fact that you aren't coming for him."

"I know that." Burnout was feeling some of his old rage resurface. "We're coming for the Daviar slitch. So how exactly does that help us?"

Lethe sighed again, a deep, tired thing. "You have been under so much pressure, I think you are over-analyzing the situation. It's quite simple. Mercury thinks you are coming for him. He'll be ready, prepared. If we cared to look, I'm sure we could easily dig up clues as to where Mercury is to be found. He wants you to find him. But he doesn't realize that you know about Daviar. He won't be near her, and so doesn't comprehend that she's in danger."

Suddenly, the tight knot in Burnout's stomach disappeared. "Damn, you're right. This is so simple, it's almost child's play, but you're right. Ryan seems to be a straight-on fighter, and from what he knows of me, he expects me to be the same."

Lethe's voice was soft. "Feel better?"

"Much. You've used Ryan's own smarts against him. If he'd tried to stop us from coming, he probably could have whittled us down bit by bit. This way . . ."

"Exactly."

With Lethe and his GPS as a guide, Burnout pulled up outside the front gate of Dunkelzahn's mansion in less than half an hour. He drove the car a half-kilometer down the road and into a tree-covered ditch. Then they made the hike back to the estate in silence and darkness.

"I think the security here is fairly tight," said Lethe. "Though I didn't worry about that sort of thing when I was here last."

"Can you give me specifics?"

"Yes," Lethe said. "There are watchers and elementals. The fence is laced with monowire and there are cameras and track-mounted drones with rotary cannons packing stun ammo. Maybe paranormal guard dogs of some sort, but nothing we can't handle."

"How do you know all this?"

"When I was here last, I possessed a member of security so that I could speak with Nadja Daviar. I read all that from his mind."

Burnout nodded. "What about the slitch? How's she rate on the danger scale."

Lethe's voice was cold. "She is not a threat. Nadja Daviar is a remarkable woman, and I would like for you to promise me that no harm will come to her."

"I can't promise that."

"I realize that circumstances might get out of your control, but I would like for you to promise that you will not take any action against her yourself. If she . . . if something happens to her during the course of events, that is unavoidable. However, I would like for you to take all the precautions available to you to ensure her safety."

Burnout nodded. "I've got no quarrel with her, and absolutely no reason to kill her. I won't kill her unless Mercury forces my hand. Or if she gets in the way."

"I guess that is all I can ask."

Just then, the sound of a big engine racing down the street toward them caught Burnout's attention. He crouched in the darkness of low-hanging pine branches across the street.

The Nightsky limo burned rubber as it turned at the entrance and accelerated down the circular drive. With a screech, the big car slammed to a halt by the door.

Burnout cranked up the gain on his low-light vision. He saw the figure of a young woman with the build of an elf. She had dark hair and wore a flowing red evening gown. She dashed up the broad steps to the house. Within seconds, she was inside, and the limo pulled away.

"Looks like someone's party didn't go quite as planned."

Lethe laughed. "Most likely Ryan has gotten word of our arrival, and has sent her to a place he believes is safe. Just as I knew he would."

"Excellent, now let's rock and roll. Give me the layout of this place."

33

Out of the darkness floated a pinpoint of white light. It swam toward him in an unsteady stream, finally reaching him and bringing pain. Ryan used his magic to channel the pain away, and the throbbing in the back of his head vanished.

He opened his eyes, and immediately shut them again.

White room. Mirrored walls.

With his eyes closed, he took a mental inventory of his body. The blow to the head wasn't the only thing his body had suffered. He had been beaten, though not severely, and his scalp itched where someone had ripped the fake datajacks off.

He was naked, he could tell that by the light breeze blowing over his bare skin from the air-conditioning and the chill of the metal chair on his back. His hands were cuffed behind his knees.

He turned his senses outward. Hearing told him that he shared the room with two others, both large, who stood behind him. Smell told him that one of the guards liked clove cigarettes and that the other wore an offensive amount of aftershave.

He forced his mind to focus, counting backward from ten. When he had centered himself, he slowly opened his eyes again.

The room was sterile white, nearly five meters wide, and half again as long. Directly in front of Ryan sat a small table bolted to the floor and holding a small deck and a telecom. On the other side of that was a utilitarian desk chair, empty. Without turning his head Ryan could see observation mirrors reflecting his image back to him on each of the three walls. His and the images of the two trolls who towered behind him, their battle uniforms looking well-used and their automatic rifles pointed directly at his head.

They hadn't bothered to clean him up. Dried blood ran down his neck to a point just above his right nipple. Ryan watched the forward observation mirror, his infrared vision telling him that two others watched him.

Ryan smiled at the two figures and mouthed the words, "Long time no see, Knight."

One figure nodded, then moved out of Ryan's line of sight. Within a few moments, a doorway at Ryan's back opened, and in the mirror's reflection, Ryan watched Damien Knight step through.

He hadn't changed since the party, and the look on his face was bemused, almost whimsical. Knight stepped around Ryan, making sure he was well out of reach, despite Ryan's handicapped position. He circled the deck, and with a sigh, sat in the chair.

Knight leaned back, crossed his legs, and steepled his fingers under his chin. For some reason, his body posture reminded Ryan of Nadja. Then he realized it was that of someone totally in control, completely in his element.

For most of five minutes, he and Knight stared at each other. Finally, Knight slowly shook his head. "I've been trying to figure out just where I went wrong with you, Mercury."

Ryan shrugged. "Maybe it was when you showed no appreciation for good aged cognac."

Knight laughed. "Touché. You're right. I can't stomach the stuff, myself."

"Then I guess you were just kidding about the offer to come to your place and sample some of that vintage Germain Robin."

Knight fixed him with an intense stare. "Yes, I think I know where I went wrong. During my dealings with you before, I formed a picture of an immaculate warrior, someone of incredible ability who had been hand-groomed by an immortal. Unfortunately, the times I had the pleasure of witnessing your crafty side, I made the assumption that Dunkelzahn was your brain, that any spark of ingenuity you possessed was programmed by your master."

He's right and he doesn't even know it.

Ryan was Dunkelzahn's weapon. Always had been. And without the dragon to wield him, to direct his edge, Ryan felt lost. Unsure.

Knight stood. "Mercury, much as I'd like to sit around exchanging pleasantries with you all night, I didn't ask you here for a social call."

Ryan smiled, tight and dangerous. "You didn't *ask* me here, Knight. You panicked."

Knight returned the smile, and if anything, his grin was even more predatory. "Quite correct. You see, you left the gathering this afternoon under some very explosive misconceptions. I've brought you here to disabuse you of those misconceptions before you do something rash and potentially . . . destructive."

Ryan kept his face impassive.

Knight sat on the edge of the desk. "I'll admit, you took me for quite a turn when you mentioned Alice and Roxborough."

"I'll bet."

Knight nodded. "Yes, a lot of your information is quite correct, though even that data is enough to get you killed. And I have to remind you, you're getting that information from a deranged vat freak and a ghost in the machine. You see, Alice flatlined and went into a coma many years ago, though both her husband and I did everything in our power to save her."

Ryan raised an eyebrow. "You're going somewhere with all this, I hope."

Knight leaned forward. "You talked tonight about holding a grudge for decades. Well, you're right. A grudge has been held, but not by me. You've been duped by Alice, but unfortunately, you played your cards so well that I fell right in line with what certain people would like you to believe."

Ryan sneered. "So you're telling me that you had nothing to do with the death of Dunkelzahn?"

Knight stood and walked around to the chair and sat again. "That's exactly what I'm telling you."

"You'll have to do a lot better than that, Knight. At least Alice and Roxborough gave me some evidence to back up their story."

Knight sighed. "I was afraid it would come down to this. And I won't deny that I often wanted the old wyrm to butt out with all his behind-the-scenes manipulation. It especially slotted me off when I had to sell him VisionQuest.

"I may have even wished for his death more than once. Frankly, he was on the hit list of all the megacorps. But we didn't all cause that explosion. I'm not even sure how it could have been done."

Ryan laughed. "Your words are like sand in the desert, Knight. There are a whole lot of them, and they're worthless."

Knight nodded. "Then I'm very sorry that you don't believe me, Mister Mercury. I can't give you the proof you need, and I can't afford to have someone as dangerous as you wandering around plotting my demise."

Knight nodded to one of the trolls behind Ryan. "Kill him quickly, and painlessly."

34

Burnout cleared the wall with a quick flex of his hydraulic legs. He landed behind some trimmed azalea bushes and fell to his belly, listening intently for the telltale sounds of alarms or guard animals.

Nothing but the distant chirping of birds and the chatter of squirrels.

Burnout had seen a number of Secret Servicemen, and he knew that if this took too long, many of them would die and he might be prevented from getting to Daviar.

That was why his plan was based on speed.

"I'm masking our auras," Lethe said. "And doing my best to make us invisible in the physical as well."

Burnout didn't respond with physical speech, but Lethe seemed to understand his answer. *Good.*

"When I was here last, she was in her office," Lethe said. "That window, straight ahead. First floor, next to the arboretum."

For the most part, the mansion was a huge red brick structure with a shingled roof, but just ahead, across a short section of groomed lawn, Burnout noticed the elaborate greenhouse. The walls were in style with the rest of the house, but the roof was made of glass or some other clear composite. The glass was held up by the huge limbs of stone trees. Very ornate and beautiful.

And very likely, complex on the inside. *A great place for a confrontation.*

Burnout scanned left and caught sight of the elf woman, Daviar, through the panes of a tall window straight ahead. It was multi-paned and most likely bullet-proof, but even plexan could be defeated with the right weaponry. Burnout didn't hesitate for a second; he sprang to his feet and launched himself into a full-out run, straight for the window.

In the thirty meters between the hedge and the house, Burnout accelerated to nearly sixty klicks per hour. He pulled the Predators and fired into the window as his legs hurtled the two of them toward the window. And Daviar.

Bullets ricocheted off the glass at first, then they cracked it. Burnout emptied both clips into the clear polymer, forming a nearly perfect circle of cracks. Then he launched himself head first into the house.

The glass exploded in a shower of glittering shards as Burnout burst through and rolled on carpeting, snapped himself up and lunged for a startled Nadja Daviar. She pulled away from him, faster than he expected, nearly reaching the door.

But his ravaged metal body slammed into her, and she crumpled beneath his weight. Alarms sounded throughout the mansion, relentless and annoying. Burnout pushed himself to his feet just as three guards in dark suits and sunglasses rushed through the door.

Burnout lifted the elf, Daviar, holding her in front of him with one large and gruesome hand encircling her neck. "Back off! Or she dies."

The woman straightened and regained her composure. Remarkably fast. "Please," she said. "Tell us what you want, and I'll make sure you get it."

Burnout allowed himself a smile. "Yes, you will."

"What do you want with me?"

"First, tell these suits to kindly leave the building."

Nadja nodded toward the security team.

"We can't just leave you in here with this thing," said one of the suits.

"You can and you will, Mister," Nadja said, her voice ringing with authority.

The suits retreated, and when they were gone, Burnout turned her toward him. She was the picture of unmarred flesh, so fragile in her unblemished beauty. And he was a tableau of gore-covered metal and bundled Kevlar III fibers. So very little flesh left, even his outer coating of vatgrown skin had mostly peeled away or rotted off.

Opposites, they stared at each other for a brief moment.

Then Burnout spoke. "There is only one person who can save you, and I suggest you get him here. He must come at once. And he must come alone."

35

Sweat dripped down Ryan's naked chest as he sat in the cold metal chair. As he readied himself for the next few seconds. In the observation mirror, he saw the big troll guard move forward slightly. Ready to pull the trigger.

Ryan tensed his legs and tried to focus. There wasn't any way he could take both the trolls, but he wasn't going to die without taking Knight down with him. He could use his telekinetic thrust to deflect the gun barrel so that the bullets would hit Knight, but timing was going to be crucial.

As the huge man pressed the barrel of the automatic to the side of Ryan's neck, time seemed to slow down. His mind was filled with the image of Dunkelzahn in his natural form. Huge and sinuous, with metallic blue scales. *I'm sorry. I've failed you again.*

Ryan was just about to make his move when the telecom on the desk came to life.

Knight held up his hand, and the troll stopped, the muzzle of his weapon digging a circular ring just under Ryan's ear. Knight hit the connect and looked at the face on the screen in surprise.

The voice that came over the line was faint, barely audible to Ryan's ears. "Do you have him?"

Knight looked up at Ryan. "It's for you."

Ryan didn't like the look of glee in the old man's eyes.

Knight smiled, and turned the telecom around, and Ryan found himself looking at an extreme close-up of Nadja's face.

Her features filled the entire screen, blocking any clue as to where she was. *She looks worried,* Ryan thought.

"Hello, dear," said Ryan. "Am I out after my curfew?"

Ryan watched as Nadja shot a glance to her left, then looked back at him. The message was clear, she wasn't alone.

She looks scared.

"Ryan, I need you to come home right now." The panic in her voice sent every muscle in Ryan's body jumping.

He forced himself to be calm. Losing control wouldn't help anyone. With as much nonchalance as he could muster, Ryan looked down at his naked condition, then back up to the screen. "Well, dear, and this might be a tired cliché, but as you can see, I'm a bit tied up right now."

One of the trolls behind Ryan laughed.

Nadja's composure came as close to cracking as Ryan had ever seen. "I'm sorry, Ryan. But it's imperative that you return to the mansion at once."

Knight turned the screen in his direction, "Miss Daviar, how good of you to call. It seems as if you just might have tuned in at a very advantageous time for everyone."

There was something in Knight's tone that bothered Ryan. It was almost as if the man had been expecting her call, as if this was just another step in a very intricate dance.

Ryan couldn't quite hear Nadja's reply, but Knight nodded. "Why, of course I'll send Mister Mercury on his way to you immediately. However, in this world of *quid pro quo,* I must ask something in return."

Nadja said something, but the only word Ryan could make out was "Bastard."

Knight laughed. "How gracious of you to notice. Still, that's off the subject. What I had in mind has to do with the disposition of your Gavilan stock."

Knight paused, then shook his head. "Something a bit more permanent. In exchange for the hasty return of your pet muscle boy, I thought maybe a two-year non-retractable voting proxy wouldn't be too much to ask."

The strain in Nadja's voice was evident, even if Ryan couldn't make out the words.

Finally, Knight said, "Very wise choice, my dear. This conversation has been notarized, and if you would be so good as to give the code for your retinal scan, we can make it legal and binding."

Knight hit a button, then grinned up at the screen. "My dear, I would suggest refraining from trying to void this agreement by claiming it was made under duress. Not only will I tie you up in corporate court for years, negating your access to the stock, I will also make sure you—"

Knight's grin widened as Nadja spoke. Then, "Well, my dear, I'm glad you see the sense of sticking to the agreement."

Four quiet beeps sounded from the telecom, then Knight looked up at one of the trolls. "Get this trash his clothes and gear, and deposit him at Dunkelzahn's mansion."

As Ryan felt the cuffs being pulled from his wrists, Knight returned his attention to the telecom. "Of course, my dear. We'll have to do this again some time. It's been ever so much more enjoyable than our usual sparring matches."

He cut the connection and turned to Ryan. "Don't even think about reprisals, Mercury. I respect you enough to know how determined and ruthless you can be when given the chance. However, you're in way over your head dealing with Alice and Roxborough. Do yourself a favor and forget them."

Ryan smiled. "We have something in common after all, Knight."

Knight looked offended. "And just what would that be?"

"We both have a long memory. You really should kill me now, because I'll never forget, and one day, out of the darkness, your worst nightmare will come calling."

Knight laughed softly. "Have a wonderful evening, Mister Mercury. Considering the circumstances I believe you'll find yourself in very soon, I doubt you'll have time to worry about petty vengeance."

Ryan just continued to smile at him until the big trolls led him out of the room. They returned his clothing and his wristphone, then drove him in an armored stepvan to the mansion.

36

Alice looked over at the flesh blob that was Thomas Roxborough. His disease had nearly run its course and his organs were coming apart. If he didn't get help soon, he would die.

Roxborough had other problems as well. His head lay across an elaborate chopping block that was situated on a huge stage surrounded by gardens of white roses and a deck of royal guards. A huge, ugly guard with a hood over his head wielded a gigantic axe.

Alice grinned her Cheshire grin. "So it comes down to this," she said. "Do you have any last words?"

"Alice!" Roxborough bellowed.

The executioner swung the axe behind his head.

"David denies killing Dunkelzahn, and I can't find any concrete evidence that ties him to the explosion."

"He had motive."

"He had some interesting things to say about that, too."

The axe rose in a wide arc over his head.

"Alice!"

"He said you were responsible for the Crash, not Dunkelzahn. Just as I suspected originally. For some reason he was reluctant to tell me."

The axe fell.

"Stop, stop! I admit it. I had something to do with it, but I wasn't alone."

The blade made a clean cut through Roxborough's neck and struck the wood chopping block with a resounding *thunk*! Roxborough's head fell onto the wooden planks and rolled over next to the fading cat.

Alice smiled down at him. "I thought you might have more to say."

"I'm still alive," said Roxborough's disembodied head. "I'm still alive."

"Surprise! Now finish your little confession, and I'll let you live a few moments longer."

Roxborough grimaced. "Okay, it begins way back with my corporation, Acquisition Technologies."

"Yes?"

"It was a small corp, but we had a drek-hot programming department. I ran it, and David Gavilan was my top code maestro."

Alice drew breath through her sharp teeth.

"Dunkelzahn had very little to do with the corporation except that he owned a small portion. Until one day, I learned that the wyrm was planning to hire Gavilan away from us. This started a little corporate data war.

"I instructed my programming team to come up with the most deadly computer virus ever constructed. My intention was to destroy the data cores of Dunkelzahn's Gossamer Threads Corporation. Nothing more. Gavilan worked on the project, everyone did."

"I don't believe you."

Roxborough's disembodied face wrinkled into a pained grimace. "Finally, the truth and you don't buy it."

"What happened?"

"We tried a small corp first to see if the virus would work. We unleashed it on Effexx Studios and it destroyed them completely. At first we were overjoyed, but then something happened. It was a complicated program, self-replicating, self-correcting, all that. It got out in the old Internet and infected hundreds of computer systems."

"I remember," said Alice. *Perhaps,* she thought, *this is finally the truth.*

"It was an accident, don't you see? We never intended to hurt anyone."

"What happened to David?"

"Dunkelzahn met with him to discuss moving to Gossamer Threads, and he saw the virus in David's mind. Dunkelzahn knew what we had done and he convinced David to quit Acquisition Technologies and go to work for the UCAS government to fight the virus. The rest of us were busy trying to hide our involvement, and with all the computer systems crashing, that wasn't too hard to do."

Alice looked at Roxborough with pity. "You deserve your fate," she said. "You deserve to be a brain in a bottle. But I never did anything wrong. I came in as an innocent . . ."

"Look, I'm very sorry. I helped fund Echo Mirage. We all fought the Crash virus."

"It mutated and grew into something else, did it not?"

"I don't know."

"Is it still out there?" Alice asked.

"Honestly, I don't know."

Alice faded herself out of Wonderland and into the shining city.

Roxborough's cries fell away into the distance. "You can't leave me like this. I'm a disembodied head, for Ghost's sake."

Alice ignored him. He was still alive. He should be thankful.

37

Ryan stood on the street, a chill wind playing through his hair, and looked at the mansion. The Dragon Heart was near, he could sense its power calling out to him.

Nadja, I hope you're all right.

Carla Brooks had arrived a few minutes earlier and had surrounded the perimeter of the mansion grounds with sec troops. She was around the other side now, getting an infiltration plan worked out in case Ryan was unsuccessful.

His wristphone beeped. He looked at the tiny screen to see Alice's liquid blue eyes. "This is not a good time, Alice."

Alice gave him a sad smile. "I'm sorry about circumstances, Ryan," she said. "This won't take long."

"Go ahead."

"I have new information that Damien Knight never thought Dunkelzahn was responsible for the Crash. Knight did not have a long-burning hatred and probably didn't have a strong motive to kill him."

Ryan just shook his head. "Now you tell me."

"I sincerely apologize," she said.

"I'll want to discuss this further," Ryan said. "But now is not the time."

Alice nodded. "Agreed."

Then she was gone and Ryan took a moment to center himself. He remembered his interrogation with Quentin Strapp. Strapp had grilled him, had made it look like Ryan could have killed Dunkelzahn, and Ryan had done the same thing with Knight.

I guess the appearance of guilt doesn't equal culpability.

Ryan took a deep breath and pushed those thoughts

from his mind. Time enough for that after Nadja was safe. He keyed in Jane's number, and her familiar icon faded onto the small screen.

"Ryan, about fragging time."

Ryan kept his voice quiet. "Give me the situation report, and this better be good."

The blonde caricature shrugged. "He's got her in the arboretum. She's tied up in the southeast corner, under the last plant table. Almost like he was trying to keep her clear of the action."

Ryan nodded. "What about Dhin and Grind?"

"With the exception of Nadja showing up, everything went just like you thought it would. Dhin is in the Secret Service van, rigging surveillance and assault drones. Grind is high up in the branches of one of the huge redwoods adjacent to the property. He hasn't had a clear shot yet."

Ryan took a deep breath. He thought about the way Nadja had looked during her call, about the hidden fear he'd seen there. He would save her, there was no other choice, but under that realization came another. He would get the Dragon Heart today or he would die trying. For the first time since losing the Heart to Burnout, Ryan had no doubts about his mission.

His indecision was gone, his uncertainty vanished.

There would be no strategic retreat this time, no fighting to a draw. He finally knew where to strike, and he was willing to sacrifice himself if necessary.

"Ryan, your gear is stored just in front of the main entrance. Get going, and we'll switch over to the Phillips tacticom on your signal."

Ryan nodded and cut the connection. He crossed the street, his every nerve on fire, his hyperaware senses going into maximum alert. He found the gear pack just to the side of the front staircase, under a rose bush.

Quickly, and with a minimum of excess movement, he laid out the gear. It consisted of light body armor, a small tacticom unit, a Vindicator minigun, and a shoulder holster with a Colt Manhunter.

Ryan suited up quickly and checked the load in his weapons. Ready and willing. He pulled the Vindicator's strap over his head, slung the ammo belt, and switched off its safety.

Then he inserted the light earpiece into his left ear and used the mimetic tape to fasten the tiny mic to his throat. "System up," he subvocalized.

"Check," said Jane in Ryan's ear.

"Check," came Grind's voice.

"Check," said Dhin, and there was an edge of humor in the big ork's voice. "Bossman, thought we'd lost you."

"Not quite. What's your position?"

"You drove past me on the way in. I'm in the black stepvan. Got a Condor II in the air to keep track of our chummer if he happens to come out, plus a Rotodrone with heavy armament package ready to rock and roll on your mark."

"Good. Grind?"

"I'm playing birdy in this fragging tree. Me and my Barret one-two-one. Can't tag him unless you move him into the middle of the room."

Ryan paused, mentally arranging his chess pieces.

"Jane?"

"Copy."

"You got control of the house systems?"

"Stupid question, Ryan, but I guess you had to ask."

"Lay it out for me."

"Quicksilver, he's smart. He's keeping to cover under the third stone tree from the rear exit. That way, he has Daviar between him and that exit, and can cover the other two at his leisure."

Grind came on. "I almost got him when he dumped Daviar under the table, but even with this high-powered scope, the infrastructure of the building is playing havoc with me. I can't get a clear shot at him as long as all those stone branches are in the way."

Ryan nodded again. The arboretum was a huge structure with two gigantic sheets of macroglass for a roof to allow the sunlight in. In the name of artistic decor, the macroglass was supported by ornately carved marble trees. Eight of them, complete with stone roots and intertwining branches, stretched upward to create a canopy.

"Jane, talk to me about the arboretum. It's got auto sprinklers in case of fire, right?"

"Affirmative."

Ryan thought about it, and suddenly everything came into focus.

"Jane, what's the oxygen content in there?"

There was a pause, and Ryan could tell the question had taken her by surprise.

"Dunkelzahn converted the arboretum into a greenhouse of sorts, said he wanted to raise orchids, so the oxygen content is higher than normal. Why?"

"You control that as well?"

"Affirmative."

Ryan grinned. "I want you to slowly increase the oxygen content."

"How high?"

"Just keep it going, but try and make it subtle."

Dhin's voice sounded concerned. "Bossman, you mind filling us in on what you've got planned?"

Ryan forced his voice to remain calm. "Grind can't get a clear shot with that roof over our boy, so I'm going to blow these stone trees sky high."

"Ryan," said Jane, "I've never asked this before, and I hope I won't ever ask it again, but do you know what the frag you're doing?"

A picture of Nadja's face filled his mind. "I've never been so sure. I'll give you the signal. Just before I blow the place, I want you to selectively activate the sprinkler systems over Nadja and myself. Turn them on full blast."

Jane chuckled. "I think I'm getting the picture. What about the Heart?"

"I'm going to take it from him before the place blows."

"I'll track it and make sure the sprinklers protect as much as possible."

Ryan nodded. "All right, people, this is one for the record books. Let's keep it clean. Grind, you know what to do."

"Check."

"If things get ugly in there, I want Nadja out. She's first priority. After that comes the Dragon Heart, then me. That clear?"

There was no answer needed, and none came. Each member of the team knew just what was at stake.

"Jane, if things don't go as planned, there are coded instructions in my safe at Assets. Follow them to the letter."

Silence.

He stood and walked quickly up the steps to the front door. There was no need for stealth. Burnout knew he was coming and had the entrances covered. There was no chance for surprise.

"Now, Jane," he said.

"Increasing oxygen content. It should reach a flammable level in just under five minutes."

With that he entered the house.

Ryan walked through the quiet darkness, and even though he knew that he was never more than fifty meters from another member of his team, he felt utterly alone. As he stepped past priceless art, he found himself growing nervous. Roxborough's self-doubt creeping in.

Ryan took several deep and cleansing breaths, trying to bring calm. But by the time he reached the sealed double glass doors of the arboretum, an edge of agitation had gripped him again. And it refused to let go.

Taking a slow breath, he keyed the palmlock, and the doors slid backward.

Humid heat smothered him, and he immediately began to sweat. The rich smell of fertile soil and blooming plant life hit him, and for just a second, he was sad that Burnout had chosen this spot. In just a few minutes, nothing would be left of the beauty around him.

It had been a while since Ryan had come to the arboretum, and for just a second, he stopped and looked around, as if he were seeing it for the last time.

Sculpted marble trees strained for the ceiling, their intertwined branches making up the supports for the twin sheets of macroglass that made up the roof. Each of the stone trees were completely wreathed in ivy, giving the impression that they were alive.

"So, we're finally alone together." The chilly voice dropped out of the air, echoing in the damp stillness.

Ryan immediately put his back to the wall, pulling the

Vindicator up to ready position. Something was wrong, something in the back of his mind told him he wasn't going about this in the right way.

"Not quite, Burnout," he said. "This is between you and me. Let Nadja go."

Burnout's laughter rang through the room, turning Ryan's blood cold. "Between you and me, Mercury? It hasn't been between you and me since you killed the Kodiak."

Ryan remembered the bear shaman, Miranda held high over his head. He shifted on the balls of his feet, slowly inching his way into the dark room. Burnout didn't give much of a heat signature, so Ryan was going to have to rely on other means.

"Jane," he subvocalized.

"Copy," came the woman's voice in his ear.

"Position."

"He hasn't moved."

Ryan took a quick, silent step, and put one of the marble trees between him and Burnout's location. "Jane, what's the count?"

"Another four minutes, but Ryan, when you blow it, you're going to have to be near the corner of the room where I can cover you with the sprinklers. Otherwise, you're going to take as much damage as he does, and I don't think I have to remind you that you are flesh and blood."

Ryan smiled in the darkness. "Don't worry about me. Just keep that oxygen rising."

There was a pause. "Ryan, you do realize that if shots are fired after the oxygen level gets high enough, the room will go ahead of schedule."

"I've already got it figured, Jane. Just be ready."

Burnout's modulated voice dropped into the room. "Mercury? Where are your friends? Don't tell me you actually did what I wanted. I would be so disappointed if you came to the party by yourself."

Ryan stepped out into the open. "I guess I'm just going to have to disappoint you, Burnout. It's just me."

There was another long laugh.

"Quicksilver! He's on the move. He's got you targeted,

and he's making his way toward you, just on your two o'clock."

"Yes, Burnout. I'm here all alone, just like that night in Aztlan. It's just you and me. You think you're chill enough to take me?"

"My, my. What's that I see? Looks like a Vindicator minigun. That's some pretty heavy rock and roll, Mercury. And what a pity, I'm totally unarmed."

Ryan turned to his two o'clock, and Burnout's metal form drifted out of the shadows and into a patch of sunlight.

Grind sounded frustrated. "Frag those branches! I can't get a clean shot. Just another two meters, and he's mine."

Ryan looked at Burnout's ravaged frame, and whistled low. "You look pretty bad, Burnout."

Burnout smiled, and in the filtered light, it was the metal smile of some chromed grim reaper. "Yeah, I ain't so pretty as I was, Mercury. I guess I owe my new look to you."

Something clicked in Ryan's mind, and he knew what had been nagging. He was alone in the arboretum, but he wasn't using the Silent Way. He had been ignoring Dunkelzahn's teachings since losing the Heart, and he knew he wouldn't survive this unless he focused on his training. On who he was.

Ryan slowly knelt down on the floor, and laid the Vindicator on the warm marble. "Burnout, it doesn't have to come to this. You know I have you outgunned, and you know from our past encounters that even in a straight fight, I can give you a run for your nuyen. But this is foolishness. We don't have to fight."

Burnout smiled. "I know we don't have to, Mercury, but I want to. I want to feel your skull crack and collapse under my fingers. I've come a long way to watch you die."

Ryan held up his hands. "Listen. You stole something that doesn't belong to you, something you can't even understand. There's an easy way out of this where both of us leave this place alive. All you have to do is put the Dragon Heart on the ground and walk away."

Burnout cocked his head, as if he was listening to

something inside his own skull. Then the smile returned. "Look at me, Mercury. You've left me with nothing. And for what? The Heart. You think I'm going to give up the only thing that makes all this worthwhile? Still, there *is* a way to end this easily."

"I'm listening."

"Why don't you lie down on the floor and let me kill you quickly. That way you won't have the shame of being beaten before you die. It would save you a lot of emotional distress." Then that scary laugh again.

Ryan shook his head. "So that's it, then. Neither one of us is going to give in."

Burnout went into a fighter's crouch. "That's it, Mercury. Let's dance, shall we?"

His movement was a blur, the fastest thing Ryan had ever seen. Burnout crossed the distance in the blink of an eye, and Ryan had just enough time to throw himself to the side as Burnout came rumbling at him like a tractor train out of control.

Except Burnout was in complete control. As Ryan leapt to the left, Burnout's right hand swung, open-handed, and caught Ryan across the chest.

The impact hit Ryan like a sledgehammer, and his body was lifted high into the air. Instinct made him roll with the fall.

Ryan came to his feet, a full three meters from where he'd been standing. His chest was on fire, and he magically channeled the pain away. When he could breathe again, he felt his ribcage, and realized that his body armor had been sliced to within a millimeter of the skin. Burnout was nowhere in sight.

"What the frag just happened?" Grind sounded completely confused. "One second he was in my sights, the next second he was gone. That fragger can move!"

"Position?" Ryan subvocalized.

"Wait a minute. Wait, I got him! Ryan, he's—"

"You still think you're a match for me, Mercury?"

Ryan spun to face the voice behind him, and just barely managed to deflect the high kick aimed for his head. The kick landed hard against his arm.

Ryan's left forearm went numb, and he rolled again,

using the momentum of the kick to push himself out of harm's way. He staggered to his feet and forced himself to center.

Burnout was casually leaning against the trunk of the tree across the large center walkway.

Ryan stepped backward until his back was against a tree trunk. He could feel the cool ivy leaves rustling against his neck.

"You like how that feels, Mercury? To have your back against the proverbial wall?"

Ryan flexed his left arm, feeling the life come back in painful prickles. He smiled. "Not so much. The big difference is that I didn't put your back up against any wall, you did. You messed in business that didn't concern you and you thought you could get away with it."

"Just get him to move another half a meter, Quicksilver, and I've got the shot." Grind's voice was soft, full of concentration.

Jane broke in. "You got another minute and a half until lift off. Make whatever you're going to do count, 'cause if you're still standing at your present position when that room goes, I don't think even you could live through it."

The feeling in Ryan's arm was back to normal, and he smiled at Burnout. "I came in here to try and settle things without anyone getting hurt, especially the innocent woman you've got tied up. But I guess that time is through." Ryan forced his will to be calm, and felt the power channel down his arms to his hands.

"All right, Burnout. You want to dance, I'll dance with you." With that, Ryan threw out his hands, sending a battering ram of force straight at the cyberzombie.

Burnout tried to move, but even with his speed, he was way too late. The magical wall smashed into him, catching him in the chest and sending him flying. The marble tree he'd been leaning against cracked with a sound like thunder and tilted slightly to the side.

The cyberzombie rolled with the impact, turning his air time into a series of backward somersaults.

While Burnout was still in the air, Ryan moved. He leapt the first table of flowers in a graceful kicking motion. As Burnout hit the ground, catlike, with his feet under him, Ryan's foot smashed into the side of Burnout's head.

Ryan used the impact to drop himself back into a fighting stance, and Burnout fell with the sound of rending metal.

Ryan pulled his Manhunter and was about to pull the trigger when he heard Jane's voice in his ear. "Ryan, no! If you spark it now, I won't even be able to save Nadja. You're too close to her."

Burnout looked up and suddenly was scrambling toward him.

Ryan threw his body backward, catching the edge of the table directly behind him with his left hand.

He pulled his legs in tightly, and pushed off with his hand, causing him to flip over back into the center walkway.

Ryan stood for a second in the silence. Once again, Burnout had disappeared on him.

"Position?"

"He's standing right next to Daviar. He knows you won't pull the trigger if there's a chance you might hit her."

"Burnout!" Ryan called. "You talk big, but when push comes to shove, your cowardice shows through. Taking refuge behind a hostage, that takes guts. Yes, sir."

Out the corner of his eye, Ryan saw the form hurtling through the air, and he turned, the Manhunter ready to fire, but he never got the chance.

With a scream of rage, Burnout slammed into him. One metal hand grabbed the pistol's barrel, another caught Ryan's throat.

As they fell, Ryan slammed his free hand into Burnout's chest, packing a magical, as well as physical punch, and Burnout's body twisted in mid-air. The cyber-zombie's momentum carried him over Ryan's head, but the metal man kept his grip on Ryan's neck, and Ryan felt himself start to black out as his body was wrenched backward and down.

Ryan's grip on the Manhunter loosened for just a moment, and it was gone from his grasp.

Damn, he's strong.

Choking, he let his legs go over his head, and he found himself on top of Burnout's prone form, straddling the man's huge artificial torso.

Holding Ryan at arm's length above him, Burnout tightened his grasp, and a sparkling blackness began to close at the edges of Ryan's vision. Ryan struggled, his hands battering at Burnout's chrome body, bashing deep dents into the scarred metal. His legs thrashing, searching for purchase.

Then, just as his strength started to fail him, his flailing hands felt the Dragon Heart, tied to Burnout's waist.

Ryan touched it with his mind, and he felt its power surge through him.

"So we meet again, Ryan Mercury."

The voice dropped into Ryan's mind like an old lover, so familiar, yet so hostile.

I thought I might find you here, Lethe.

38

I'm sorry, I'm sorry, I'm sorry. The words had become a mantra in Lucero's mind and she couldn't shake them. She was back in the dark stain, at the metaplanar outcropping of stone. She sat at the edge of the newly reconstructed wedge of blackness, her back propped against the body of a young boy, his smooth skin cold against her spine.

Directly in front of her, Señor Oscuro was pulling another docile young girl toward the new altar of corpses. The pretty raven-haired child slipped on the blood of the latest victim and dropped to her knees.

It had taken Oscuro a fraction of the time to create the new wedge-shaped stain near the tip of the outcropping. He worked with a renewed vigor that made Lucero ill, spilling blood and carving up corpses against the music. Pressing forward until the dark barrier came very close to the singer of the song.

The black line edging just around the source of the light.

Now, with all the grace of a prince at a royal ball, Oscuro gently took the girl's hand and helped her to her feet.

I'm sorry, I'm sorry, I'm sorry. With each repetition, Lucero imagined that the blood stain in her soul grew fainter and fainter, until it was nearly gone. Gone also was her strange blood lust, the twisted, manipulated manifestation of her craving for the power the blood could bring.

Lucero shivered in revulsion when she thought about the things she had done, when she thought about how

Oscuro had magically turned her lust for blood power into some strange, sick obsession for the blood itself.

She knew now that Oscuro had been using her all along. Everything he had done, and everything he'd caused her to do, had been a trick to keep her soul riding that fine line between light and darkness. He had managed to maintain that balance so Lucero would remain functional as the link between the real world and this one.

But was the stain on her soul really growing lighter? Could the mantra truly erase her sins?

She could tell by Oscuro's ease of movement. Before, when the black spot on her soul had lightened, it had strained Oscuro to the limit just to complete the sacrifices. Now, Oscuro moved as if he were taking a relaxing walk through a quiet park.

I'm sorry, I'm sorry, I'm sorry.

As the raven-haired girl lay back on the bloody mound of dead bodies, Lucero became aware of her own scarred hands, clutching her knees. She was rocking back and forth in beat to her litany of apologies.

Oscuro looked over at Lucero and grinned, a track of spattered blood dripping down the side of his face. His violently shadowed face watched her, not the sacrifice, as he raised the gore-covered blade and let it fall.

The young girl's head nearly came away from her body as the knife cleaved the delicate skin, splitting tissue and cartilage with equal ease.

Oscuro had brought a real *Chac-mool* with him this time, and he bent to catch the spurting flow of life in the black granite bowl.

"We are almost there, my child, we are on the edge of the bridge," said Oscuro, his gaze still fixed on Lucero. "Soon, all of your struggle, all of your suffering will reach fruition. Soon, you will have the release you crave."

Even the sound of his voice made the bile rise in the back of Lucero's throat.

I'm sorry, I'm sorry, I'm sorry. Lucero rocked faster, the words echoing in her mind until they started to run together, to become a blur of supplication.

Oscuro turned from the still twitching body, and

delicately picked his way over the jumbled tangle of life-less limbs.

He reached the last small section of the uncompleted wedge. Very near the power of the song, at the sharp edge of the outcropping, right next to the tip. But instead of finishing the wedge and bringing the dark stain to the tip of the spike, Oscuro turned back to Lucero. "Come, my child. This is a grand moment, a momentous occasion. I think it would be fitting if I shared it with the one who made it possible."

Lucero continued to rock, continued her mantra as stark horror filled her soul.

Oscuro smiled softly. "As you wish, my dear. I can understand how this glorious achievement might be a bit overwhelming for one so young." With that, he turned back toward the tip of the outcropping and raised the bowl.

No! Lucero struggled to her feet. She had to stop him, she had to keep him from completing the wedge. Dread filled her, and her soul quaked before it.

She staggered across the corpses, stumbling with every step as the flaccid limbs of dead children seemed to catch at her flesh, to block her steps.

Oscuro held his position, *Chac-mool* raised high, until she was only five meters from him. Then he tipped the bowl.

The thick burgundy liquid poured out, searing the cracked earth with its stain. Completing the wedge. And as the wedge closed, Lucero could hear Oscuro say in a deep booming voice, "My masters, Darke welcomes you."

A tiny sliver of darkness had edged past the singer and reached the tip of the outcropping. A mere splinter. Yet it was enough.

An icy chill crept into her limbs then, a dark, barren, numbing cold that froze her mid-step, that clenched all the muscles in her body as her very flesh revolted against the touch of pure evil. This was despair at its true depths, this was hatred in its most refined form. The only thing that kept her from losing her mind completely was the muted sound of the music.

Lucero's stomach muscles seized up and she vomited

blood. It splattered on the ground, mixing with the blood of those who had died before, and began to sizzle. She continued to wretch and gag until nothing more would come out of her. With a shaking hand, she wiped the muck from her chin and slowly raised her head.

Oscuro knelt before her, a bemused smile on his dark face. "Impressive, no?"

Lucero wanted to vomit again, wanted to spew her insides all over this hateful creature in front of her, but she was too weak to even spit in his face.

His smile turned to a grin. "And, as they used to say back when I was still young, you ain't seen nothin' yet."

Oscuro stood, and walked behind her, and it took every ounce of strength for Lucero to sit back and watch him. He stood as close to the tip of the spike as he could and raised his arms in welcome. "Masters, Darke bids you to come. Crush the light that has held you back for so long. Come and take what is rightfully yours."

At first, Lucero thought she was hallucinating. The mean cold deepened for a moment, and it felt as if she were suffocating, then something moved at the corner of her vision. She turned her head, just in time to see one of the corpses, a brown-haired girl, stagger to her feet.

The girl's head toppled to the side and stayed that way, the half-moon wound on her throat gaping like a hangman's leer. Then Lucero became aware of movement all around her as the dead came to life and pushed themselves to their feet.

With a quick movement, Oscuro lifted the sacrificial dagger from the altar, and raised it. With two deft slashes, he cut diagonal wounds along his upper left forearm. Then he transferred the knife to his opposite hand, and repeated the process on the right forearm.

No blood flowed from those wounds. Oscuro began chanting in a tongue Lucero couldn't understand, but that hurt her ears.

Several of the zombie-corpses around her began to transform. They doubled over in pain as huge sharp bristles of spiny black hair pierced out of their skin. Their legs and arms changed into furry tentacles, multiplying until there were four on either side of their now-hideous bodies. Their heads flattened, and massive insect mandibles jutted with a gooey crunch sound from the base of their jaws as their eyes split and divided. That was all Lucero had time to see, because at that moment, she was slammed with the full force of the evil across the Chasm. It was a raver's madness, a lunatic's cruelty, a rapist's glee at the subjugation of all it surveyed.

I'm sorry. I'm sor—

As Lucero's consciousness faded, the knowledge that her sins had allowed this to happen struck her with desperate force. The hollow, cadaver sound of Oscuro's laughter echoed around her as his new forces made a slow advance toward the light.

Lucero knew it was only a matter of time before the song was silenced. The light quenched.

And like herself, the beauty turned to ugliness.

Abomination.

39

On the floor of the arboretum, Ryan straddled the cyborg body covered in gore, feeling as if time stood still as Burnout's cold metal fingers squeezed down on his throat. Blackness crept in like ink on the periphery of Ryan's vision as the power of the Dragon Heart surged through him.

Suddenly, Ryan felt Lethe bring his influence to bear, pushing against Ryan's hold on the Dragon Heart.

Ryan knew Lethe wasn't able to use all of his magical strength, because Ryan would never have been able to resist the spirit's full force.

Lethe, why are you doing this? I thought you wanted to help.

"Help you to attain the Dragon Heart so you could keep it for your own? I would much rather this man of wretched metal have the Heart. At least he can be reasoned with, at least he is honorable."

Ryan struggled to understand what Lethe was saying. Then he understood. *Lethe, I know what you're thinking, but you're wrong.*

"Am I?" The deep voice was grave. "Even now, I can sense your desire for the Dragon Heart."

Yes, I have a desire for the Heart; its power is seductive, and any man could justify that desire by saying how much good he could accomplish with it. But if you can sense that desire in me, then you've got to be able to sense the fact that I will not keep the Heart for my own.

There was a short pause, and Ryan became aware of Burnout's grasp on his throat, of the cyberzombie's slow-motion movement to bring the Manhunter on target.

"Even though I sense what you say is true, why should

I surrender this man, who for the small price of your death, will put forth his entire effort into helping me transport the Dragon Heart to Thayla? You, on the other hand, might still succumb to your own base desires."

Ryan grew desperate. The barrel of the Manhunter was swinging toward his chest, as if in slow motion, targeting the spot where his armor had already been damaged.

Lethe, there is more. Things you don't know. Listen to the truth in my mind. There are only two people on this planet who have the knowledge and the trustworthiness to carry the Dragon Heart across to the astral plane. Two mages specified by Dunkelzahn. Neither of them would have anything to do with Burnout. Everything we are fighting for will have been for nothing.

In that moment, the odds were put on the scales, the risks were calculated. Ryan could sense the spirit's thoughts turning as Lethe made his decision.

"You have still not convinced me that you are devoted to taking the Dragon Heart to Thayla," came Lethe's reply. "I will honor my agreement with Burnout."

Ryan couldn't breathe, and he felt the power of the Dragon Heart fading with the last of his strength. Tiny splotches of black touched his vision, like droplets of dark oil on his eyes. *I'm going down.*

Burnout targeted the Manhunter, his finger poised on the trigger. But he didn't fire. "I have detected the rise in oxygen," he said. "Any spark would blow this whole room. I think I'll move outside before I riddle your flesh with bullets."

Into Ryan's mind came Dunkelzahn's voice. *A follower of the Silent Way uses the terrain to his advantage, Ryanthusar. Uses all his assets in a fight, even those that seem to be lost.*

Grind's voice came dimly, as if from a great distance, yelling, "Get off him, Ryan! I've got the shot! Get clear!"

"Negative, Dhin," came Jane's voice. "At his current position, Quicksilver is not covered by sprinklers. Even if you don't hit him with the sniper gun, he'll buy it in the explosion."

Ryan felt the zen of the Silent Way creep over him as he centered himself. It had been too long since he had felt this way, ever since Roxborough had taken control. Now, as he focused, his spirit meshed with his body in perfect synchrony. And he knew what to do.

Ryan closed his hands over the Dragon Heart, hanging from Burnout's waist in its cloth sling. He brought all of his strength to bear, making sure that his grip was iron-tight.

Then he concentrated and used his telekinetic magic. Ryan nudged Burnout's trigger finger with a focused magic push.

The Manhunter roared, and Ryan could see the muzzle flash just as he heard the distant sound of Grind's heavy-caliber sniper rifle.

Ryan felt the Manhunter bullet blow through his armor and throw him back, knocking the breath from his chest.

Then everything turned the nightmare orange color of Hell. The exposed flesh of his face and hands began to sizzle and cook as he flew through the air. The pain was too great, the force too strong.

Ryan lost his grip on the Dragon Heart.

The skin of Ryan's eyelids split and began to bleed as he closed them against the roaring wall of flame that engulfed him.

His blistering ears could hear the sound of glass shattering above him as the roof blew outward.

Ryan drew on every reserve of strength he possessed, and focused to hold his flesh together.

And he heard the sound of something heavy, something metal, hit the floor just beside him, and he knew it was Burnout.

Something pushed Ryan violently across the room and into the soothing cool of the sprinklers. Jets of cold water, which at first simply turned to steam, finally fought their way through the fire on Ryan's skin to gently caress his wounds and soothe them.

Then it was all over.

Ryan opened his eyes, which were covered with a film of red, making the purgatory scene in front of him even more lurid. *Am I still alive?*

The small pockets of flame that still remained were hissing and smoking under the constant spray of water.

As Ryan rolled slowly, trying to get to his feet, he could feel the huge blisters on his cheeks break open on the blackened marble floor.

Across the room lay the motionless, charred body of Burnout like some child's fallen nightmare, a huge hole in his chest from the sniper round.

"You have won, Ryan Mercury." Lethe's voice was weak, distant.

You saved me? That push into the water spray was you?

"I saw your willingness to sacrifice yourself. I see the truth that you have changed."

Thank you, Lethe.

"Just fulfill your promise. Take the Dragon Heart to Thayla."

I will. But I could use your help.

"I have used up the last of my strength."

What do you mean?

"Ryan Mercury, we all make mistakes, and we all pay for them. When this fragile mortal coil dies, I will die with it."

Don't die, Lethe. You have to help me take the Dragon Heart to Thayla.

No response.

Lethe?

There was a crash behind Ryan, and Secret Service agents stormed into the room, weapons ready. Grind followed a minute later and rushed up to Ryan's side. The dwarf took one look at Ryan and spoke into the air. "Jane, get that DocWagon crew in here pronto. Quicksilver's so fragged up I'm not sure why he's still alive."

The only answer Ryan could hear on his melted earphones was distant static.

"Ryan?" The voice came from behind him.

Floating into his vision came Nadja. She was sopping wet, her ruined gown clinging to her. Her black hair was plastered to her soot-smudged face. Standing there, like some war zone survivor, Ryan thought she was the most beautiful thing he'd ever seen.

40

In the swirling darkness of the interface between Burnout's meat body and his cyber, Lethe found the silver cord—the trail Burnout's soul left as it struggled to find an exit from the magic that held it trapped. The cord draped downward into Burnout's inner darkness.

Without hesitating, Lethe plunged into the blackness, following the cord as fast as he could.

It didn't take him long to find Burnout's essence.

To Lethe, it looked like a small human boy, with skin of liquid silver that shimmered as the boy trudged slowly downward.

"Burnout?"

The boy did not run, did not slow his descent.

"Burnout?" Lethe said, again.

The boy turned slowly and looked at Lethe with dull, tired eyes. Eyes that spoke of a weariness no child should have to suffer. "There is no Burnout here. He is dead. I am all that is left. Now leave me alone."

Lethe moved closer. "If you are not Burnout, then who are you?"

The boy turned away, but called over his shoulder, "My friends call me Billy. Billy Madson."

Lethe continued to follow him. "Where are you going, Billy?"

"Go away. I'm going to rest. I'm so tired."

Lethe thought about it for a moment. There had to be something that would draw Burnout's soul back to his metal body, something this young boy would find enticing.

Then it came to him.

"Billy, you want to see a magic place?"

The small figure stopped. Turned. For a moment, Lethe could see the excitement behind the exhaustion in the boy's eyes. Then a look of suspicion crossed the young face. "What magic place?"

Lethe came up close. "There is a place in the metaplanes, a spike of mana. There's so much magic there that it fills your whole spirit."

Billy's eyes narrowed. "I've heard of that place. A lot of people died there. What's the magic in dying? I mean, if you're dead, how're you going to enjoy it?"

Lethe laughed. "Billy, I can show you a side to that place that very few people ever get to see."

"Oh, yeah?"

"Look." Lethe formed an image of Thayla in his mind. He drew from his memory of her song, of the sheer perfection of her beautiful magic. He showed Billy the power of the white light that radiated from her.

The small boy drew breath as the vision took him.

After a minute, the vision faded.

The boy looked up at Lethe. "You've been to this place?"

Lethe nodded.

"And this is a real place, not just something you made up?"

Again, Lethe nodded.

"It's wonderful."

Lethe laughed. "Yes, it is. Would you like to see it?"

A small fire seemed to light behind the weary eyes. "You could take me there?"

"We can only go together. You have to come back with me, back the way you came."

The small boy looked upward, his eyes trailing the silver cord that stretched out of sight into the darkness overhead. Then he looked downward, in the direction he'd been heading, and such longing filled the boy's eyes that it made Lethe's heart hurt.

"But I'm so tired," said Billy, in a tiny, child's whisper.

"I know you are, Billy. But this place is worth it. I promise."

They stood there like that for a moment, then Billy looked up and faced Lethe. "All right, if you promise."

Together they struggled back up along the silver strand.

41

Ryan woke to the sound of crickets.

For a long moment, he didn't open his eyes, he simply savored the feeling of clean sheets beneath him and the smell of fresh air.

Even the dull pain in his chest and on his hands and face was welcome.

I'm alive.

He opened his eyes to silvery moonlight peeking through the miniblinds. The window was open, and the blinds rocked gently in the soft breeze blowing into the room.

Ryan felt good. Sore, tired, spent, but good nonetheless.

He was in one of the small guest rooms in the mansion's west wing, the walls were a soft magenta with oak wainscoting stretching up from the floor for about a meter.

A nice, simple room, compared to the luxury of the rest of the place. It suited Ryan just fine.

Ryan turned to the oak night stand next to the bed, and there, lying on a cushioned bed of real velvet, was the Dragon Heart. Ryan could feel its power, feel the pulse that drew him to it like the proverbial moth to the all-consuming flame.

Ryan stretched out a bandaged hand and clumsily grasped the Heart. He pulled it to his chest.

With a thought, he tapped into its power. Instantly, he felt the healing of his body accelerate at such a rapid rate that he found himself sitting upright without any complaint from his chest.

Ryan looked down and saw a piece of elegant stationery resting next to the velvet.

With care, Ryan peeled the bandages off his left hand. Even though the skin of his hand was fully healed, small, circular scars remained. He felt his face. It was covered in bandages as well.

He picked up the paper. There was a note inside, and he recognized the handwriting immediately. He leaned back against the pillows and read the flowing script.

> My sweet Ryan,
> I hope I am able to be there when you wake, but if not, I wanted you to know how much I love you, Ryan Mercury. I love you more than I can say, more than I will ever be able to express.
> There are still dark days ahead, for both of us, but I know we will succeed. You have a mission that you must finish, I understand that, but even when the path seems dark, know this: there is one who loves you more than life itself.
> I'll wait for you, Ryan. Unfaltering, unwavering, because I know you will return, just as I knew you would come for me in the arboretum.
> With all my love, Nadja.

Ryan smiled, feeling the tightness of his newly healed skin.

He looked down at the Dragon Heart and thought about Nadja's words. She wasn't completely correct. He didn't have to leave if he didn't want to.

Ryan felt the Heart's power fill him.

I could keep it.

The idea made him giddy, just as it had the last time. When he had been consumed by Roxborough's personality and had decided to keep the Heart. To have all this power at his command, the wonders he could do.

Then, without bidding it, Miranda's face slipped into his mind. Her final request had been to make sure her sacrifice had meant something, that all the ruin and destruction hadn't been for nothing.

Ryan knew he was more than a little responsible for her

death. He looked down at the new scar tissue on his hand, and that hand balled into a fist. Those scars brought the image of Nadja, soaking wet, nearly killed because of Burnout's desire for the Heart.

And my own.

As long as he kept it, he knew that wouldn't stop. There would always be those who desired it, and one day someone would come along with enough power to take it away from him.

Then it would all have been for nothing.

Ryan felt the Dragon Heart's power wane inside him. With it, his desire to possess the artifact faded as well.

Ryan looked out the window at the beautiful sunshine.

"Don't worry, Dunkelzahn, you're going to get your way, as usual. Even dead, you're still going to get your way. But there's a difference this time, you bastard. I'm not doing this for you anymore. I'm not doing this for some holy crusade to save the fragging world either. I'm doing this for me, Dunkelzahn. You hear me? I'm going to finish this thing for me, and for everything and everyone I hold dear."

Ryan smiled to himself. "But you knew that, didn't you, old wyrm? You knew this would be the only way I'd take on the mission. By making it my own."

Ryan carefully set the Dragon Heart back on its velvet bed, and watched the breeze gently rock the blinds. "Be at peace, you old lizard."

Ryan smiled, as a single tear fell from his eye to be quickly absorbed in the bandages on his face. "I miss you."

42

The steady drizzle of rain spread a glossy sheen over the mirrored glass skyscrapers of Wonderland City. Alice brooded, her head bent as she watched the ground, seeing the reflection of the buildings in the shiny black of the street.

She stopped suddenly, taking a long drag from her cigarette. She gave up, admitting to herself that she didn't know what to do. *I need outside counsel.*

Wonderland placed the call for her.

"Hello?" came the man's voice, remarkably alert considering what he had been through. And his image came on-line. White bandages covered his head and face, though his silver-flecked blue eyes shone like glittering jewels.

"Ryan," Alice said. "Are you all right?"

"I've seen better days."

"I need your advice."

"You need *my* advice?"

"I don't know what to do with Rox."

"What have you done already?"

Alice told him about locking Roxborough in Wonderland, about torturing him with his own disease, and when she was finished, Ryan sank back into the pillows of the bed he was in.

"I know exactly what to do," he said. "The only thing worse than anything you've already done.

"What?"

"Let him go," he said.

"What? Ryan, are you insane?"

"Send him back to his miserable life."

"But . . ." Alice couldn't believe that Ryan of all people would want Rox released.

"Think about it, Alice. He hates his life, hates being trapped in the Matrix. It's his clockwork asylum. A mechanical prison of his own creation. All I want is to make sure he doesn't continue his spirit-transfer experiments, and you've already wiped that data."

"I also had his head scientist transferred to Saeder-Krupp."

Ryan laughed. "Perfect."

Alice was silent for a few minutes. She took a drag from her cigarette as she thought about it. Maybe Ryan was right. Roxborough would never be happy unless he was in a physical body, and Alice had taken away his ability to do that. At least for many years.

She looked at Ryan. "All right, I'll let him go. I know his system inside and out now, and I've riddled it with back doors for myself. He'll never be able to lock me out unless he isolates himself so completely that he's totally alone."

"He hates being alone more than anything."

"Exactly."

"Glad I could be of help," Ryan said.

"Perhaps I can return the favor."

"What do you mean?"

Alice had not meant to share her knowledge of Ryan's mission, but she owed him, and Alice made a point of repaying her debts generously. She had accidentally misled him with the bogus Damien Knight information, and she wanted to make up for that. From what Alice knew, which was almost everything, Ryan's mission was far from over, and it was going to get a lot more dangerous very soon. He could use all the help he could get.

"Just be cautious, Ryan. There is data to indicate that Dunkelzahn and Harlequin were long-time associates, perhaps friends, perhaps enemies. Going way back."

"Alice, how do you know this?"

Ryan, come on, I have access to nearly every source of information in the cybersphere. Harlequin is very powerful and quite possibly a long-time enemy of the dragon. He's high on my current list of assassination suspects."

Ryan shuddered. "Thanks for the warning, Alice, but I need to ask his help. Dunkelzahn specified it."

"I know," Alice said. "I just wanted you to go in with your eyes open."

"I appreciate it."

"Get some rest, Ryan Mercury. You'll need it."

Ryan leaned back in his bed. "I'll do that," he said, "Give my best to Roxborough. I just wish I could see the look on his face when he realizes you've wiped all his data."

"I'll record it for you," Alice said. Then she disconnected and felt a thrill of excitement race over her skin as she thought about Rox's reaction. She was anticipating the joy Rox would feel when he found himself back in his own system. Home. And then the severe disappointment that followed when he realized that his hopes for escape from the Matrix were crushed.

Alice smiled the Cheshire grin of the Cat, jumping up and down in excitement. *This is going to be so much fun.*

ABOUT THE AUTHOR

Clockwork Asylum, Book Two of the Dragon Heart Saga, is Jak Koke's fourth novel. His fifth, *Beyond the Pale,* will complete the story of Ryan Mercury and the Dragon Heart that began in *Stranger Souls.*

Koke has also written two other novels set in FASA-created universes. His first, *Dead Air,* was a stand-alone book in the Shadowrun® world and was published by Roc Books in 1996. His second, *Liferock,* is his only fantasy novel so far and will soon be published by FASA Corporation as part of its Earthdawn® series.

Koke has also sold short stories to AMAZING STORIES and PULPHOUSE: A FICTION MAGAZINE, and has contributed to several anthologies such as *Rat Tales* by Pulphouse, *Young Blood* by Zebra, and *Talisman,* an Earthdawn® anthology.

Koke invites you to visit his web site at http://www.sapermedia.com/koke/. You can also send him comments about this and any of his books care of FASA Corporation.

He and his wife, Seana Davidson, a marine microbiologist, live in California with their four-year-old daughter, Michaela.

MEMO

FROM: JANE-IN-THE-BOX
TO: NADJA DAVIAR
DATE: 20 AUGUST 2057
RE: THE LEGEND OF THAYLA

Dunkelzahn's Institute of Magical Research just unearthed this document. Thought you'd be interested. Text follows:

Ages ago, before written memory began, lived a queen of great beauty and even greater heart. Thayla reigned over a rich green valley nestled between two mountain ranges that rose like spikes into the heavens. Under her rule, the land she loved prospered, and her people lived their days in joy.

Each morning Thayla greeted the rising sun with a Song. She sang in a voice as clear as the air and as bright as the great burning orb itself. Nothing foul or dark could prosper in her land, for her voice was too pure for such abominations to bear.

One night an army of dark creatures made to enter the valley, seeking to overrun the prosperous land and corrupt it with their vile presence. Thayla rose that morning as she always did, and upon seeing the black army, sang. Her voice filled the valley with power and hope.

The evil horde, shown the depravity of their existence by her voice, had no choice but to flee. And as they did—running and flying with wild abandon for refuge beyond the valley—one black soldier slowed and, for the briefest of moments, listened to Thayla's Song.

Days passed, and the terrible army remained beyond the valley, fearful of the Song. Finally, driven by their dark masters, they surged forward again. And again Thayla sang.

As before the foul creatures fell back blindly, unable to stand even a few pure notes of her voice. But again the lone, tall warrior with hair and eyes of dark fire lingered and listened, if only for a few moments, before fleeing the valley.

The next time the creatures approached Thayla's domain, less of the army came. The rest were unable to marshal the will needed to enter the valley. But again, the lone dark soldier fell back last, so that he could hear her Song.

Finally, not one of the black army would come. Not even the terrible threats of their vile masters could push them forward. But still a single warrior in ebony and red armor would slip into the valley before each dawn and listen, and after a time, watch as well.

The black figure advanced to where he could see Thayla standing high upon the terraces of the great sprawling city that surrounded her palace. And he would watch her every morning as she rose and greeted the new day with the Song. And as he listened, blood flowed from his ears and his skin blistered from the powerful purity of her voice, but he would not turn aside. He would not flee from her Song. And so he stood, listened, and watched.

Then one night, the dark warrior slipped into the city as Thayla slept. He crept into her citadel, sat at the foot of her bed and watched her.

When she woke and found him there, she called for her guards, but none were strong enough to move the dark warrior. She called her sorcerers, but none were wise enough to banish him. She sang to drive him away, but though his body and spirit were wracked with pain, he stood strong and firm, enraptured by her beauty.

Unable to drive him away, the great Queen Thayla decided to ignore him. Though he stood at her side, she ate without speaking to him. Though he ran alongside as she took her horses out for exercise, she did not look at him. And though he stood silently nearby as she slept, she did not acknowledge his presence.

Each morning she would rise and greet the sun,

singing loud and strong so that the dark army waiting beyond the valley could not enter. And each morning he stood beside her and cried tears of blood and fire at the pain and joy her voice gave him.

And so this went on for some time. Thayla slept, sang, and performed her royal duties. But the black warrior stayed at her side, and slowly the land began to darken from his presence. The animals of the field sickened, as did the people. The crops would not grow, and dark and terrible clouds filled the sky over the valley.

Thayla knew the black soldier was the cause of all these things, and so she asked him to leave. He did not even answer her. She tried to trick him into leaving, but he would not be fooled. Then she tried to force him away, but he could not be broken. Finally, she begged him to leave.

"But I do not wish to leave," he replied. These were the first words he had ever spoken to her, and his voice was like dried leaves blown on the autumn wind. "Your beauty is like none I have ever seen."

"But you cannot stay," she told him. "Your presence is destroying my land and my people."

"I care not for your land or its people," the warrior told her. "I care only for you."

Faced with his determination, Thayla wept. Slowly her people died. Finally, she called her greatest advisors together and told them what they must do.

"As you know, the presence of the dark warrior is destroying our land and our people," she said. "However, he will not leave my side. We cannot make him leave, and so *I* must leave the land and take him with me."

Her advisors wailed at her words. "But you cannot! It is only your voice that holds the black army at bay! If you leave, we will certainly die!"

Thayla nodded, for she knew this to be true, but said, "I will leave, but my voice will remain." And with that she charged her most powerful sorcerers with the task of placing her voice in a songbird that would greet the rising sun each morning as she had.

They searched the land and found the finest song-bird of all. And as the sun rose, they performed the ritual. When the first light appeared the next morn, the bird sang with Thayla's Voice, and the Song held the dark army at bay.

The sorcerers rejoiced at this, but when they turned to congratulate Thayla, she and her dark shadow had gone. They searched the land but could find neither of them.

But the Songbird rose each morning. And with a voice as pure as the clear air itself, it sang the Song, and the black army trembled in its tracks, unable to enter the valley.

AN EXCITING PREVIEW FROM
BEYOND THE PALE
BOOK 3 OF THE DRAGON HEART SAGA
BY JAK KOKE
COMING FROM ROC MARCH 1998

His name was Billy Madson, and he was a boy in the body of a machine.

A boy with a guardian angel hovering around him. Protecting him. Calming him when the vicious memories came rushing back, the violence and the killing. Memories of his previous incarnation—a cyberzombie who was called Burnout.

The angel surrounded and buoyed Billy. The angel was the only reason Billy still lived. The angel's name was Lethe, and he had saved Billy's life. He had shown Billy the images of terrible beauty, blinding light and a song that brought tears to the boy's eyes. A voice of such power and purity that even Lethe's memory of it, filtered through Billy's mechanical body and into the recesses of Billy's mind, had moved him back from the edge of death.

Back among the living.

Now, Billy lay on his back, shackled unceremoniously to a metal operating table. Technicians and doctors had probed and studied him, apparently interested in the technology of his body. A few hours ago, they had left the room, leaving him attached to machines that monitored his brain patterns and the electrical activity of his cyberware.

The room was quite secure, he knew. His mind had automatically analyzed it for avenues of escape. He had done this without thinking, the possible scenarios running like a subroutine in the back of his mind, and he had marveled at himself for it.

I am trained to kill and to destroy. A combat machine.

"Someone's coming," Lethe said, his soothing voice dropping into Billy's mind through a device in his cybernetics called the IMS—Invoked Memory Stimulator.

Billy opened his eyes to the darkened room. It was night and moonlight shone through the barred and fenced-over windows, the crisscrossed shadows rippling over the floor and table next to him. Like hatch-marked silver.

"Not the same as before," Lethe said. "I sense stealth and barely contained aggression in those who approach."

Billy yanked at the heavy bands that anchored his legs, arms, chest, and head to the table, but he couldn't even turn his head, and much of his connection to his cybernetics had been disrupted by the doctors. "Can you tell if they're coming to kill us?"

Billy sensed laughter through the IMS. "No, my friend, I can't read minds. I can only sense auras. Here they come."

The door to the room opened and someone entered, perhaps several people. Billy could hear them only when he cranked up the sensitivity on his cybernetic ears to their maximum. He could sense the slight pressure shift in the room as well.

"*Señor, aquí!*" The words were barely audible, subvocalized into a throat mic or headware, but Billy understood what they meant. "Over here, sir."

The Azzies have found me, finally.

Several people surrounded him. Billy couldn't see them and suspected that they had hidden themselves magically. He felt pressure against his chest and a compartment popped open. Then something was jacked into him, running diagnostics.

Billy knew that in his past life as the cyberzombie Burnout this had happened to him on a regular basis. Just a routine systems check. The portable deck was speaking to his brain, telling him exactly what parts were malfunctioning, what parts worked and how much damage he had sustained in his quest to destroy Ryan Mercury.

A quest that now seemed so distant, so remote as to be unimportant. In fact it had been Ryan Mercury who had brought Burnout so close to death that he had lost his identity. Or rediscovered it. His previous incarnation died in the massive fire in Dunkelzahn's arboretum, and Billy was not sad about it.

Perhaps Ryan Mercury did me a favor by almost killing me.

The irony did not escape Billy.

The diagnostic program indicated that his homing signal had been destroyed, probably when he had fallen into Hells Canyon. Another confrontation with Mercury that seemed like eons ago even though it had only been a week or so.

"Remarkable," whispered one of the invisible people standing over him. "He has sustained a huge amount of abuse, but he lives on. I think we should abort termination and take him back with us."

"*Si,*" came the response.

The paralysis started in his toes and moved up rapidly, system by system through his knees, legs, waist. Up through his torso and chest it traveled, the sheer absence of feeling. No tingling numbness, just a digital erasure of his sensory perception.

His taste turned off with a click, then his sight, hearing, until finally he was alone inside a vast ocean of darkness. A brain in a sensory deprivation tank.

Lethe, he thought.

Yes, Billy?

Could you show me Thayla again?

Billy felt the spirit smile inside and suddenly the darkness gave way to a brilliant light. The silence yielded to the glorious song of the goddess Thayla who stood on a cracked plane of rock. The light shone from her like a beacon against the darkness, a wondrous sun in the blackest firmament. The song and the light were one and the same. Her voice rang out, rising and falling in beautiful melodious waves, washing over him like warm surf. Until he cared not who he was and why he was there.

He merely wanted to stay forever.

Lethe's memory of Thayla was flawless, the sensation of the experience overwhelming Billy until he knew that he must join his guardian angel in his quest to help Thayla. The beauty must not be destroyed.

But we're in no position to help, he thought. *When we wake, we will be in Aztlan.*

If *we wake.*

MORE EXCITING ADVENTURES FROM
SHADWORUN®

ENTER THE SHADOWS SHADOWRUN®

☐ **WORLDS WITHOUT END by Caroline Spector.** Aina remembers the world of centuries ago, but now she's in the Awakened era of shadowrunners and simulations, magic and metas. And she may have brought an ancient nemesis along with her. . . . (453719—$4.99)

☐ **JUST COMPENSATION by Robert N. Charette.** Andy is happy as a shadowrunner wannabe, but when he accidentally gets involved with real runners, the game of Let's Pretend is over. So is his safe, corporate life. (453727—$4.99)

☐ **BLACK MADONNA by Carl Sargent and Marc Gascoigne.** Michael Sutherland is a hardened decker who's been around. But when a panicked Renraku Corp enlists his services, he quickly realizes this is no ordinary crisis—he's up against an immortal elf, who's engineered the most stylish and sophisticated electronic virus ever to destroy a computer system. (453735—$5.50)

☐ **PREYING FOR KEEPS by Mel Odom.** When ace shadowrunner Jack Skater leads his team of commandos in a raid on an elven ocean freighter, things get a little sticky. Yakuza hit men crash the party, and a Japanese shaman whips up a titanic sea creature just to make sure nobody gets out alive. And as a ghastly virus hits Seattle, unleashing hordes of homicidal cannibals onto the streets, Skater and company have to bring in some artillery just to stay alive. (453753—$5.50)

☐ **DEAD AIR by Jak Koke.** It's fast and furious inside the Combat Biker maze, where armor-plated hogs and juiced-up rice grinders blast, pound, and pummel each other for points. But it's barely up to speed for Jonathon and Tamara, two elven bikers at the head of the Los Angeles Sabers. (453751—$5.50)

☐ **THE LUCIFER DECK by Lisa Smedman.** Life on the streets of 21st-century Seattle can be tough, especially for a young ork like Pita. And it gets a lot tougher when she witnesses a corporate mage murdered by the violent spirit he just conjured from another dimension. (453788—$5.99)

Prices slightly higher in Canada

Buy them at your local bookstore or use this convenient coupon for ordering.

PENGUIN USA
P.O. Box 999 — Dept. #17109
Bergenfield, New Jersey 07621

Please send me the books I have checked above.
I am enclosing $_____ (please add $2.00 to cover postage and handling). Send check or money order (no cash or C.O.D.'s) or charge by Mastercard or VISA (with a $15.00 minimum). Prices and numbers are subject to change without notice.

Card #_____ Exp. Date _____
Signature_____
Name_____
Address_____
City _____ State _____ Zip Code _____

For faster service when ordering by credit card call **1-800-253-6476**

Allow a minimum of 4-6 weeks for delivery. This offer is subject to change without notice.